Through the Hourglass

Lesbian Historical Romance

Through the Hourglass

Lesbian Historical Romance

Edited by
Sacchi Green
Patty G. Henderson

2015

Through the Hourglass: Lesbian Historical Romance
A Lizzie's Bedtime Stories Anthology

© 2015 by Sacchi Green and Patty G. Henderson. All Rights Reserved.

ISBN: 978-0692559567

This Book is published by
The Liz McMullen Show Publications
Thelizmcmullenshow@gmail.com
www.thelizmcmullenshow.com
First Edition: December 2015

Credits:

Editor: Sacchi Green and Patty G. Henderson
Copy Editor: Adrian Blagg
Book Cover: Boulevard Photografica/Patty G. Henderson,
www.boulevardphotografica.yolasite.com

This book is a work of fiction. Names, characters, places, and incidents are a product of the author's imagination or are used fictitiously. Any resemblance to actual events, locales, or persons, living or dead, is coincidental.

Our Stories

Introductions

Megan McFerren   1
VOLVUR

Heather Rose Jones   13
WHERE MY HEART GOES

Patty G. Henderson   31
IN FULL MOON LIGHT

Priscilla Scott Rhoades   47
EMMA

Susan Smith   63
SAFFRON AND FENNEL

Cara Patterson   89
PROPRIETY

Doreen Perrine   109
A YEAR OF SILENT PROMISE

Connie Wilkins   133
THE BRIDGE

Lexy Wealleans   151
CAPTAIN MY CAPTAIN

R.G. Emanuelle   171
THE RUM RUNNER AND
THE SHOWGIRL

Jean Copeland   199
NIGHTINGALE

Our Stories *cont.*

MJ Williamz   219
MY ELIZABETH

Aliisa Percival   237
WITH A SPARK

Allison Fradkin   251
WITH BALL DUE RESPECT

Ann Bannon   267
BEEBO BRINKER (Excerpt)

Lee Lynch   279
HONEYDEW MOON

Author Biographies   299

Introductions

Patty G. Henderson

We live in a harsh world. Technology rules and love is sometimes born and nurtured via an iPad, iPhone, or social media sites. Where is the romance?

Lesbian fiction has its share of erotica anthologies, where passions, sex, and lust take center stage over tender romance. I yearned to see an anthology that captured those days gone by, where romance was sometimes slow and tender, but seething with passion beneath the velvet, satin, and proper restraint. I approached Liz McMullen with an idea to do an anthology honoring lesbian historical romance. It would be a first, and we would travel through history, telling tales of lesbian romance like the sands through an hourglass.

I was honored that Liz wanted to see those stories too. And I do hope that readers who take the trip back in time to sneak a peek at lesbian love in the distant or exotic past or in not-so-distant times will be left all the more enriched and entertained.

Sacchi Green

Through the Hourglass has been very much a group effort, so both Patty G. Henderson and I want to share our thoughts here, and publisher Liz McMullen will outline the charity aspect at the heart of our project. What could be more appropriate for an anthology focusing on historical stories of lesbians than helping organizations that benefit senior lesbians right now?

History, to my mind, is the greatest story ever told—or too often left untold.

Women loving women have been a fact of life for as long as love and women have existed. Who's to say some of those sculptors of full-bodied stone or ivory goddesses weren't women? We have always been here, in every era and every area of society, even though our stories have so seldom been told.

Fiction has its own power to deepen and intensify our perceptions and beliefs. Stories that show lesbians in well-researched historical settings, with passions fully recognizable today, rescue our past from invisibility and affirm our place through all time, past, present and future.

The writers here are, of course, the real hearts and souls and inventive minds of *Through the Hourglass*, and their stories speak for themselves.

We begin in the Old World with Megan McFerren's "Völvur", set in the Iceland of the 990s where the old Nordic beliefs have not yet given way to the newly arrived Christian missionaries, and girls called Wand-bearers still run free as messengers between the worlds.

Six hundred years later, in the mid-1500s, Heather Rose Jones's "Where My Heart Goes" takes us to the Renaissance, where a woman's royal privilege is offset by being a pawn of political intrigue and succession, but her heart is still her own to give, however long it takes.

By 1692-93 in the New World, we find the brutal misogyny of the Salem Witch Trials pitted against the unbreakable bond between two women in Patty G. Henderson's "In Full Moon Light". Then, two centuries later during the War Between the States in "Emma" by Priscilla Rhoades, a young woman passing as a man finds love in an unexpected setting before inevitably taking on the duties of a soldier.

Meanwhile in Europe, also during the 1860s, Susan Smith's "Saffron and Fennel" depicts an aristocratic widow taking on a man's role in order to pursue archaeological exploration, and, with the scientifically trained daughter of a botanist at her side (and in her bed), discovering traces of women loving women as long ago as the early Cretan civilization. Just twenty years later, the characters in Cara Patterson's "Propriety" struggle, with tenderness and wit, against class distinctions and the obligations of an Austrian Archduchess.

Back across the sea and half a century later, in 1910, Doreen Perrine's "A Year of Silent Promise" paints a complex scene of art and longing and the roughly beautiful coast of New England. Just a few years later, The Great War changes the world forever, and by 1917, an ambulance driver wounded in body and spirit by trench warfare in France encounters a free-spirited artist in England at "The Bridge" by Connie Wilkins. "Captain My Captain" by Lexy Walleans takes us forward four years to the postwar England of 1921 and another seacoast, where recovery and loss and memories of adolescent games of piracy affect the lives of childhood friends.

The between-wars era of prohibition in the USA forms the colorful backdrop in 1928 to "The Rum Runner and the Show Girl" by R.G. Emanuelle, followed by a cluster of stories sparked by the drama of WWII. Jean Copeland's "Nightingale" portrays the struggling nightclub scene on the home front, while MJ Williamz's "My Elizabeth" depicts women like Rosie the Riveter building war planes, and Aliisa Percival's "With a Spark" varies the theme with a celebrity visiting a Canadian bomb-building factory for a patriotic fund-raiser. Just a year later, in 1944, the characters in Allison Fradkin's "With Ball Due Respect" pitch witty banter and score with each other as team members in the All-American Girls Professional Baseball League.

The post-war decades bring us to times so recent that some of us remember them, and those who don't know someone who does, but they still belong to the history that formed who we are today. Ann Bannon's *Beebo Brinker* is an icon of lesbian literature, and here we have an excerpt from her book with all the grit and moody tension of Greenwich Village in 1962. Lee Lynch's stories, too, have inspired us for years and continue to illuminate our world, and her evocative story "Honeydew Moon" is the perfect conclusion to our anthology, with an older, established couple in the 1980s sharing their memories of romance and struggle during the 1950s with young lesbians just beginning their adult lives.

All these wonderful stories, with their passion, adventure, variety, and attention to historical details, have come together because of Patty G. Henderson's original proposal.

From Publisher Liz McMullen

A portion of the proceeds for *Through the Hourglass* will go to these charities that directly serve LGBT senior citizens: Services & Advocacy for GLBT Elders (SAGE) and The Gay & Lesbian Association of Retiring Persons, Inc. (GLARP).

SAGE works to achieve a high quality of life for LGBT older adults, supports and advocates for their rights, fosters a greater understanding of aging in all communities, and promotes positive images of LGBT life in later years. Learn more about their mission and services by visiting their website: www.sageusa.org

The Gay & Lesbian Association of Retiring Persons, Inc. (GLARP) is a non-profit corporation formed in 1996 by co-founders Mary Thorndal and Veronica St. Claire to call attention to the aging issues in the GLBT community. They are currently working on creating a retirement community for LGBT seniors. Visit their website to learn more about the organization and their mission: gaylesbianretiring.org/site.

Völvur

Megan McFerren

They call us *halju-runnos*—hell-runners.

The missionaries gasp when they hear it. Quick fingers mark some rune unknown to me, from their heads to their bellies and across their chests, and they do not speak to us again. No matter. We laugh when they cower at milk-sweet girls only eighteen, nineteen winters alive, our hair unbound and childish, because what have they to fear from us?

Plenty, in truth. And in moments like this, I see how we've earned that name.

The earth itself opens up beneath our feet. Bare heels dig into black soil, lichens and moss exploding outward beneath our toes. There are few enough woods left in Iceland untouched by the reavers who use the trees for their ships to go a-Viking, but this one is ours, and we know it by heart. I duck a branch and grab the trunk, slips of birch flying free beneath my fingers as I spin from it and turn in a new direction. It doesn't help. I hear the laughter of the other girls behind me giving chase, and in my delight, nearly stumble over an upturned stone from the last time we played like this.

My legs are longer than most of theirs. I've grown tall and sturdy as oak, hair stiff and golden as late-summer straw. But gods, they are persistent, howling laughter like wolves after a stray lamb. Lambs, though, are not so clever as I am, and vaulting over a fallen tree, I skid sideways down a hill, feet turned to stop from losing control. Sharp rocks catch my skin, but I pay them no mind now, rolling to my stomach and flattening.

I listen, no sound near me but the rush of my own breath and the hum from my heart, hammering. Their voices seem further away, but they may have split—one band in one direction, one in the other—and so I try to hold my breath to quiet it. The soil is still dawn-damp where I cling to it. I gather my wits again.

Our own people call us *völva*—wand-bearers. The missionaries' name isn't wrong—we do run, and not only in the woods to burn off energy before a long day sitting stoic with herbs and ritual. No, we are the messengers between worlds, between highest Asgard and our own Midgard, between the plains of Vanaheim and woods of Alfheim, and to fog-thick Niflheim and lower still, to Hel, where those dead reside who have not been plucked by the gods in higher branches to join them. Hela, in her kingdom beneath the World Tree, waits for us to visit and return, sharing messages between living and dead, past and present and future. I have not seen her yet, but they say that half her face is pale as fresh cream with hair black as raven's feathers, and the other half foul with decay and hollowed by rot.

I imagine each side is beautiful, in its own way.

"Brynja."

She draws my name out like a song, a *galdr* of our very own, and when I shiver, it's little to do with the cold earth

2

pressed against my belly.

"Eydis." I greet her as if it were the temple we were meeting in rather than the wild woods, as if my dress wasn't darkened with dirt from our rough and joyous games, as if there weren't bits of branch stuck against my hair. I roll to my back, writhing until the rocks press less painfully into my spine, and regard her standing at the foot of the hill. "How—"

"Because I know you," she answers, clever grin quirking one corner of her lips. "Don't I?"

"You know everyone. Too well."

"Blame the gods for that." Unhurried, she picks a careful route up the slope, feet pressing into summer-soft mosses that squish between her bare toes. "But I know you best. I don't have to seek you out in goat entrails."

"I would hope you wouldn't find me there," I laugh, plucking a leaf off my dress. "Maybe I should court favor with the *alfar* to hide me when you come looking."

"Would they listen? They're fickle, and you run like a wild horse through their home."

"Of course they would listen. I could talk a frost giant to Muspelheim."

I declare this with a certainty that widens her grin, her lips an archer's bow drawing over her broad white teeth. We have always been a people prone to bragging, although it's typically the men who do it—and gods save us, do they ever. But our bravado dictates our actions, which we must then fulfill so as not to be liars, and our bragging spreads our legend. And we, myself and the witches, are just as free to speak and act as the men are. Our heads are bared, no betrothal ensnares us; we are married to forces greater than any man who would quiet our voices.

"Brynja Bold-Tongue," she calls me. "Hair flaxen as

Sif's own and all the sense of Loki who stole it."

Pressing earth-stained fingers over my face, I muffle a laugh. The sky is iron grey through the branches that vein it, and in the distance, I can hear the ocean in its ceaseless whittling of the fjord's jagged rocks. When she stands above me, it is as though the sun has parted every cloud and come to rest only on me. Her hair is like a hearthfire, radiating warmth in copper curls that have never known a comb. It's lucky to have red hair—Thor does, and he looks on favor with those who share it.

Sometimes I think all the gods look on her with favor. It's the only way I could explain her.

"Surely they've found new quarry by now," I tell her, resting my hands against my stomach. The muscles tense beneath my fingers as she turns her head aside as though to listen for their voices, and hearing none, brings her dark eyes back to me. "You see? I wouldn't be worth turning over."

"But I know how you love hearth-duty," she teases. "Sitting up until dawn to stoke the fires so the crones don't fuss about their aching bones."

"I am kind enough of spirit to allow others to share that joy."

"Truly generous," agrees Eydis. "But what victory is mine, then, if not to hear your grumbling all night?"

"You might choose to hear another sound from me all night instead," I whisper, grinning.

She snorts and tosses her hair like a stroppy horse, but her eyes narrow in pleasure. "I get that already."

She isn't wrong—she rarely is—but the words still brook a shiver, like cold sudden rain across my skin. With her, I feel more moved by the gods than by any sea or storm, temple or glen. Eydis makes my ribs feel too small, my breath shorten, and all at once I feel as though I might crack like a jug, splintering and spilling heat across her feet. I rest a hand against her slender ankle and trace the delicate bones, following the swell of her calf through the soft scarlet hair that grows there.

I only reach her knee before she hums, and my hand stops. The hunt has not gone from her yet, mischievous and snared by a possessing thought as if during a *blot*. My own skills pale in compare, though my *galdr* are strong of voice and the runes are generous to me in their knowledge. But Eydis, she I have seen become other beings entirely: gods and men, elves and monsters. I have seen her eyes go mist white as she spoke truths that a farm girl could not have known. Seeress and *seidh* speaker, the gods whisper in her ear as if she were their own daughter, and so when a mood catches her, it is all I can do to follow where it takes her.

"You've won me already," I remind her, as if by voice alone I could bring her thoughts back to me. "You won me the night we both arrived from the farms, and you were the only one to come and sit with me at dinner."

"But still you ran," she teases, and I know there is no arguing with her until her curious mood is sated. I miss the softness of her skin the moment she steps away from me—my hand feels empty, my chest hollowed, though she is only a step or two away. "There is a practice."

"There is *always* a practice," I groan, flopping back onto the ground again with a wince. I pluck out a rock and toss it skidding down the hill, as she takes up a thin birch branch from the forest floor.

"There is a practice," continues Eydis, "in the regions west of the Rus, where boys chase girls with strips of goat hide." She shrugs out of the woven wool shawl that hid her snowdrift shoulders and tosses it aside.

"For what purpose?"

"Because they are awful." Her teeth flash as she turns another grin to me before shaking her head. What little sun is left turns to molten gold in her hair, and I strain to hear her preternatural wisdom rather than let myself imagine burying my face in her curls and whispering torrid, terrible things to her.

"Why, really?"

I roll to my stomach, arms folded beneath my cheek, and she wanders slowly back again. "They lash the girls' legs with them, and send them scattering, laughing, dripping goat's blood down their skin."

"When we make sacrifice, we use boughs to spray it all across the carvings so the gods can have it. It's all a mess," I tell her. "It pleases the gods. Do they do it to make the girls willing?"

"One assumes that is why boys do most things," grins Eydis.

"I wouldn't be particularly inclined after being flogged with bits of goat."

Her laugh finally breaks like the sun through clouds, glittering off the swift meadow brook of her voice. The fullness in my chest is nearly painful, and I squirm as if that might make it easier to love her so much. A funny thought, really, since I'm sure that loving her couldn't be any simpler than it is already.

"Brynja, think on it again, before you run away in your thoughts as you did on your feet." Eydis's scolding comes with the birch branch pointed at me. "Why do we give offering that way to the gods?"

"Because the *kona* tell us that's how it's done."

"No," she insists. "Why do we really?"

I grasp for Eydis's ankle and miss, then lunge again and hook a finger in the hem of her woolen dress. Reeling her towards me, I slip my arms around both her legs so she can't escape again. Her thigh is soft beneath my cheek and I shiver, suddenly warm.

I yield to her questions.

I yield to her.

"Because it brings their presence to the temple to receive the sacrifice," I answer obediently. "Because it makes the gods alive in Midgard, in the shapes we carve for them."

"Yes," Eydis whispers. I could moan when her slim fingers touch the messy knot of my hair and loosen it with one clever twist of her wrist. Her fingernails drag along my scalp, through my hair, and up the back of my neck. I do moan then, shameless, against the rough wool of her dress. "So when those girls are given sacrifice, does it not make them into living goddesses, too?"

"I'm sure the boys would tell them so."

"Brynja," she sighs, stamping an impatient heel against the ground.

"Yes." I give, I give, I always give, and I laugh against her leg. "Yes, maybe so."

Scraping against my thigh, the tip of her claimed wand follows high enough to catch my skirt. The white bark is spotted through with black — Freya's favorite tree, and she the goddess as much of ourselves as of our temple. It seems appropriate, then, that Eydis would tease me with a symbol of that fair lady, and so I do not stop her when she skims her birch branch higher. She follows the curve of my hip, bared where my skirt has slipped.

Whatever path her mind follows is once again obscured to me. My own want for her, stirring deep

7

between my legs, blinds me to anything beyond what is just before me. Her, her, always her. Since we sat beside each other as younger girls, freshly wrenched from far-flung farms and told we were to become messengers across nine worlds. Since we first shared a bed, pressed tight only for heat beneath each other's skinny limbs. Since we discovered that mouths can be warmer still than hands.

I press my forehead to her leg, my cheeks ember-hot as she taps the branch against my backside just hard enough to sting. "Eydis," I laugh. "I needn't bloody you with hide to make you a goddess."

My hands run high up the backs of her legs, and they tighten against her lithe thighs when she leaves another mark on my skin. It's enough for me to flinch, hissing between my teeth. I shift away from her gentle torment to sit on my knees instead, clearing out the rocks from beneath with a quick hand. My fingers are cold when I bring them to rest on her bare legs again, just beneath the curve of her backside, and her spine draws tight into a shiver.

Her eyes are shadowed by the wild drape of hair around her as she stands over me. Despite being shorter than me, despite being lean and fierce where I've instead grown broad and strong. I sit before her in joyous reverence to worship at her body as readily as I do her mind.

Eydis tosses the branch aside, insolent little goddess, and frames my face with her hands.

Freya should envy her.

I bend when she bends me. I move when she moves me. And so when she lowers her mouth against my own, my lips part to allow hers passage against them. Every breath I held in aching for her releases at once, every coil of tension she twisted into my belly unfurls. Rising to my knees, my hands seek her hair, soft as new lamb's wool, and I twist my fingers into her curls as if I was not already entirely ensnared.

Our tongues touch, just a brush, but it's enough that she makes a sound like a songbird, sweet and high and trembling. I cannot stand it, even this distance, and I catch Eydis by the knees to drag her, laughing, against my lap. She spreads her legs wide over my thighs, fingers smudging earth across my cheeks, and our brows touch.

"I want to see them," she whispers. My brow arches and I grasp her wrist. Her palm tastes of green grass and her fingertips of bark, her bones those of birds. I place her hand against my breast—enough to overfill her gentle grasp—and sigh when she thumbs across a peaked nipple.

"Not those," Eydis murmurs, laughing scarlet-cheeked, her eyes tidepool bright when she slips her arms around my neck instead. "I've seen those. I have them."

"Already you've lost interest in me," I mumble. Holding her around the waist, I tilt her back until she lets her body loosen, head lolling comfortably and neck bared for my mouth to explore with lips and tongue and teeth. "What do you want to see, Eydis Spirit-Speaker? Tell me and I will show you."

"Anything?"

"Anything," I swear, and as if our words were heard, the wind rises, quivering the trees and pulling at our hair and dresses. We do not fix them. We let our thighs press bare together, she astride my lap, and only when our skin heats do I realize that we are both moving, little motions to ease the tightening pleasure between our legs. "You see? Even the *alfar* want us to be bare."

"I want to see the girls," Eydis answers, laughing when

9

she sees the dark look I send her. "Not like I see you, but—their people, the Rus, all of it. I want to travel, Brynja, I'm tired of being here. Three winters long and what else is there to know? The gods talk to us now, not just through the *kona.* We should be teaching them rather than stoking their fires."

Nineteen winters alive and each of us, years before, sent here to become seers and *seidr*, soothsayers and spinners on the Norns's tangled loom of destiny. And have we not become that? The *volva* wander—we travel between farms and villages, through fields and mountains, past seas and lakes, to seek out those who need our conveyance between other worlds and this one.

Eydis speaks truth, and though the temple is comfortable and safe, it is hard to imagine that the gods have destined her for only that. She will make peace between families long bloodied in feuds; she will bless babies newly born and ships newly built. Crops will grow bountiful in her footsteps, and she will be treated with welcome and the highest seat wherever she goes.

"And what of me?" I ask, my hands stilled against her back, searching her eyes for news of my fate, and knowing that she must see it. It is a selfish question, but I hardly care when the thought of watching her go is enough to sunder me. I hardly hear her speak again over the tidal rush of my own blood in my ears.

"Come with me."

I swallow hard when she runs the backs of her fingers down my cheek. "You don't need me for any of this. The gods move in you. They move *you*."

Her eyes soften in the corners and she studies me as if in confusion, the crease in my brow, my lips parted slack. "I don't need you for that," she agrees. "I need you for me."

I nearly send us both down the hill when I press my head against her shoulder and squeeze her tight, skinny body bending against my own. "Eydis–"

"Who else is going to bring me back from *seidh*-saying? Who else will keep me from wandering off chasing *alfar*?" She answers with a little laugh, running her hands through my hair, down my back, the cause and ease of every shiver that shakes me now like winter winds. "Yours is the voice that carries through all nine worlds and brings me back to this one. Back to you."

She laughs when I can do no more than nod, again and again, and kiss her, again and again. "Brynja," she chides, tilting her head aside with a grin. "Where is your bold tongue now?"

"You have conquered it. You have your victory in its silence." I laugh too, knowing that if I do not, I will weep for joy instead.

Where My Heart Goes

Heather Rose Jones

Siena had fallen. The news spread quickly along the roads to Florence, to Milan, to Venice. It came to me in Parma on a pale spring morning with the clatter of a messenger's hoofbeats in the courtyard. After I paid and dismissed him, I hurried across the piazza to the cathedral to pray, clutching the pendant with Laudomia's portrait between my hands as if it were a holy relic. *Mother of God, let her be safe; let her be alive.* It had been nine years since we had spoken or written. Nine long years of my own making—I could admit that now. It was like the stain of sin on my soul that she might have died without forgiving me. Now all that was left to me was to wait and pray, but the only words that came to my lips were from that last poem she wrote for me: *May it not please God that I should ever live without my treasure! Ah cruel fortune, will you not arrange for my body to go where my heart goes?* And I remembered when we first met, twenty-two years before.

I never believed Laudomia Forteguerri when she called me goddess and praised my beauty. I knew what I was. I always remembered how they spoke of me as a girl in the Low Countries when I was still "the little bastard", before my father the emperor recognized me and betrothed me to a Medici and I became *Madama*. After that it wouldn't have mattered if I'd been hunchbacked or squint-eyed—though I wasn't. I was only very plain, with a bit too much of my father's lip and chin for beauty.

I never believed her when she said I was beautiful, but I believed her when she said she loved me, though I never knew why. It was easy to know why I loved Laudomia—everyone loved Laudomia. I loved her from that first day I saw her on the hot dusty road winding out of Siena as we passed Villa Olivia.

We should never have met. Rebellious Siena had not hung banners in my honor as so many towns had done on the road winding down from Verona through Mantua and on to Florence. I was tired—not tired of the gifts and fine gowns and being made much of. I was tired of sitting stiffly for hours before a crowd of strangers who spoke a tongue I couldn't understand. I was tired of the constant presence of my betrothed: a man whose mercurial temper frightened me, though he always spoke me fair. Florence—that queen of cities that I would next enter as a bride—had welcomed me with cheers and song and endless banquets...and sidelong looks of pity, and whispers and glances toward my future husband that were filled equally with hate and fear. But he had stayed behind in Florence and now I was only tired. I saw no other fate before me. I was eleven years old.

We were still five days from Rome. Siena had fallen out of sight behind us among the winding hills when a splintering crack was followed by men's shouts and women's screams. The first wagon of our cavalcade had lost a wheel and driven a second off the road into a ditch. Madame de Lannoy drew aside the curtains of my traveling chair and said, "You needn't fear, there's nothing lost. But it will be some hours to repair the wheel and they need to unload the wagons to set them right. Would Madama like to take the air?"

I liked Madame de Lannoy, who had been set to teach me what I would need to know as Duchess of Florence—and even more as the emperor's daughter. But a question from her was to be thought of as a command, and so I stepped down from my chair and looked to see where we had stopped. Just above the road stood a red-roofed villa, like many I'd seen dotting the hills all through Tuscany. Low walls spilled down toward the road, showing glimpses of tall junipers and close-clipped laurel trees. In the stillness of the noonday heat, once the uproar of the accident had faded, I could hear the sound of music and laughter from the gardens beyond. And when the men in charge of the wagons returned from the villa in company with a wheelwright and smith to survey the damage, they were followed by a small crowd of bright-gowned ladies, peeking curiously through the side gate from the gardens.

I still remember how Laudomia looked to me then: tall and elegant, her dark hair braided up with pearls and her eyes bright with laughter. Only seven years older than me, but so assured! She spoke quickly with Madame de Lannoy in Italian—which I still stumbled to understand—then turned to me and opened her arms with a smile as bright and inviting as a statue of the Madonna. Madame de

Lannoy said, "The Signora Forteguerri has invited you to take your ease while the wagon is repaired."

Some said it was only one more move on the chessboard—that knowing who I was, Laudomia had calculated what my friendship might someday be worth. That was a lie. Every moment of that brief visit is burned in memory. They sat me on a chair beside the fountain, with my ladies and Madame de Lannoy standing by to make certain of the proprieties. Three girls were singing to the strains of a lute while another pair danced. Laudomia made me a garland of roses with her own hands and then a garland of poetry with her own mouth. And when two men began a jesting debate on the movements of the spheres, Laudomia bade them speak only Latin so that I might understand.

I had stepped outside the world into a garden of delights as only a painter could imagine, where no time passed and no cares could reach us. But all comes to an end, and at last my chamberlain came to tell us that the wagons were ready. I needed no prompting from Madame de Lannoy to give my thanks for their hospitality and welcome. And before Madame could think to protest, Laudomia had bent to kiss my cheek and said, "Write to me and I will send you the little verse I made for you." From that moment my heart found a second home in Siena, wherever my body might lie.

She was beautiful—of course she was beautiful. But it was her soul I loved: that bright soul that burned like the Tuscan sun. And because of that, I believed her when she said she loved me too.

The Sienese villa faded like a dream when we arrived in Rome. But the pomp and splendor was left behind when we arrived at Naples. I became a girl again, with tutors and

16

lessons and endless study. When I was set to learn to write in the Italian tongue, I asked Madame, "Would it not be proper for me to write to Signora Forteguerri to thank her for her kindness to me?" And Madame consented.

Castel Pizzofalcone, Naples, 18 August 1533—My most esteemed Signora Forteguerri, I hope you will not laugh at the mistakes in my writing. The time I spent in your garden made me very happy. I beg you please to send the poem you made for me as you promised. Your friend, Margaret of Austria.

I did not see Laudomia again for five long years. Can one fall in love only through the written page? She sent me that first poem, followed by others. I read them to myself in moments when I was alone. I knew the words by heart before my Italian had mastered their meanings. I never wrote to Laudomia about important things. My letters would be read by many eyes before they reached her. I didn't tell her of my hopes when His Holiness died and it seemed the Medici marriage might be forgotten.

Castel Pizzofalcone, Naples, 2 December 1534—To the noble and wise Signora Forteguerri, It gave me great joy to hear of the birth of your daughter. I have sent with this letter a set of coral beads for her and hope that you will accept them. I have been reading the book you sent me of the Marchesa di Pescara's poetry, but I think that yours is better.

I said nothing when my father the emperor came to Naples or of the whispers that he would now marry me to the new pope's grandson. I pretended not to hear the rumors that my betrothed Alessandro had murdered his

17

cousin.

Castel Pizzofalcone, Naples, 15 June 1535—My most honored friend Signora Forteguerri, I thank you for the new verses you sent. It pains me to think that there is nothing I can write in return that would give proper recompense. As my own talents are so small, I send instead this small volume of Erasmus who, like me, comes to you from far to the north.

———⚜———

There was no need to tell her when I was wed to Alessandro de' Medici, so I only described the beautiful red velvet *zimarra* I wore when I entered the gates of Florence at midnight with rows of blazing torches lining the roads, and how kind all the people were, and what they served at my wedding banquet. I didn't tell her how one by one those around me were replaced by Alessandro's creatures.

Palazzo Ottaviano, Florence, 28 October, 1535—My beloved friend Signora Forteguerri, I write to ask your advice on what may seem to you a small matter. Monsignore Giuliani has asked to dedicate a volume of poems to me. They tell me I should permit it to be polite, but I do not think he is a very good poet. It may be that you have spoiled me for any other verses than yours. What would you advise? I wish that I could ask Madame de Lannoy, but she has returned to Naples. I long to have my friends about me and wish that I could see your face once more.

———⚜———

There were no letters to Laudomia in the confusion after Alessandro was murdered. She would not have expected that. I didn't tell her how Cosimo de' Medici kept me safe until my father the emperor removed my household to Prato and I could breathe again.

Palazzo Datini, Prato, 4 August, 1537—My dearest friend Signora Forteguerri, I have given thanks to God that you are again safely delivered of a daughter. We are settled comfortably here, though we have not the elegant refinements of Florence. If you know of a musician who could lighten my days, I beg you will send him here. I long to see you again. We ride out hunting in the hills above the town, and I sometimes wish to turn my horse's head south and not to stop until I come to Siena. If only I could join you in your garden, I think my heart could be at rest.

It was not Alessandro's death that weighed on my heart but the question of my next marriage. An ordinary widow might use the black veil to turn away men's eyes and thoughts, but I could never be ordinary. There was a new Farnese pope, and popes have ambitious families. Once again, I was to be the bridge to Rome and this time the choice fell on Ottavio Farnese, the Holy Father's grandson.

Palazzo Datini, Prato, 10 October, 1538—My beloved friend Signore Forteguerri, I am summoned to Rome at last. My noble cousin Cosimo de' Medici will come to fetch me, and I have begged him, as a sign of the affection he holds for me, that we might break our journey in Siena. Letters cannot take the place of your beloved face, which I hold in memory as if it had been yesterday. Please write to tell me that I may come. There is so much I cannot write in these pages that I long to say to you.

She had not changed in my eyes—I think she could never change. And if I had still been a girl of eleven in her mind, I saw that fall away as she greeted me on the steps of the villa and quickly discarded the stiffness of *Madama* for the warmth of *mia amica. Angelic beauty would not delight me more,* she had written me, and she made me believe it. Villa Olivia was given into my hands for my stay, and I in turn sat Laudomia at my right hand and her husband at my left.

After that first day, we left formality behind. The olive-dotted hillside called to my restless spirit, and we climbed up above the formal garden into the orchards. My ladies trailed behind, and we settled on a marble bench with the entire countryside spread before us.

"You're too young for widow's black," Laudomia laughed and twitched my skirts aside to sit as closely as clothing would allow. "Sixteen is far too soon to leave gaiety behind. Do you mourn Alessandro so deeply?"

"I rejoiced when I heard he was dead," I said. Here there was no one to overhear. No need for anything but truth. "Alessandro was a monster and Ottavio is a brutish boy. If a black veil would keep all suitors at bay, I could pretend to a broken heart. But I am an emperor's daughter; no one cares for my heart."

"I care." Laudomia took up my hand and pressed it to her lips. "You are the sun that graces these poor hills."

I didn't believe her, but I believed the longing that stirred within me. Words didn't matter. I only knew that she had no reason to say them except for love. My answer stumbled in confusion, uncertain what I desired. And then my ladies finally came in sight on the path, panting from the slope and looking affronted that I had outpaced them. The moment passed.

"How old were you when you were married," I asked Laudomia.

"Scarce seventeen."

"And are you happy?" I knew it wasn't a question one should ask. I had never looked to marriage for happiness.

"Marriage suits me," Laudomia said, but that was no true answer. "I love my children and my husband is kind." There was an empty space within her reply, and she searched my face for something to fill it. I didn't know what I might give and so I stood and we retraced the path back to the villa.

Laudomia's friends came to Villa Olivia the next day. Like bees they descended on the garden: poets and philosophers, musicians and artists, learned men and beautiful ladies. Though the year was beginning to turn, we filled the space around the fountain with couches and cushions, and tables spilling over with fruit, and braziers to keep the hint of chill away. There was wine and witty conversation, games of chess and dancing. Laudomia sat at my side again and held her cup for me to drink and slipped sweet grapes and comfit cherries between my lips until we giggled like girls. This was what I'd tried to build at Prato. Perhaps I would succeed in Rome.

"They've come in your honor," Laudomia whispered behind her hand. I knew better: they came to bask in Laudomia's sun. And like the sun, she bade them bloom and they obeyed.

"A poem!" one man entreated her. "We must have a poem from our Muse!"

"And which muse shall you have?" Laudomia answered playfully. "Shall I be Clio and recite histories for

21

you?"

"It is for you to choose," he replied with a bow.

"Then I shall be Sappho, the tenth Muse for you—my own translation." She turned to me and I felt her hand shake as she passed me the winecup. "I think he is a great man—like to God—who sits beside you." She held my gaze, and I felt her words like fingers on my skin. "Meeting you, I cannot speak, or see, or hear—I tremble and turn pale."

And I, too, trembled.

Later, when the twilight turned to true night and the gardens turned chill, when the dishes had been cleared from the tables and the braziers were being put out one by one, Laudomia took my hand and said, "I have one more poem to offer you tonight, if I may?"

She led me to my chamber, and our ladies unlaced our gowns and laid them aside and saw that the sheets were warmed and scented before retiring. Then she whispered verses closely in my ear—*I know well that you left heaven only to show me divine things*—and made poetry of her hands and lips playing across my skin, with even the finest linen of our *camisias* too great a barrier to allow.

The wind was chill the next day, and we made our garden in the hall with dancing and playful debates. At night she came to me again and taught my tongue new words. All thoughts of Rome and popes and marriages left me for days at a time. But time was a serpent in our garden. Too soon I was driven out of paradise.

"Write to me," I begged as they repacked the wagons and the men of my escort crowded the courtyard on restless steeds. "Write to me in Rome and remind me that you love me."

"I will tell the whole world I love you," Laudomia whispered. "And when you are acclaimed the queen of

Rome, do not forget your poor friend who longs for you."

⁓

Villa Madama, Rome, 6 June 1539—Carissima Laudomia, It is a fine thing, I find, to be the first lady of Rome. Ottavio troubles me not at all and I trouble him even less. The Farneses are not well loved here, and the people of Rome find it no fault in me to hold them at a distance. My father the emperor has named me Duchess of Camerino and Penne and given the governorship of Abruzzo into my hands. I am finally able to begin to order my life as I see fit. Your friend the painter Franzetti presented himself to me and I have set him to work on the frescos we discussed. In a year, the gardens here will be worthy of the guests I hope will fill them. In everything I do, my dearest wish is to honor what you have seen in me.

Laudomia was true to her word. She wrote poems for me openly now, her passion couched in the ordinary praise of princes. *Flow, ancient Tiber, and reflect the image of a brighter truer sun!*

⁓

Villa Madama, Rome, 10 January, 1540—To my beloved Laudomia, I send the portrait you requested by this messenger. I would not have delayed so long except for the need to find a worthy artist. Would that I could send myself! In summer when I travel to Camerino, I will pass your way.

⁓

Villa Madama, Rome, 23 November, 1540—Mia Carissima Laudomia, I beg you will pay no mind to the news you have heard and will visit me here as you have planned. The Farneses have been badgering me about that silly boy Ottavio, but my father the emperor is pleased, I think, that I keep him dangling. I keep the golden chain with your portrait always close to my heart, but the image will be a poor substitute if I cannot have the substance.

And Laudomia came as promised. I held a great banquet in honor of the astronomer Piccolomini who had dedicated his books to her, but it was truly to honor Laudomia herself. The people of Rome smiled to see us ride out together and called us *inseparabile.* It was a golden season—but seasons turn.

Villa Olivia, Siena, 1 March, 1542—My beloved friend Marguerita who allows me the joy to call her so, When I heard of the terrible news from Algiers, the one consolation that remained to me was to think that now we would both be widows together. I rejoice to know the rumors were mistaken and you are not doubly bereft of husband and father. You may not think it, but life can be hard for a woman left alone, and I at least have the comfort of my children. I pray for your continued health and that you may find some small space in your life to think of me. If you are able, I pray your steps will bring you to Siena soon. I know not when I may find myself in Rome again.

24

It was the next year before I was able to answer her plea. The gardens at Villa Olivia seemed to be in mourning themselves, the paths sodden with dead leaves and the branches bare, though it was only the late winter that made it so. We sat in her chamber with only a few ladies in attendance, listening to a mournful air. Laudomia was full of somber silences, and I knew nothing of the cause until I asked what I hoped would lift her heart.

"Join me in Rome," I urged. "Your life is your own now; share it with me."

She shook her head. "My darling Ghita, it is impossible."

I took her hand and warmed it against my cheek. "Nothing is impossible. Your daughters are married, your son is in the care of his grandfather. What is there left to keep you here? Who could need you as much as I do?"

"Marguerita, there is talk."

And what of that, I thought, but she laid a finger across my lips.

"They say you are bewitched—that enemies of the Farneses have made unholy bargains to keep you and Ottavio apart. They look for a place to lay the blame...and we have made no secret of our love. For now, the world holds us blameless: you are famed for holding yourself chaste from men and my love is praised as pure and noble. But what would they say if I came to you in Rome now?"

All my protests were in vain.

"Marguerita, you must be wise. Silence the whispers. Give your husband a child. It is long past time. And I...I will marry again. It is the only way."

That night when we were alone, I wasted the precious hours in rage and lamentation, but she would not be moved.

25

In time it becomes a sickness, I think—the desire to turn every step into a bargain. All my life I had been bargained away to others, and I learned to set my own price. I gave myself to Ottavio and gained nothing except a swelling belly. I paid my debt twice over, with twin sons quitting me of what I owed my husband. Should I not be rewarded with more? The Duchy of Milan was, perhaps, too much to ask. My father the emperor had turned his heart elsewhere. So I asked for something smaller. And I stumbled, not in the asking, but in writing to Laudomia before that gift too was denied.

Villa Madama, Rome, 24 February 1546—My dearest and most beloved friend, Soon, if my plans prosper, there will be no distance between us. My father is pleased to hear of my sons and I have asked him, in return, to grant me the governorship of Siena...

I had not thought what it might mean to her, beyond a chance to be together. I had not understood that every drop of blood within her veins was of the Noveschis, the founders of the Sienese republic who still clutched tightly to the dream of freedom. Laudomia's reply cut like an icy wind.

Villa Olivia, Siena, 3 March, 1546—To her grace the Duchess of Camerino, Is my home no more than another pawn upon your chessboard? Come to Siena as friend and guest or not at all.

Perhaps she should have made allowance. Perhaps I should have begged forgiveness. Perhaps and perhaps: the matter lay uncrossable between us, like the Alps in winter, for nine years. For nine years, I neither saw nor heard from Laudomia, not when one of my sons died, not when I was finally confirmed as Duchess of Parma, not when we both found ourselves besieged by enemies.

———

All of Italy was suspended between the Empire and France like a dog between two bones. But the bones had teeth. Siena was not the only city to cast their lot with France, and for that my father the emperor unleashed the Medici who hungered to extend their reach south. And my foolish husband, thinking I could stay the worst if it came, made secret treaties with France that earned him only empty promises. We, too, had a greedy neighbor, and my father gave Gonzaga license to lay siege.

I thought of Laudomia throughout that ordeal, hearing how she had lent all her wealth to build fortifications and had led a thousand women of Siena in defense of the city. The months dragged on, and Gonzaga fumed outside the walls of Parma while my father gave him orders to let wagons through that I should not starve. I thought how Laudomia knew no such mercy and wondered if she went hungry. When the tide turned once more and Gonzaga was ordered back to his kennel, I wrote in secret to the leader of the forces outside Siena.

Palazzo del Vescovo, Parma, 13 June, 1554—To my beloved friend, Cosimo de' Medici, Duke of Florence, It has been long years since I knew your kindness in those dark months after Alessandro was murdered, but I have never forgotten. I beg you, if there remains anything in your heart of the love you felt for me, to show mercy to one I hold more dear than life itself. Within the walls of Siena there is a lady of grace and beauty and more perfection than can be imagined. Her name is Laudomia

Forteguerri...

❧

Siena had fallen and I waited, hardly daring to hope. The news came at last as I walked in the garden on a warm day in April. The walls shut out everything but the twittering of sparrows. When the messenger was announced, I thought it must once more be news from Ghent where Ottavio had gone to make peace with my father. But then I saw the man wore Medici livery and my heart stopped.

"Madama," he said, bowing deeply and holding out a sealed letter. "My lord the Duke of Florence sends greetings."

My fingers trembled so that I could scarcely break the seal. I scanned the first few lines, passing over the empty salutations. *For the sake of our friendship, I send you a gift that I found within the walls after the surrender.* I read no further. "Where?" I demanded.

"In the wagon," he said. "Madama, there are conditions. You should read it all."

But I had picked up my skirts, heedless of dignity, and ran through the corridors to the courtyard to pull aside the curtains from the back of the wagon that stood there. Do not think that I would not have recognized her. I would have known her at the ends of the earth or the depths of hell. But I think she had been very near to the latter. The hand she reached to me was gaunt. I could feel every bone, and when I helped her from the wagon, only my arms kept her from stumbling. I buried my face in the hollow of her neck and could only sob "Holy Mother of God be praised" over and over again.

⁓

There were conditions.

"I am exiled from Siena," Laudomia said as I plied her with comfits and fresh oranges and every dainty thing she had forgotten could exist on the face of this earth. "From Tuscany—from any place the Medici hold sway. I should have been imprisoned, he said. To make an example. But then he asked if I would swear to accept exile, and he brought me out of the city in secret at night and set me in a wagon…"

I took her hand and stroked it. "And your husband?"

She shrugged. "He fled to Montalcino with the others. Hope maintains them, but I think France will do so no longer." Laudomia looked up at me, her hollow eyes full of uncertainty. "What is to become of me?"

I had asked the same question for myself so often in the dark of night, praying for guidance. Would she be willing to follow my path? "We are reconciled with my father once more, for the moment. He has traded peace in Parma for the custody of my son. I have been told to make ready to bring Alexander to him in Brussels. I have thought—" This I had not yet spoken to any mortal soul. "I have thought to remain in the Low Countries. God knows I cannot even see my own fate, but will you share it with me?"

She smiled, a thin smile like the winter sun striving against clouds.

⁓

A year passed before we set out: a cavalcade to rival

the one that had brought me to Italy twenty years before. This time I shared my traveling chair, not with the stiff and formal Madame de Lannoy, but with the lady of my chamber. As the roofs of Parma disappeared behind us I said, "There is a garden at the palace of Coudenberg, walled in with hedges of yew and eglantine. In the spring the paths are lined with crocus and hyacinth. The scent of apple-blossom from the orchards drifts through the air like angel song. In the summer, it will be filled with music and poetry. Will it please you, do you think?"

Laudomia nestled closely against me. Her arm curved about my waist and her lips brushed my neck as she whispered, "My heart goes there; it gives me joy to follow."

In Full Moon Light

Patty G. Henderson

People were running, their angry voices shouting holy verses to the heavens. Prudence Crandall ran among them, not part of the call for punishment, merely caught up in the mob that seemed to carry her along like a wave of moving flesh.

"Witch. Harlot. Wicked woman!" Their voices pierced the cloudy and murky Salem morning.

Prudence knew where they would end up. Gallows Hill. Gallows Hill, a place Prudence only heard in whispers. A place they hanged women convicted of witchcraft and consorting with the devil. Prudence never knew what to believe. She'd spent all her childhood in a cramped home for abandoned children. She'd never known the love of a mother or a father, only the cruelty of the harsh Puritan ways. She knew only that a man by the name of Crandall had begged she be given shelter. Had that been her father? She barely spoke for fear of retribution were she to say something wrong. No, Prudence only developed her speaking skills when she braved escape and ran, ran like a

31

wild animal into the forbidden deep woods of Salem. She found life, salvation in the woods. She found Abigail.

Gallows Hills was worse than Prudence imagined, even in a fevered state. The stench of urine and other bodily fluids seemed to emanate from the actual wooden planks. She would never forget the stink of the bucket room at the orphan house. Filled to the brim with days of use that rarely got emptied, buckets of urine and waste sat the length of the room. It was a smell she had not learned to expel from her nostrils.

The light rain of the morning had made the ground thick with mud and muck. Her shoes, riddled with holes, were heavy with wetness.

The people huddled and stood staring at the older woman standing atop the wooden flooring, the hanging rope swaying in the intensifying wind that blew in from the harbor like an ill omen.

She recognized the frail old lady atop the gallows. The woman's eyes darted across the crowd like those of a hunted deer. Mary Simpson had been a widow for as long as Prudence could remember. She'd kept to herself and had more cats than most considered prudent. The cats did no harm and seemed to bring joy to the old woman's life.

Prudence swallowed down the fear in her throat. What could the dear Goody Simpson have done to deserve a hanging? Surely, she could not have been accused of witchcraft?

Two men, stone-faced, lean and commanding in their severe black coats and hats, stood beside her, a Bible in each their hands. Prudence did not recognize them, for she rarely came into Salem Village after first escaping, fearing she would be recognized and thrown into the gaol. She pulled the hood of her threadbare cloak further down her face.

"Goodwife Mary Simpson, you have been accused and convicted of performing spells of witchery and of consorting with familiars. What have you to say before your sentence is carried out in the name of Our Lord Almighty?" The man closest to the old woman spoke in a loud, solemn voice.

Prudence stood spellbound by the spectacle before her. She knew there was danger the longer she stayed and that Abigail would be worried and scold her dearly once she got back, but she could not break free. She'd never been witness to a hanging. Her heart bled for poor Goody Simpson. Was there no one to stand up for her character? Her innocence?

The desperate sound of the old woman's voice brought Prudence out of her thoughts.

"I am your neighbor, your friend, dear good people of Salem. You know I am not a witch but merely an old widow. My husband was a carpenter and helped build some of your homes." Her eyes pleaded as she searched the crowd below her. "Ye know who I am. Ye knew my husband and we both sat at your holiday table and gave thanks for the food and the shelter. Please, I am not a witch!" Her last words were a raspy screech.

Prudence was frightened. The crowd surrounding her shifted but remained silent, mumbling amongst themselves. But not one voice was raised in defense of Mary Simpson.

The other Elder standing beside Goody Simpson spoke loudly, pointing a finger at the old woman.

"Name the witches, witch. The Lord, in his greatness, might offer mercy to your soul if you provide his servants with the names of other witches." He paused, and suddenly flung the heavy Bible he held upon the chest of Goody Simpson. The old woman nearly fell over from the blow.

"The names, witch, or suffer the fires of Hell for all eternity." His voice boomed across the hill.

"I will name them," her weak voice rang out. Her body trembled as if she would fall apart and faint.

It was then that Prudence ran. She ran, shoving and elbowing her way through crazy people, ran through the stinking road, ran as fast as she could into the mighty woods, never looking back. She had to get away from the ugly scene she'd witnessed. The fear began to gnaw at her. Goody Simpson had been close to her beloved, Abigail. Would she name her? The old woman would be tortured until she had no choice. The thought of Abigail's name thrown into that crowd of hungry animals was enough to cause her to scream as she ran. What if they came for Abigail? What if they came for her? She ran faster, looking behind her to make sure no one had followed.

As the humble wooden cottage with the thatch roof came into view, Prudence slowed her pace and looked once more behind her. She had to make certain no one had found their safe home. She practically ran through the door, rushing to stand, out of breath, in the center of the tiny room

"They've hanged Goodwife Mary Simpson!" she said, taking deep breaths and exhaling. "No one stood to proclaim her innocence."

The tall, lean woman with wild, unruly midnight hair rose from the wooden chair, leaving the large cauldron she'd been stirring. It bubbled quietly over a steady, burning fire.

"Calm down, Prudence, or you'll lose your breath

entirely." She smiled, and eyed Prudence with deep gray eyes.

"But Abigail," continued Prudence, not able to contain the anxiety she felt. "They..." she paused, re-living the images of the Puritan Elders standing atop the hanging scaffold like scavenger black birds. "Those horrid men forced names from her lips, names of other witches. Lies. She lied, believing it would save her soul. And your name..." she paused again, her eyes wide with fear. "Your name was surely upon her lips."

Abigail drew Prudence close, slipped strong arms around her waist, and kissed her softly upon her lips.

"Now, my darling Prudence, have I not taught you to avoid the masses in Salem Town and in the Village? They will do us no good, only harm."

Prudence sank deep into Abigail's embrace, savoring the scent of herbs and earth in her Abigail's simple blouse, and relishing the heady feel of safety in her lover's gentle voice. Yet the thought of Abigail, or even herself, standing atop Gallows Hill, was too strong to allow Prudence rest.

"Will they come looking for you, Abigail? You did not see the bloodlust in those men's eyes or hear the hate in the voices of Salem's own people, people you have aided as often as did Goody Simpson."

Prudence searched Abigail's calm face. How did she harness such power to remain without fear, without panic or doubts?

She'd known Abigail Black was considerably older than she when Prudence had come barging into the poor and modest cottage deep in the Salem woods. Prudence had escaped the cruel Fogg House, where orphaned children were put to work as slave labor, spinning wool, chopping wood, and tending to the Fogg family duties. In turn, they were given a threadbare blanket, lumped in a crowded room to find space where you could find it on the floor. The food was shared among them, but there was so little of it that many went hungry.

Yes, she'd run from the Fogg House. Old man Fogg had set his bloated eyes on her, and she wasn't about to wait to find out if the rumors of what he did to teenage girls were true or not. She ran. It mattered little if she was caught and punished by the Foggs or thrown in jail. Prudence had to make a break for a chance at freedom. She ran into the woods. Ran into Abigail Black's house and into her arms.

"Come, my darling girl," Abigail said softly as she guided Prudence to the chair in front of the glowing hearth. "Come, sit here with me." She cast Prudence a sidelong glance, a sly smile upon her lips. "Look what I've prepared for supper."

Prudence followed Abigail and inhaled the aroma of the scrumptious stew in the pot. Little frothy bubbles floated at the top, the strong smell of chicken and carrots making her stomach growl. She'd forgotten how hungry she was.

But how could she eat when Salem was hanging innocent women and coercing lies from their lips in order to incriminate other innocent people? What villainy and evil had come to Salem? Prudence knew Goody Simpson was no witch. And what was a witch anyway? Was it something the Puritans had invented for some kind of sick revenge on those they wished to remove from their village? Was it the land and property people like Goody Simpson owned that the fearmongers coveted? Prudence was convinced that their lives were in mortal danger.

Abigail sat down, pulling Prudence into her lap and

gently running her hand through her golden locks.

"Have I not provided for you, given you my love, my heart, my body, my home, and kept you safe from harm?" She eyed Prudence with a gentle smile in her eyes.

Yes, Abigail had done all of those things and far more. She had saved Prudence. She owed her lover her life. Prudence cuddled further into Abigail's strong arms.

"And you know I am not unappreciative. Please forgive me if I appear ungrateful. I just worry so about your safety." She kissed Abigail lightly on the lips.

Abigail took Prudence's face in her hands. "We are safe. We will never part. They cannot harm you if you are at my side, our hearts united, my darling. Just know this and be at peace."

Abigail returned Prudence's kiss hungrily, wrapping up her small frame and crushing her tighter. Prudence felt the fire grow inside her. Abigail suddenly raised Prudence into her arms, their passion flaming hotter than the blaze that burned in the hearth. Prudence clung to her lover, her legs wrapped around Abigail's waist. As they stumbled toward the small bedroom, Prudence entertained one fleeting thought of the boiling pot left behind.

"But supper—"

Abigail covered her mouth with lips that tasted like fire.

"Supper can wait."

<hr />

After a night of lovemaking, a full belly of steaming chicken stew, and blissful respite from the horrifying scenes at Gallows Hill, Prudence woke to the cranky rooster outside and an empty bed.

Why had Abigail not awakened her? Was all well? Alarmed, Prudence dressed hastily in a plain gray shift, wrapped the white apron about her waist, pulled back her hair haphazardly, and rushed out the cottage door.

It was true that the sunshine of the *morning after* always made things feel beautiful and right, especially as she spotted Abigail in the small garden a short distance from the cottage. The sun managed to sneak through the towering trees in the thick forest and cast bright rays that sliced down in a shower of light on the little patch of garden.

Abigail was on her knees, her well-worn bonnet atop her head, planting new squash. Prudence exhaled and rushed out to grab the tall woman from behind. She wrapped her arms around Abigail's shoulders.

"Why did you not wake me? I would have been out here by your side, although I would have preferred helping myself to you in our warm bed."

Abigail smiled wide and tucked in the loose strands of blond curls left dangling around Prudence's face.

"But then we'd gotten not a shred of work done and lost the whole of the morning sun to plant and feed the chickens." She pointed to the small fenced area beside the cottage. "Go on now, feed the chickens or we'll have no eggs or fowl on our plates."

Prudence frowned but knew Abigail was right. Playing in bed was far more satisfying than tending to the land, but out here in the wilderness, you made the best of what the land gave you and worked hard to bring the fruit of those labors to bear. It was a cruel environment, but Abigail Black seemed to have worked magic on this little piece of land. How she made anything grow out here was beyond Prudence's understanding of farming. But then again, she knew nothing of what it took to grow crops. And she had no idea where the chickens had come from or the vegetables, corn, and fruits growing in the garden. She only knew that Abigail provided for both of them, and she was honored to be able to lend her help in whatever was needed. It had all been here when she showed up at Abigail's door, and it wasn't polite to question her. Quite frankly, Prudence didn't care. This was the closest thing to a patch of heaven on Salem's good earth, and she wasn't about to go poking into the how or the why.

Prudence reluctantly left and worked her way to the fenced pen, took a pail, filled it with the feed from a barrel, and began spreading the food to the handful of chickens and the raucous rooster. She was thankful Abigail had no pigs. Prudence would not relish the caring or feeding of pigs.

She'd almost finished feeding the chickens when she noticed Abigail walking slowly towards her, casting careful eyes toward the outskirts of the woods. Prudence, uneasy, went to meet her at the fence.

Abigail's face was calm, but her deep dark gray eyes revealed apprehension, and her lips quivered with an unnatural smile.

"Do not be frightened, dear Prudence. There is a man at the wood's edge, believing he is hidden behind an elder tree. We are no longer alone here. Please act as if we do not know he is there and finish feeding the chickens. I will await you inside."

With her emptied basket in hand, Abigail left her and disappeared round the cottage, leaving Prudence alone with chickens and a stranger hiding in the woods with prying eyes. He was most likely spying for the Elders of Salem Village. With heart ready to explode from her chest,

Prudence managed to finish the feed and tried her best to not run like a scared rabbit back to the cottage. She did her best to appear routine.

Once inside, she found Abigail wiping the dirt from her hands, bonnet flung on the floor. It was Abigail who would calm her. It was Abigail who would save them. This Prudence knew and believed.

"Do you think he is from Salem Village?" Prudence asked, holding back the fear.

Abigail nodded. "He is most assuredly from the village. No one gets lost out here. They come for a purpose, good or harmful." She rushed toward Prudence and wrapped her up in her arms. "But now is not the time to turn our backs in fear, my love. I need you to listen to and follow my words. We will always be safe. No harm will come to you as long as you are mine."

She tipped Prudence's chin up to face her and looked deep into her eyes. "He will bring them to our humble home. They will come as accusers, and there could be many who will come with them. The blood lust in Salem is boiling, and I cannot promise that we won't be taken away to gaol. But I can promise that as long as we are not separated, no harm shall come to thee."

Abigail kissed Prudence softly. Prudence had never felt more secure than in the arms of Abigail Black. She'd never doubted her and wasn't going to start. She hugged her and clung to her, inhaling the fresh scent of the earth on her clothes.

"I will go with you to the ends of the earth, my darling Abigail."

"I am no witch. I am Godmother to half the newborns in Salem Village. I give you ointments to soothe your burns and the pox upon your flesh." Abigail eyed the crowd of women and men with steely grey eyes. "Your women have become fertile and have birthed healthy and plentiful children for Salem because you came begging for my fertility potions."

She pointed into the crowd at no one in particular. "And you now come with pitchforks in your hearts to falsely accuse me of witchcraft? Well, I say to thee, you are all as guilty as I then, for each of you who have come to my door in the middle of a dark moon have partaken of witchery." The scowl of contempt that twisted her face was so fierce that some women pulled back. "Witches, the lot of you, then!"

Yes, they had come. A near dozen men and women from Salem Village and two of the black-clad Elders Prudence recognized from the hanging. They came knocking on their cottage door that day at sun's setting. Some of the women, most hiding behind their husbands and other men, had once come to Abigail seeking aid in childbirth, and many others had come seeking help. Never in her wildest dreams did she imagine they would turn on Abigail and come as accusers.

The Elder with the stone face and tight jaw glared at Abigail, not wishing to relinquish the situation after her strong and intimidating words. He pointed his own finger at her.

"Abigail Black, you stand accused of using witchcraft. There is proof from statements of the Godly citizens of Salem Village that you did indeed engage in unnatural magic, achieved only by turning your soul over to Satan and his evil. By the laws of Salem Village, you are entitled

41

to a trial—"

"There will be no trial and I will not leave my home. I am innocent. My soul does not belong to your God or to your Satan. My soul is mine and is as free as the air we breathe and as eternal." She cast her steely gaze upon the crowd once again, then turned to the Elders. "Now, be gone before I set the wrath of my familiars upon you."

Several of the women covered their eyes and scurried off. Some of the men looked lost, crowding closer to the frozen Elders. It was nearly dark now, and the deepening night cast crooked shadows on the faces of the men with the tall black hats and wide brims.

"You will face the judgment of God Almighty, Abigail Black, as will that child whom you have consorted with unnaturally and brought to Satan as a servant of his ways," said the shorter, frog-faced Elder. His jowls bounced in anger. "You two will not escape the gallows."

They turned away in a huff, and all disappeared like furtive, twilight wolves into the darkness of the woods. Prudence followed Abigail closely as she slammed the door shut behind her.

"Abigail, you don't really have familiars, do you?" Prudence had to make sure her lover jested.

Abigail turned and smiled, a smile that seemed too sad to Prudence.

"Not in the plural, darling Prudence." The twinkle in her eyes confused Prudence.

"But, you are not a witch...Abigail, their accusations, they say witches consort with familiars from the devil and all sorts of horrible things."

Abigail pulled her close. "Darling, I am not a witch. I am not the witch they have created from their warped religious fervor and obsessions. I am not a witch who even

42

knows of what devil they speak..." She lowered her gaze and looked at the floor, before pinning Prudence with her dark grey gaze, her voice a low, husky whisper. "Why don't I show you what you need to know before it is too late."

Abigail took her lover's hand and guided her to the small cabinet near the hearth. There was one panel on the cabinet that was not a door but a panel of decorated wood. Abigail crouched down and suddenly began to chant words Prudence did not understand, and waved her hands and fingers in mysterious motions.

Prudence inhaled in shocked surprise. Before her appeared a secret door where there had been none. She looked from Abigail to the new door in the cabinet in stunned silence.

"A spell of illusion to hide the most important thing a witch will ever own." Abigail held her gaze while she flipped open the door and pulled out a weathered, leather bound book, held shut with leather ties. "My Book of Shadows. My book of life."

She held the book in her hands and offered it to Prudence. "Forgive me my sweet darling, for not revealing my true path. I had to be sure and the time right..." She paused, a wistful smile upon her full lips, her eyes moist. "That time has come, for the both of us."

Prudence was struck mute. In confusion, she looked to her Abigail, her savior, for answers.

"You...you told them you were not a witch, yet this is surely magic that I behold."

"I did not lie, my sweet child. I am not the witch they seek to hang. I have explained that to you. I practice the old magic of seers and healers and pagans of long past. I worship no god, no deity, no devil. And I do no evil." Abigail pressed the book to her chest and came to stand before Prudence. "You must not doubt me or allow distrust to fester. It could part us and I will not be able to keep you with me." Her gaze bore into Prudence, a pleading tear trickling down her cheek.

Prudence reached up to wipe it away. "You have been as an angel sent from above to give me life and everything I need to be happy. How can I doubt you now?"

The kiss they shared was deep and filled with longing, and when the two parted, Abigail took Prudence's hands and placed them upon the rough leather of the book, while she held the book from beneath. Her gaze remained intently upon the blue of Prudence's eyes as she whispered ever so lightly.

"Together we are bound, souls forever, in spirit, in flesh, in eternity, in time, by blood and by heart, by body, light surround, dark departed, death defeated." She paused and smiled gently, and nodded toward the book. "Repeat my words, my precious Prudence, and we shall live without fear always."

Prudence's knees trembled and she feared she would buckle from the beating of her heart and the heat enfolding her entire being. Now was no time to distrust Abigail. She knew with all her heart that Abigail would never lead her to ill deeds. Prudence repeated the words Abigail had spoken.

As she uttered the last word and it faded into the shadows of the barely lit cottage, Prudence saw a slight shimmer come across the cover of the book Abigail had called The Book of Shadows. Her hands still upon it, the cover felt warm and then suddenly cooled. What had happened? Was it magic? But what did Prudence know of magic? She was confused, yet still marveled at how safe she felt.

"I must bury this book deep on the outskirts of Salem Village heading north, away from Salem, for we shall travel by the light of the full moon that will grace our heavens in several days. I will be able to claim it back at that time. You will stay here while I do this task and wait for me. But beyond tonight, I cannot keep you from the horrors that await us, my Prudence."

Abigail kissed Prudence once more. "They will come for both of us tomorrow and they will put us through every cruel mental and physical torture they feel will allow for a show of power and their own perverted justice. They have their trumped spectral evidence and will convict us. It is their way. They will hang us at Gallows Hill, dearest Prudence—"

Prudence shivered uncontrollably. "But no, you said—"

"Shh, no, darling..." Abigail covered Prudence with kisses to quiet her fear, her confusion. "I promised we would never be apart, that we would walk away in freedom from this place, from this time. Believe me. Do not let go of my hand. Never."

Prudence buried her face in Abigail's chest, her tears running free. And she never let go of Abigail's hand.

<hr />

Abigail Black and Prudence Crandall were hanged on Gallows Hill. And they remained silent in the face of death and in the prayers uttered for their souls. Prudence and Abigail refused to have their faces covered and instead, confounded the arrogant Elders by standing steady, both holding hands. Their hands were so tightly wound together, that not even the hangman could separate them.

In the evening, on a night where a full moon blazed cool in the darkest sky, when the two men came for the bodies to dump in the shallow graves away from consecrated cemeteries, they ran away instead, screaming in fear to the church, seeking prayers for their souls. But the Elder and the minister were already dealing with a most perplexing and vexing situation.

Apparently, Good Servant William Fogg was nearly mad with fear, thinking he'd been possessed by the spell of the witches Abigail Black and Prudence Crandall.

"Has the witchery taken your very souls, men?" the Elder pleaded. "How can what you three men say be possible? Both Abigail Black and her unholy consort, Prudence Crandall, were both hanged until dead for their practice of witchcraft. We both saw it, the entire Village saw them hang." His eyes were wide with frustration as he searched the faces of the three frightened men. "Mr. Fogg is feverish with tales of seeing both witches floating along the road, their feet barely touching the ground below. And you two cannot find their bodies! Has Satan taken hold of all of Salem?"

Fogg was blathering, barely focusing, his eyes glazed over. "I swear to the Lord in Heaven or my soul may he take this night. I saw them, the both of them, nearly dancing with glee, and Abigail Black holding a big book. But the Lord smite my eyes, they were floating I tell you. In full moon light I saw them floating down the road north of Salem Village."

Emma

Priscilla Scott Rhoades

My father had wanted a boy to work our farm in Mush Creek, South Carolina, and when my mother had borne me, her fifth girl and last child, he was furious with us both. As time passed, I proved to be more like a son than a daughter in nearly every way. Yet my father resented me even more for my boyishness and took every opportunity to express his displeasure in words and gestures and with his belt.

For her part, my mother remained passive, suffering from the Consumption that would end her life too soon. To her credit, she taught us girls to read and write and to regard knowledge as a good in itself. When I was thirteen years of age, she gave me a secret book entitled *Fanny Campbell, the Female Pirate Captain.* I took it to the fields to read, safely away from my father's watchful eyes. When I had finished, I felt as if I had been emancipated from male tyranny. My infant soul had been impressed with a sense of my mother's wrongs, and now I vowed never to let myself suffer the same fate.

When I was seventeen, my mother passed from this

earth. She had not been buried a month before my father promised my hand in marriage to a widowed neighbor many years my senior. With no one to take my side, I saw no alternative but to run away. I cut my hair short, put on my father's clothes, rolled up at cuff and elbow and his boots made snug by double socks, and fled from the MacIntyre Farm.

⁓

Mr. Foote is a short fellow, a foot shorter in height than I, and of less sturdy frame. He dresses like a man of some importance in a bleached-white shirt, dark trousers, and a frock coat. Introducing himself by his full title—Mr. Thomas Albert Foote, M.A.—he asks my name. This is something I have not considered, and I offer the first thing that springs to mind.

"Frankie Campbell," I say.

"And you are here about the position?"

"I am, sir."

He is referring to the advertisement in *The Highland Messenger*:

HELP WANTED. Young man from 15 to 17 years of age, able to tend a garden, take care of a horse, and generally make himself useful. Contact Mr. Foote, The North Carolina School for the Deaf, Morganton.

"And your age?"

"Seventeen, sir."

"And where are you from, Mr. Campbell?"

"From Mush Creek, South Carolina."

"You are a long way from home, young man. What brings you to Morganton?"

"Work," I say. "My mother is dead of the Consumption, and my father has gone off to fight in the War." This first is true enough, but the last is a necessary lie. At this information a frown creases all the features of his face.

"Terrible thing that," he says. I believe that here he is referring to the War of Northern Aggression. "And your qualifications?"

"I can outwork, outshoot, and outride any boy I've ever known," I tell him. This is God's truth, although I suspect he would be more impressed if he knew the whole of it.

"I see," he says. "Well, Mr. Campbell. Do you know anything of this institution?"

I admit I do not. He seems not a bit surprised by my answer and goes on, almost before I have finished speaking.

"During the summer of 1843," he begins as if he has given this speech many times before:

"I conceived the idea of attempting to establish an institution for deaf-mutes in North Carolina. At that time I was the principal of the Virginia School for the Deaf in Staunton..."

And here I listen as Mr. Foote explains how he had so impressed the North Carolina Legislature with his demonstration on the proper way to educate a deaf-mute that they were inspired to pass a bill requiring the building of such an institution in this state.

"The first day of May 1845 the School was opened with seven students," he continues.

"Today we house thirty-nine—twenty girls and nineteen boys aged six to seventeen. Our students are enrolled in vocational classes that include sewing for the girls and shoemaking for the boys. At this School we use the Language of Signs as the ordinary means of communication. You will not be required to learn American Sign Language but if you so desire, instruction will be arranged with one of our older students."

"Yes, sir," I say. "Does that mean I have gained the position?"

"It does," he replies.

⚬

My room is in the basement of the School's three-story brick building, on the Boys Ward. I have been given a uniform of trousers and a shirt, both butternut in color and sewn by the School's girls, along with an undershirt, drawers, wool socks, and a new pair of brogans, pegged and stitched by the School's boys. I have worn the same clothes since I left Mush Creek and am sorely in need of a change. But before I am allowed to dress, I am shown a tub of hot water, into which I am expected to immerse my naked self. At this demand, I adopt a modest demeanor, pretending to be a youth unaccustomed to revealing himself to others. I have assumed the role of a boy for so long that it seems most natural to me by now, and only on occasion am I reminded that I do not have a boy's body. Mr. Foote accepts my dodge without question.

After I am clean and dressed, I am told my duties, which seem to follow most closely the "generally make himself useful" portion of the advertisement in the *Messenger*. It appears that I will be asked to do what most urgently needs doing on a day-by-day assessment. Like the students, I will be awakened each morning at 5:00 a.m. and fed breakfast in the Dining Hall. Following breakfast, students will attend classes, and I will begin chores. As good Christians, we are all required to attend Chapel each day at 9:00 a.m. Lunch is at noon, dinner at 6:00 p.m. After dinner I am free to do as I please until lights go out at 9:00 p.m.

There is something else I should know, Mr. Foote says. "Staff are not to fraternize with students," he admonishes and checks to see if I have appreciated his meaning. "There is a line to be drawn," he adds in case I haven't. I assure him I will not cross this line. Furthermore, I am accustomed to keeping to myself and will use my free time wisely. "For private study," I assure him. I sense that he does not entirely believe me. Yet he nods in seeming acceptance. He hands me a Bible, a journal of blank pages, a quill pen, and a bottle of ink, saying these are mine to use in reflection and personal betterment. And with that my new life begins.

This being the Journal of Frankie Campbell, today being the tenth of June in the year 1861, I write here now. I have been in the employ of the North Carolina School for the Deaf in Morganton for one week. During this time I have surmised that I am well-suited to my duties, which are many and varied. After living under my father's hand for so long, life here is a great deal less punishing.

The School sits on an estate of many acres, and as there is light yet in these summer evenings, I have taken to walking the grounds and into the woods after dinner. I find great comfort there in the sounds of Nature, whose music soothes me when I feel most alone. I sometimes think of Mush Creek and wonder if my father has given chase. I know his fits of rage, and my absence has surely provoked his anger. But my thoughts rest uneasy on him, and they soon return to more soothing things—the river on rocks, the call of a screech owl.

The seventeenth of June. Mr. Foote informs me that he expects a new student to arrive today. I am at work in the Rose Garden when I notice the approach of a buggy bearing two figures. I return my attention to pruning, and when I look up again I see her coming toward me down the path. A white dress billows around her like a sail, and in her hand she carries a white bonnet. At her elbow strides a gentleman bearing a protective, paternal air. They walk by me, and I observe her as she passes.

What I notice first are her eyes, which glance my way. They are gray and green and in the morning light they seem almost transparent. Then her mouth: her lips are not painted and yet they are red as cherries. I am drawn to those lips as if by some magnetic field. Her hair is dark and parted in the middle, pulled back and tied with a white ribbon. Her skin is pale as wisp of cloud. At the sight of me she blushes.

"Morning," I try to say. My mouth seems to have filled with wet cotton. I bow in courtesy and then remember my rank. I dip my head a little lower. *Staff are not to fraternize with students.*

The rose in her cheeks deepens to the color of summer apples.

"Morning," the gentleman allows, nodding in return.

Mr. Foote appears, holding the door for them as they enter.

"Dr. Leventhorpe," I hear him say. "And Emma. Welcome. I trust you had a good journey..."

Emma. I am left standing among the buds and thorns, dumbstruck as my fellows.

She is a beautiful youth of sixteen who has been deaf

since childhood. "Spotted fever," Dr. Leventhorpe tells Mr. Foote in explanation. Her mother died in the labor, and so the country doctor has raised his only child alone. Dr. William A. Leventhorpe is soon to be Officer Leventhorpe, as he has just enlisted in the First Regiment Infantry, Company G. He and the rest of the Burke Rifles will march out to Virginia on the twenty-fourth. There is no one in Burke County he trusts to watch over his deaf daughter, and he fears that she will be unsafe in his absence. Mr. Foote assures Dr. Leventhorpe that Emma will be in good hands here at his School for the Deaf. I learn all this by standing at the door to Mr. Foote's office, where I pretend to polish wood.

Emma may remain at the School until she comes of age in two years, but surely the War will be over before then. They both agree that the Union will cease its offensive against the South once Mr. Lincoln comes to his senses. When that happens, Officer Leventhorpe will return to the School to take Emma home.

The eighteenth of June. Growing up as the youngest of five girls, I watched as each of my sisters took a husband and left my father's farm. They were not bad men, the men my sisters married; yet they were men nonetheless, and I saw no appeal in any of them. The delight my sisters found in Romance escaped me, and I thought of girls who indulged in such illusions as silly, light-headed things. I never pictured myself with a male, the mere thought of which turned my stomach inside out. Certainly, I never pictured myself with a female either, as such imaginings were unnatural and against God's law, or so I had read in the Bible.

Now everything has changed. My sisters had told me that when it was my turn for Cupid to pull back his bow, I would be powerless against his darts. I had thought such musings nonsense—until now. Now a gold-tipped arrow has pierced my heart, and on that arrow there is a name inscribed: Emma.

The twentieth of June. I make my first visit to the School's Library today. There I find *Theory of the Signs* by Abbé Sicard, an illustrated book of the deaf alphabet. I also find a collection by my mother's favorite poet, Robert Burns. I note these in the Library's ledger as "borrowed" and take them to my room.

My room is small, yet it assures me of a privacy I have never known. In the evenings when I have finished my walk, I study the Language of Signs by candlelight until I hear "Lights out!" I struggle to shape my hands, which feel calloused and clumsy. I fold my fingers to my palm—A. I hold them straight up—B. I cup them to form the letter C...

I picture Emma's hands, the skin so pale and smooth it nearly shines, the nails clean and white. Sometimes at meals, I watch her from across the room as she Signs with the other girls. Her hands sweep the air like wings, like birds fluttering from her wrists. I think of Emma and I read again the words of the poet:

But Delia on thy balmy lips
Let me, no vagrant insect, rove;
Oh, let me steal one liquid kiss!
For oh! My soul is parched with love.

The twenty-first of June. Each morning at 8:30, a break is given for students and staff to prepare ourselves spiritually for Chapel. During this time I sit on an iron park bench in the Rose Garden. It is a fine time of day; the summer air is not yet too warm, the dew is still on the buds, and my mind turns easily to pleasant things. Nature is more God to me than Yahweh, though I dare not share this sentiment with anyone.

Today Emma joins me in the Garden. She sits on the bench, her hands silent, looking at the roses, not at me. Shortly before the hour of nine, the Chapel bells ring out, vibrating the air with their call. As if heeding its summons, a lone cardinal flies off in the direction of the church. Emma and I rise together and walk to Chapel.

The twenty-fourth of June. Emma has taken the habit of joining me most mornings in the Garden. I see my opportunity and compose a note.

Dear Emma,

Please allow me to introduce myself. My name is Frankie Campbell. I am seventeen years of age, and I hail from South Carolina. I have served in the employ of Mr. Foote since the third of June as a "Jack of All Trades." I would like very much to learn Sign Language and toward that end have borrowed a book from our Library. Nonetheless, I struggle.

Therefore, I ask your assistance. Would you, kind Lady, be willing to tutor me in the beautiful Language of Signs? I await your reply.

Yours most truly,

Frankie Campbell

The twenty-fifth of June. I receive a note in response. Emma writes that she was unsure if I was Deaf or Hearing but now that she knows, she will be delighted to tutor me in Sign. We arrange to meet each Monday in the Garden for our lessons. She signs it, "Sincerely."

The first of July. I am afraid I am a poor student. I have mastered only one motion that I make with great repetition. I drag my right hand up the inside of my left arm to indicate that I wish Emma to Sign more slowly. Then I rub my fist over my heart to say, "Sorry." In truth, I am happy just to be near her. I watch her hands move like butterflies in the air, and I forget all else.

The eighth of July. I am learning the alphabet as well as a few words and phrases. Yes, no. Male, female. What? When? Why? Who? Good morning. How are you? In addition to "Slow down" and "Sorry," I have learned "Silly boy." This last is Signed often of me.

Sometimes I pretend to have trouble just so she will touch me. Then she cups her hands around mine, molding my fingers into shape. Her hands are soft as a mother's touch. I want to tell her how I feel, but I dare not.

The fourteenth of July. Mr. Foote takes me aside after Chapel today. It is his observation that Emma and I have been enjoying each other's company, he says. He trusts that I am not taking advantage and reminds me of the School's rule against fraternization. I explain our arrangement and assure him we have nothing in mind but the furthering of my education. He seems to believe me only slightly.

The fifteenth of July. Today we do not study at all. Emma has received a letter from her father that has upset her. Her hands flutter wildly. I interpret only a little. "No" and "mad" I see. And then "I am not a baby! I am a female!" I Sign, "Yes, yes." I try in my broken language to tell her about my father. She watches as my hands labor to form the words. Then she looks deeply into my eyes. What she sees there I cannot imagine, but I feel suddenly exposed. We have known each other only a short while, Emma and I, and yet I trust her for reasons I don't understand.

The twenty-first of July. I do not believe the Bible to the Letter of the Word, but as it was one of the few books my father allowed, I have read it through and can quote it chapter and verse. Today the reverend tells the story of Ruth and Naomi, while at his side a boy interprets in Sign. I know the story, but I hear it as if for the first time.

In the foreign land of Moab, the reverend says, an Israelite named Naomi has suffered the death of her husband. Before long, the same fate falls on her daughter-in-law, Ruth. Widowed in a strange land, Naomi has no choice but to return to her people in Bethlehem. She tries to persuade Ruth to return to her own people as well, the Moabites. But Ruth clings to Naomi, saying:

Entreat me not to leave thee, for whither thou goest, I will go; where thou lodgest, I will lodge; where thou diest, will I die and there I will be buried.

Seeing that Ruth is steadfast in her resolve, Naomi says nothing more, and the two women travel to Bethlehem where the Bible says, "they are gladly received."

I listen to this sermon, and I think of Emma and me, and I suddenly see: we are Ruth and Naomi. *Entreat me not to leave thee. Where thou lodgest, I will lodge; where they diest, will I die and there I will be buried.*

The twenty-second of July. It was not his intention, but the reverend has lifted a veil from my eyes. Today I see clearly that it is the nature of the human heart to feel unwhole until it finds its mate. My heart has found Emma, and I must be true to myself by revealing my true self to her. Whatever follows, I must be prepared. If I am rejected, I must accept it stoically. If she reveals my masquerade and I must leave the School, I will. But I place my hope in Emma that she will be my Ruth.

The twenty-ninth of July. I have given a letter to Emma.

My dearest Emma,

It is with trembling hand that I take pen to paper to

write this letter. My dear Emma, I have a confession to make. After I have made it, I fear that you will no longer be my friend, that we will no longer share the sweet intimacy of our meetings in the Garden. But of that I cannot be concerned. I must be true. I must tell you something. I am not who you believe me to be.

I have told you of my father and his cruel hand. Of how I fled our farm and found my way here to this School where Providence placed you within my sight. But I have not told you the whole of it. The truth is this. It was not Frankie Campbell who fled Mush Creek. It was Nellie MacIntyre. And I am she.

This confession perhaps explains many things. What it cannot explain is the love I feel for you. I did not expect nor wish these feelings, and I tell you no falsehood when I say I do not understand them. I know only what I feel. I feel for you as Ruth felt for Naomi, as Robbie Burns felt for his Delia.

I will stop now. I know this has come as a shock. I will give you time to consider your response.

Yours most truly,

Frankie

The thirtieth of July. I wait. Nothing from Emma.

The thirty-first of July. Still nothing from Emma.

The first of August. Still nothing.

The second of August. Finally. Emma finds me at work in the horse barn. I am surprised; she is supposed to be in Sewing Class. She flies at me like the Devil himself. Her hand goes up as if to Sign but then swings back and out. It lands with great force on my cheek. She stands for a moment without moving, watching for my reaction. My fingers hasten to my face, burning with the sting of her slap. Then she turns and runs away. I am stunned, left

58

foolishly rubbing the place where she has struck me.

The nineteenth of August. Emma no longer comes to the Garden. I see her in the Dining Room, but she refuses to meet my eyes. It is torture to be so near and yet to be deprived of her company. I cannot bear to wonder what she thinks of me now.

The twenty-sixth of August. At last, a message.

Dear Frankie,

I cannot deny that your confession came as a shock. Yet I too confess that in some small way I was not surprised. You have always been a most gentle boy, and now I understand the source of that gentleness.

We two are female, you and I, and it is the disposition of the female to be tender. I love you, my dear Frankie. But for reasons of our gender, I cannot love you in the way you hope.

Do not be afraid for your position with the School. I will keep your secret. I will not betray you.

In friendship and with much affection,

Emma

P.S. I am sorry I slapped you. I have never slapped a boy until now.

P.P.S. I say "boy" with intention. I call you boy although I know you are female. You are "boy" as well.

The twenty-eighth of August. "I cannot love you in the way you hope." I did not know I bore so many tears. Perhaps to give vent to my long pent-up feelings, I do nothing but weep hour after hour until it would seem that my head is a fountain and my heart is one great burden of sorrow.

The thirtieth of August. I have read Emma's letter it seems a thousand times, but I read it once more. This time I read it afresh. Emma is still my friend "with much affection." She finds my manner gentle. She considers me a "boy." I am the first boy she has felt enough passion for to slap—a compliment of sorts, I decide.

⁓⁓⁓

It is a new month, September. I am feeling better. The wind off the mountains brings with it the first hints of autumn and change. My tears have dried; the fountain is empty. My heart seeks a hopeful future. I make an important decision.

The ninth of September. I am proud to report that the Army of the Confederate States of America is one soldier stronger as of today. I have enlisted in the North Carolina Infantry, Sixteenth Regiment, Company E. They call us The Burke Tigers. I am Frankie Campbell, Private, Tiger. We march out the sixteenth of September to join the Army of Virginia. I have given notice to Mr. Foote. I have not told Emma.

The eleventh of September. Gossip finds its own course. Emma knows I am leaving even before I tell her. I am in receipt of a note.

Dear Frankie,

Or shall I say Private Frankie? So, you have enlisted without even talking to me first. I cannot lie and say I am pleased. But I respect your decision. Father will be proud of you. I will write and tell him.

And I will write to you, Private Frankie, wherever you go. And you must promise to write to me in return. I will miss you.

Always yours,

Emma

The twelfth of September. I am sad to leave the School,

but I am eager to turn the page on this chapter of my life. I know I will never again love anyone the way I have loved Emma. But I must leave behind what has been and start anew.

The fifteenth of September. Today is my last day with the School. I have traded my butternut uniform for a uniform of gray. The reverend blesses me and wishes me God's grace. Mr. Foote shakes my hand and tells me I have been an exemplary employee. He regrets to see me go.

I will miss my room with its solitude and time for private reflection. I pack my journal and my few belongings in a rucksack. I have saved Emma's notes, and these I fold and tuck within. When I look up the door has opened, and Emma has slipped inside my room, where she is not allowed. This is so unlike her that I am taken by surprise. She closes the door behind her.

"I want to say goodbye," she Signs.

"Yes," I Sign.

"You are a handsome soldier," she Signs.

This pleases me. "Thank you," I Sign back.

"I will miss you, Frankie."

"And I you."

I will miss her eyes most, their lovely gray-green clarity. She hesitates as if unsure. Then the most unexpected thing happens. I watch as Emma moves across the room, light as an angel, and all at once her lips are on mine. We kiss: the sweetest, most tender of kisses. After a while she pulls away and strokes my face with a delicate hand.

"I love you," she Signs.

I am astonished, as I am sure my countenance expresses.

"I love you, too," I Sign. Then I cross my hands over

the most vulnerable place on my person. "With all my heart."

⚜

The sixteenth of September. My fellow soldiers are waiting for me at the Railroad Depot downtown. As the Captain calls my name, I step into line. "Present, sir!" I say in my deepest voice.

If I try very hard, I can still feel Emma's kiss on my lips.

Saffron and Fennel

Susan Smith

She kept a monkey with light blue fur on a jeweled leash, his long, curious fingers trained as carefully as a child's to pluck saffron. She, Ariadnh, would rest the leash on her rounded forearm among bangles of gold and jasper, languid, beautiful enough to make the saffron itself sigh and bend closer. When the court women went forth from the palace at Knossos to the fields above the Great Goddess's shrine, along came the monkey, chattering, running to the end of his leash, eager to gently murder the slender flowers that formed the very lucrative crop. Saffron, blessed saffron, whose tender radiant stigmas formed mutably into medicines and perfumes, spices and cosmetics, and noble assistants to love—the tiny thing, the thread, that makes beauty of the larger whole. Some saffron was sold off island, to the shores of Mycenae, to Egypt and the Levant, even to the coast of the cold islands in the North, where amber came from. Always some was kept for the Gods.

Like all things in Crete, a portion of the best, the

unblemished, belonged to the divine ones, the eternal ones. Zeus had been hidden as a child on the island and favored it still; their sleek trading ships with bright painted eyes ruled the waves. Above all was the rule of Rhea Magna Mater, the Great Mother. She of the labrys, the snake, and the bull. The priestesses of the Great Mother were frequently from the royal house, trained from girlhood in the processions, the dances, the hymns, the rites of ax and bull and blood. They would dance in the shrine courtyard, feet spurning a carpet of crocuses and lilies, a snake twining each arm, short jacket tight against upper arms, breasts openly presented by the formal dress, seven layered skirt flouncing in the bright Cretan sun. The royal women of the ruling house in Knossos were the very set of fashion and the envy of the world. If a woman from Crete wore a new jacket, amber and cinnabar earrings, jet and faience bangles, a net of gold and seed pearls in her glossy black hair, all the Aegean would desire exactly that within a month.

Chief among these women was Ariadnh, hair coiling like hyacinthine snakes about her shoulders, eyes like a night at sea, darkness moving liquid under the sheen of the Pleiades. Cousin to the queen, dancer before the shrine, she was one of the blessed Mother's priestesses called the Melissae after the sacred bees that fed the infant Zeus with honey in the cave on Mount Ida. The court women of the House of the Double Ax swarmed forth to pick saffron in the fields that flanked the Mother's shrine, above the cliffs where the sea rang and boomed against the crags. Thus the blue furred monkey on Ariadnh's gemmed leash, picking wild saffron from the hilltop above the shrine, started the stone rolling down to the beach.

The beach was a ribbon between rock and wave, a shelf

where the bull leapers trained, carrying large rocks rounded by the surf into the waves to strengthen their legs. Kitane, the bull leaper, was on the beach working with her team, laughing against the waves, heaving a great stone back into Poseidon's embrace. The pebble, dislodged by the monkey on the cliff above, gained speed as it clattered down the slope and struck her in the right shoulder, rebounding from the curve of muscle. Kitane thought at first that she'd been stung; bees drowsily filled the fields above and might on becoming lost venture down to the shore.

She looked up, and saw it was not bees but Melissae, women of the court calling out to a naughty monkey balanced on the lip of rock and chattering, refusing the summons. In a heartbeat another head silhouetted against the brilliant blue sky, chiding the monkey. Ariadnh with the sun behind her.

<hr />

The Times of London, 1845-

In the advertising section of the paper, between a notice for work as a governess and a clergyman's daughter seeking an engagement, ran this advertisement:

Peculiar Situation: Desired a respectable steady young woman of good character and industry to serve as travelling companion and assistant to a respectable Lady. Must have a fair hand at landscapes and scientific drawing. Knowledge of Greek and archaeology are exceptionally well desired, artistic temperament is essential. Must not be averse to theatre. Testimonials as to character and suitability

unnecessary if you give the correct impression. Orphans preferred.

Lucy Braddon put the paper down, stung by the note. It was tailored for her, she felt, and might just be a joke or sport of some sort. To fall on it the very afternoon she returned from her botanist father's funeral was grim enough humor that it must be staged. Lucy fit the requirements in every particular, though her Greek was fair; she was now an orphan and in need of a situation. She had travelled widely with her father, keeping his scientific journals and adding detailed drawings of specimens.

Robert Braddon was accounted an eccentric, a kind way of referring to a man who thought his daughter needed an education and might even profit by it. No woman was accepted at the Universities, of course, so it was left to his own tutoring. He had kept her with him on his journeys after the death of her mother, not exactly sure what to do with a daughter. Thankfully this suited her temperament and fine, keen mind. Fascination with the natural world, the autodidacts' eclectic blend of fact and insight, and the kindled light of a fierce intelligence Lucy got directly from him. Her elegant, surgical hand at drawing came from her mother. Many were the evenings this set of skills caused her father, looking up from reviewing his notes by oil lamp in a tent and finding his daughter, raw honey hair bound impatiently back as she bent over recording the samples from that day's work, moments of pride mixed with the bitter knowledge that the world would not be kind to her. She was not one of those respectable young ladies brought up to sit in drawing rooms and practice the pianoforte.

There would be no emerging into society for her; as a daughter of the staunch middle class it was her duty to find a position and support herself, failing the achievement of a husband and losing the protection of a father.

A husband was something Lucy had spent years running full tilt from, the very prospect anathema to her nature. Over the years some men had approached her father, but the peripatetic and Spartan lifestyle of father and daughter eliminated fortune hunters. Lucy had a spring day's loveliness with her pale honey hair and her father's bright blue eyes, delicate rather than lush, retiring rather than inviting, but enough men found that enticing. None of them stirred anything in her but a revulsion that ranged from mild to consumptive. Some women are born to be spinsters, she reasoned, to live in the country and keep dogs. It would never do for her to share a man's bed and board, no matter how well set he might be. So, at the ripe age of twenty, she had embraced the hope of her spinsterhood, fully willing to spin like Arachne even if she had to undo her work every night like Penelope. Her father had not neglected her classical education, even if her Greek was slight.

In a week a letter came to her rooming house.

Mademoiselle Braddon-

I found your briefly sketched background to be intriguing and, as in all things, I follow the sting of intuition to the furthest possible ends. If you are willing, meet me at my country house in Blackbird Lane, Bromyard on Tuesday, the 5th of June. I find the best possible chance of understanding and sympathy occurs when eyes meet eyes. I will explain the nature of the position and situation I offer over tea. We must be civilized while we are still in England; once we sail away from these green shores, we might take on all manner of other strangeness and customs.

-Eulalie Parthena Urania Wakefield, Lady Washerford.

⸻⸻

Heading for the grand staircase from the Queen's megaron, Ariadnh passed through the doorway under the bright blue mural of dolphins frolicking, past the light well and the crimson cedar columns along the balustrade. Ceremonial shields of cowhide and bronze adorned the walls, interspersed with the labrys symbol of the Goddess. She felt a powerful arm circle her waist and pull her behind one of the cedar columns.

"I will be late for the procession." She twined her arms like snakes around the bull leaper's naked shoulders.

"They haven't brought the great red and white bull up from the field. We have time. Kiss me." Kitane pulled the priestess in close. Ariadnh did with abandon, one hand holding the back of Kitane's head, just under the clubbed braid banded tight with golden clasps the bull leapers wore. Both were clad for the ritual, Ariadnh in priestess' garb, Kitane in the tight wasp-waisted kilt all her kind wore, male and female. Green scales framed with gold border formed the kilt, cinched by a wide leather belt covered in bronze plaques. Leather buskins bound her ankles, and rock crystal and bronze bands circled her upper arms and wrists. Both women burned bright in the madness of youth and adoration. The bull leaper drank honey from the lips of the Melissa.

"Will you seek me tonight after the banquet?"

Kitane shrugged. "I might have other offers." She didn't try to hide her grin.

After the bull ritual, the successful bull dancers were eagerly sought out as lovers, the sheen of power still clinging to them. Ariadnh put her lips to Kitane's ear.

"I will give you reason to never glance at another, as long as you live."

On June the 5th, Lucy Braddon was shown into Lady Washerford's library by a butler. Standing by the mantle was Eulalie Wakefield, Lady Washerford, kindly absorbed in closely reading a small book, allowing Lucy to form an opinion of her before they spoke. Lady Washerford wore her hair rather carelessly, as if she'd just come in from riding in a strong wind. It was such a deep auburn as to look brown in shadow, and glowing red where it caught the firelight. Her dress was otherwise conventional, if ineffably elegant; down to the perfection of the cameo broach at her throat. Lucy wondered what the image might be, but it was nestled in the lace of Lady Washerford's collar. She was tall and of a strong stature, the type of woman rarely called beautiful and easily called handsome. Lucy guessed her to be in her thirties.

Lucy stood, waiting to be noticed. Lady Washerford seemed unaware of her presence. The fire popped and hissed.

"Are you familiar with the *bean nighe*?" Lady Washerford turned the page, not looking up at her yet.

"Pardon, Madame?"

"*Bean nighe.* Gaelic. Along certain rivers you must be careful, if you come upon a monstrous woman washing bloody clothes in the stream. If you recognize the clothes it means you are going to die. Terrible omen before a battle. The Washer at the Ford." The red book slapped shut; Lady Washerford looked up at Lucy. Her eyes were the most magnificent black Lucy had ever imagined, deep as the night sky. Her voice was in contrast rather rough, what might be termed, Lucy thought, husky. The sound of it disturbed the ear and then reshaped expectations until the listener had been molded to the sound and left enthralled.

"I was not aware." Lucy's hand touched her collarbone absently.

"One of my husband's ancestors stomped about Scotland oppressing everyone until he saw the Washer at the Ford. The family title derives from this. Or so the legend goes." Lady Washerford took Lucy's hand and led her to one of the chairs before the fire. "Now, is that a myth, or is it true?"

Lucy sensed that this was no idle question. She considered carefully. "Don't all myths have within them the core of truth?" Lady Washerford had not released her hand. Now she clasped it in delight.

"Just so! Just so, my dear. Do you mind travel?"

"Not at all. I spent most of my life travelling with my father on his expeditions."

"Ever been to Greece?"

"Twice, though for short stays."

"And you have no aversion to theater? Acting, I must add."

"I can't imagine anyone having such an aversion."

"Chilton!" Lady Washerford stood. "Miss Braddon will take the peacock room. Thank you." She turned to an amazed Lucy. "You will accept the employ, I believe."

"I would be grateful."

Lady Washerford accepted the tea service that Chilton brought in, then waved him out of the room. "How do you take it?" Lady Washerford poured out two cups of tea.

"Any way you serve it."

"Miss Braddon—"

"Lucy."

"Very well, Eulalie. I have a feeling, and I am accused of always heeding my emotions over my reason, that we will get on splendidly. You needn't always agree with me; that's not what I am seeking in a companion."

"What are you seeking?" Lucy accepted the bone china cup, a delicate spray of crocuses and lilies enameled along the outside.

"An assistant to accompany me on an archaeological dig in Crete. Someone to do the drafting, the scientific recording. Someone with an artist's eye and a scientist's touch."

Whatever Lucy might have been expecting, this wasn't it. "I did specimen drawing and kept the journals for my father," she stammered.

"Mm. Botanist, wasn't he?"

"Yes." It hadn't been long enough; the spear went right through her heart at his mention. Lucy's eyes fell.

Lady Washerford put down her cup and took Lucy's hands in both of hers. "How horrid of me. It can't be two weeks since his funeral. I am so very sorry, my dear. I will strive to lift the shadow on your heart."

Lucy cast about for a change in topic. "Will Lord Washerford be joining us on the expedition?"

It was the first time she heard that dark and heady laugh, the unbridled bark of humor escaping from Eulalie's throat. "Cecil has been dead these thirteen years, poor old monkey. I've been a widow since my first year of marriage. But yes, he will be joining us on the journey."

The night before they were to take steamship to the Italian coast, Eulalie, with Lucy's help, had undergone a great transformation. Her magnificent auburn hair was sheared away by Lucy, who hesitated with the blades in hand, feeling the weight of the beautiful braid slide across her palms. Then the blades closed, and the short crop of unruly auburn became a boy's crown, then a man's.

"Women travelling alone are in for a great deal of potential trouble. Even with the masque we maintain, Eulalie Wakefield would not be allowed to head an archeological dig. I might be allowed to accompany one, if my husband were rich and present. Therefore, and I am certain you will understand and be of perfect sympathy, my husband Lord Washerford must accompany us."

Eulalie ran her fingers through it, looking at the glass. "I will have to wear a hat; it will never stay down. What do you think?"

"I think you look like the most handsome man who ever lived. Your face is suited for it, if you will allow me to say so."

"Your great transformation begins as well, my dear."

"Am I to be a boy?"

"No. But a respectable young lady cannot be travelling with a man unless—"

"I am his wife."

So it had been. Cecil Wakefield took passage, accompanied by his wife. Now the salt wind bit at Lucy's cheeks as she stood along the rail of the steamship's upper deck. She felt the presence behind her before the hand, gloved in dove grey, touched her arm. "My dear."

Cecil Wakefield, Lord Washerford, was a rather dashing figure to the other passengers, a man of adventure and mystery. He wore brand new Italian suits, didn't play cards or smoke cigars in the gentleman's lounge, but doted uxoriously on his young bride, a sweet and very lovely honey colored girl. Off to Crete for some exploring, he was heard to say. His laugh was frequent, his devoted young wife always on his arm. It was the firm opinion of the Bulgarian mistress of the Roman captain that they had not been married long; they had the gentle air of newlyweds, and clearly the lady was entirely besotted with her lord. Presuming the journey to be a coded honeymoon, the other passengers allowed them greater leeway and let them have some privacy. Now, at the rail, might be glimpsed the pair, the lord holding his wife's hand, the two dreaming out toward the rise and spray of the waves off the bow. How charming an image of matrimony.

"It is in the Iliad, the Catalogue of Ships. Homer lists all the kings and princes and nobles sending ships to Troy, and their home ports. A hundred cities he lists from Crete! Think on it; if Homer was right, then there is a great civilization on Crete waiting to be discovered. Buried beneath the dusty feet of Time, the sandals of the rude Mycenaeans who came to burn and loot and conquer. The Palace of Minos, the Labyrinth." Lord Washerford looked out over the night sea with a sigh, as if the coast of Crete were visible before the ship's keel. As if the drums of war summoned forth the ships, again, to avenge the insult to Menelaus before the walls of Troy.

"Troy itself isn't a real place. Might Homer not have been indulging in the romantic poetry his listeners expected?" Lucy pulled the night-black eyes back to her. A thrill shot through her. She was enjoying being Mrs. Wakefield, Lady Washerford, more than she could say. Matrimony had seemed a pitiable state to her, but now she pitied all the world who did not have this person's light of intellectual fire and passion directed toward them. Pitied all who were not wife to Cecil Wakefield even if, particularly if, he was Eulalie. They had, even when alone, quickly adopted the habit of exclusively calling one another by endearments to minimize the risk of being overheard. Or so they asserted.

"My dear, I think Troy is real as well."

Lucy took in her breath. "The Iliad is real. Achilles, Hector, Hecuba, Priam—think of it!" She held the dove grey gloved hand in her excitement.

"In some part, surely. Dionysus might not stalk the hills outside Thebes, Athena might not stand atop the Acropolis, but when you have stood in the high city and looked out toward the sea, when the sun reveals the plain below in a gilded pouring out of light on the olive groves and vineyards, how can you not feel the presence of the Gods just behind you? Athens is real. I expect the Cretan cities to be as well."

"Why begin in Crete then? Why not strike out for Troy?"

"Two reasons. One, Homer is remarkably vague about the exact location of the city and plains of Ilium. Two, I have been to Crete. Last season, a farmer tending his vineyard turned over what turned out to be a dressed stone. Underneath was a terracotta figurine of a woman with snakes bound about her arms, and this." From inside the greatcoat Eulalie drew out a ring. The band was simple bronze, but it held an intaglio done in carnelian. Lucy took the ring and looked closely at it.

"Three figures, one before and one behind a running bull, and an acrobat leaping over the bull. Is this from Theseus and the Minotaur?"

"Something associated I would guess. It is my

contention that this is the bull dance, a rite of the Cretans. Perhaps for their Goddess. Can you tell me anything about the acrobats?"

Lucy held the ring up to the moonlight. "Very little. They are all stylized, all dressed alike."

"I need to find this vineyard again. I think a tomb is nearby, perhaps for a bull leaper. If I can find evidence it would be the first in history to prove the Cretan civilization isn't just a fancy of Homer's. That, my darling one, is our goal."

"The core of truth in the myth. We begin with Crete, then perhaps Troy. Why not Mycenae, Agamemnon's seat?"

"That is how I know you are the perfect companion for me, my dear; you take up my madness and run with it so I must chase after, like a child drawn by a kite."

A storm pitched the ship like a child's toy, keeping everyone below for two days, until Poseidon's rage had abated and the air hung still on the gray wasteland, murmuring down to silence. They came across a smaller vessel from the Italian coast, bound for Sicily, damaged beyond repair in the toss and crash of foaming waves. The Roman Captain, sentimental with satiation from his Bulgarian mistress, kindly welcomed the bedraggled extras aboard for the short leg of the journey, a Berber family from North Africa, a Venetian and his dogs, and an older Englishman. Lucy popped her head out of the cabin door for desperately needed air just as they were embarking. The night was still, the stars out again, the sea a sheet of glass as the new passengers wrung out sodden clothing. The Englishman took off his coat and twisted it violently, sending a waterfall onto the deck. He glanced up at Lucy, who quickly withdrew behind the door.

"We've taken on some new passengers. Poor wretches stranded by the storm."

"I expect just till Sicily." The auburn head was bent over a map and notes. "Inland from Heraklion. Just a few kilometers. I purchased the digging rights from the farmer last season for a fortune."

Lucy sat down next to her on the bed. "That should occupy us, looking for the tomb. Once we have evidence we publish it in one of the journals of the scientific societies and raise money to mount a full expedition to seek the cities. Oh darling, it is wonderful!"

Eulalie looked up from the notes. "I would lay my life down that I was your darling from the way you say it." Lightly said, with a smile to soften any sting, but Lucy felt it and dropped her eyes.

"It is a masquerade, I know. For the work."

"Wear a masque long enough and it reveals the person beneath. Come now, no sadness."

Lucy felt her face drawn up, a touch on her cheek, for all the world a devoted husband comforting his wife.

"Would that I were your wife!" The words escaped before she could reason with them, a burst of passion pent up in close quarters for too long. It was entirely true even as it was entirely impossible, but suddenly Lucy understood the stories, and poems, and longing letters written from wives to husbands, the myths of devotion and completion. What then was the core, the truth within? That she longed to have her, Eulalie Wakefield, Cecil, Lord Washerford, as her female husband. It didn't matter that nature and religious opinion stood in the gap and shouted against it. It was the drum of her blood, leading on the ships to conquest. She longed to lie in Eulalie's arms, every night.

"You may be, if you dare."

The words stopped Lucy's heart. It was partly the freedom of the masquerade, giving the bridge for them to begin, partly feeling so deeply that nothing under heaven could move her from where she was. "I would dare anything with you at my side."

Eulalie picked up the carnelian intaglio and placed it on Lucy's finger. "Be my most beloved. My wife."

That night, the masquerade became a face of the eternal truth, and Lucy lay in Eulalie's arms, wife and beloved.

All the passengers departed in Sicily, with Lord and Lady Washerford eagerly striding down to the dock to meet their next ship, a much smaller sailboat bound for Greece. The old Englishman followed them, deliberately Lucy thought, but seeing her looking back he exited abruptly in the opposite direction. A coincidence surely, a tourist lost on his journey.

When she thought she saw him again in Athens, she put the idea aside as a mirage or fancy of the heat. The spray of the Aegean leapt under the keel of their ship, fleeing away like a wild horse from Piraeus across the narrow way to the island. Crete before them, Lucy quite forgot about the man. He had never even spoken to them. They landed at Heraklion, from there renting horses for the last few leagues.

The vineyard was on a gentle rise, the remains of a stark crag that had long fallen into the sea in one of the great convulsions that shook the island over the millennia. Volcanic soil from the eruption of Thera threaded with the local limestone. The rough, terrible youth of that cliff Time had ground down into a mellow hill with the mantle of age upon it, crowned with vineyards where surprisingly large, drowsy bees kept the grapes. Beyond was an olive grove, trees old enough to have witnessed two thousand years march by. The remains of a Venetian fortress weathered away into dust between the trees. Every season, the plow overturned a Roman coin, a piece of Ottoman cannon, shards of pottery more ancient than both. The ages lay on one another like sated lovers.

They stopped at the farmer's home, a building of white washed walls of gypsum under a flat tiled roof. He greeted Lord Washerford delightedly, revealing to Lucy that he had had no idea his lordship was married. The land in the vineyard was ready for the dig, a few local men solicited for aid. Lord Washerford paid very well, but wanted to keep the crew small. They were of course given a small whitewashed building of their own for their use, a converted animal shed hastily kitted out with rough chairs, a long table, and a bed. Most nights, Lord Washerford explained, they would remain with the dig, in tents. Not unlike the life Lucy was used to with her father, the snap of canvas in the breeze from the ocean, a cot to rest on and an oil lamp to see by at night for the compilation of the day's finds.

The workmen didn't mind, spending most of the day lounging in the sun for a week's pay while the odd English lord ran about. It was frustratingly slow for Lord Washerford, but to Lucy it was the golden heart of her life. Each day spent in combined work, seeking the great finds, the evidence, shoulder to shoulder together. Each night spent reviewing and noting the day's work, meticulously, and talking about everything.

"I sat in Churchill Babington's lectures at Cambridge until the other students threw me out in a rage. Archaeology was no study for a female mind! It made little matter that I endowed an expedition to Karnak. Donation is one matter, participation another. Did you know that learning weakens the female constitution?"

Lucy, gilded bronze from the sun and alive to the tips of her fingers, shook her head. "I had no idea I was so frail."

"You are stronger than a team of oxen, my dear. They called me the Roaring Infidel."

Lucy looked down at the sketch in her hands and smiled. "Well, it is apt. This trench has yielded us nothing. Do you want to position the next at an angle from the first?"

Cecil, Eulalie, stood up and tossed the notebook on the cot. "Blast it! I was so sure that the original find was a paving stone, part of a sacred way. An approach to a temple or tomb. But the landscape has changed so much over the centuries. How do we know what we seek isn't under the sea? We can't just peer into the ground like a looking-glass and say, 'oh, here is where the Cretans built, we shall have our dig there!'"

Lucy covered her mouth to keep from laughing. The fit of temper was glorious to her, another chance to see how very much Eulalie trusted her. Clasped to her bosom in abandon at night, at work in the sun all day, every moment was more than she thought life would ever grant her. Aphrodite became her patron. She would die before going back.

The flash of insight struck, handed to her whole from years working with her botanist father.

"Look for fennel!"

"Why?" Eulalie turned toward her, hands on her hips.

"Fennel has exceptionally long roots and likes to appear in places where the soil has been turned over the years. Find clumps of fennel and we will find the past."

"Fennel is our looking-glass! My dear, you are brilliant." Eulalie strode to her and kissed her soundly.

Fennel clustered in tufts on the edge of the rise, a waving crown for a dreaming green head. They started digging, and the dressed stone came free at last from the ages. Lord Washerford struggled to keep an iron grip on his wild enthusiasm and move slowly, agonizingly slowly, to document every inch of soil lifted away. Thankfully his young wife was there, sketching every day, cataloging finds by oil lamp at night. The stones, their soil veil pulled back, lay exposed to the sky for the first time since civilizations long past had fallen away from man's collective memory.

It became clear that, more than just a sacred way, it was the roof to a chamber-tomb. Lord Washerford shoveled alongside the workmen, his enthusiasm infectious, uncovering the keel-shaped vault and stone lintel, the bronze bound cedar doors long since gone down to dust. The dromos was revealed, halfway into the hillside. Late afternoon revealed the limestone walls of the fore-hall lined with gypsum benches. Beyond the doorway was a limestone slab. The last rays of the sun showed the tomb itself still sealed. Evening forced a halt.

Lord Washerford broke out bottles of wine, toasting the diggers, the tomb, the sea beyond the rise, and his devoted Lady. He poured out a libation to the residents of the tomb, distributed bonuses, and declared that tomorrow at first light the limestone slab would be moved. The workmen departed for the evening, drunk and happy.

In with the sifted soil they had uncovered a chalcedony seal showing two figures and a lion, pottery pieces that gave evidence of Egyptian origin, a gold ring with a motif of ecstatic dance by female votaries in a field of lilies. And above the limestone door, still sealed against time, were stylized stone bull's horns and the image of an apotropaic double ax. Lucy recorded it all, the sketches of the doorway and the outer hall, the dromos, the lintel with symbols intact.

"Tomorrow," Eulalie said, pacing like a lion on a leash. "Tomorrow we let in the sun and greet our Cretan hosts. The symbols, the bull's horns, the labrys!"

"Yes, beloved. From the position of the tomb in the landscape, I would wager that it isn't the end of the sacred way, but positioned alongside. The road wound beyond it."

"Beyond it, into the sea. Whatever knelt on the crag of that cliff has long since fallen into the waves, perhaps in an earthquake. We might owe our intact tomb to that great earth-shifting. The land fell away, the remaining ruins were covered."

"You are on the cusp of greatness."

Eulalie seized her up and spun her about in an impromptu dance. "We are! Well, Cecil Wakefield is, when he publishes his results. I never would have found it without you."

"I wonder if it is possible to die from too much happiness. I don't know how to live with it. Do you suppose it will ever be possible to publish under our own names?"

"My imagination runs backward, my dear. I leave the dreaming about the future to you."

"Do...do you think we might spend the night in the cottage? But I know you must want to stay with the tomb."

Eulalie looked at her closely. "One night of privacy might be acceptable. We have been consumed in the journey; surely on the cusp of success we might celebrate a bit. After all, this is our honeymoon."

The whitewashed walls allowed a change of pace, a letting down of walls kept up in company. Lucy couldn't believe that she'd asked, on this night, or that Eulalie had accepted and understood. But this night of triumph she wanted to lie naked in her husband's arms and drink other wine. Lucy dreamed of fish playing between the columns of a lost temple, of ecstatic women, hair flying, spinning before the open colonnade holding stalks of fennel, of a magnificent red and white bull charging. In the morning Eulalie dressed again as Cecil. Lucy helped her knot the cravat, button the waistcoat. Even at a dig certain things were expected, of men, of women. They hurried to the site, expecting to find the workmen waiting for them. Silence lay over the tomb, dew gleaming on the leaves of crocuses in the field on the rise's left flank. Tools lay scattered, pickaxes and shovels tossed about randomly. Limestone shards littered the formerly cleared fore-hall. The slab was destroyed, sledged into pieces. A limestone larnax sarcophagus had been dragged half into the light, tipped over, the lid levered off and the contents scattered. Bones and the dust that had been cloth spilled from it. The tomb had been looted.

The shock was too great for Lucy to compass, a blow she couldn't feel yet. She looked immediately at Eulalie in horror. If they had spent the night at the dig, if she hadn't asked to go back to the shed, they would have heard the destruction. Perhaps even been able to stop it. Guilt ravaged her.

Eulalie was looking not at the tomb, but away from it. At the edge of the dig site stood the old Englishman from the ship. He was looking at Eulalie with a mix of anger and contempt, his mouth drawn up and back like that of a foaming dog.

"Mrs. Wakefield."

He wasn't speaking to Lucy.

For the first time, Lucy heard Eulalie become every inch the frozen aristocrat.

"Ambrose. The last I heard you were on the foreign service in Africa. What are you doing in Crete?"

He walked toward them, picking his way between the scattered tools. "I had heard my dear old friend Cecil Wakefield was travelling to Crete when he has been more than a decade in the grave. There must be some mistake."

"I think there have been many mistakes," Eulalie said, and the tone froze Lucy's marrow.

"So I waited to get a good look at the wretch impersonating my friend, abusing his good name. Never could I have imagined this, this unnatural charade."

"You lack imagination, Ambrose. You always did."

"You were always a hellion, Eulalie, but to make mock of Cecil's good name, to ruin this young girl, to play at man's work?" He gestured widely at the site.

Lucy took Eulalie's hand. Ambrose noted the movement and shook his head.

"This unnatural rebellion is finished. I have given out word that Cecil Wakefield is dead and an imposter is abroad. Your workmen have been paid off and dismissed. I gave them their freedom to take their own bonus."

"You *bastard.*" The aristocratic control was cracking.

The old man stood, wide as an elephant, pulling light from the landscape into him. On his jacketed shoulders rested all the power and authority in the world, the reminder to Lucy that no matter the joy they had taken these past few weeks, his world still held all the trump cards. Everything they had could be taken from them.

"And if you continue, I will ruin you and your consort."

This broke the dam and brought out the lioness. Eulalie stormed forth, her right hand crashing into Ambrose's teeth. She stood over him, trousered legs spread wide. "Breathe a word against her and I will kill you with my bare hands."

On his back Ambrose was deflated like a pricked bladder. "How dare you, how dare you! This is not yours!" He looked his age, grey haired and fragile suddenly. The illusion of power had melted. The angry child remained.

Eulalie stepped away and turned her back, dismissing him. She walked into the tomb. Lucy waited until he climbed painfully to his feet and shuffled away, his image sinking into the curves of the road. Lucy followed Eulalie into the shadow. The sun cut across the floor in a triangle, showing where the limestone box had stood, a few large clay jars broken and shattered about the edges of the small rectangular room. Eulalie was on her knees, hands full of bones and dust, weeping.

"Gone. It is all gone. We will never know."

"Darling." She knelt and gathered Eulalie into her arms, crying herself. "Can you ever forgive me?"

"For what?" Eulalie sounded genuinely bewildered. "It is you must forgive me. Ambrose is right. I care not a whit for my reputation. But you will be destroyed. "

"You think I am worried about my reputation? I am an orphan; I have no father to shame. And there is no shame, for me, in being known as your wife."

"Cecil's wife. I was a fool to use his name. Of course someone would realize he was dead eventually. We would never be able to publish our findings."

"Darling, look," Lucy said. The triangle of light had shifted subtly around them. The sun now revealed the tomb's walls. The contents were stripped, but the walls remained. Lime washed frescoed walls in brilliant blues, deep scarlet, gold, and saffron. Eulalie stood, mesmerized. There were figures marching in a line, bearing tall jars, lilies and crocuses; women with bare breasts, arms wreathed in snakes, long, serpentine hair down their backs in curled locks.

"It is a procession. See, the jars, the flowers are offerings. Look at the clothing! The statuette was true, see how the women are clad. The men in kilts and jewelry. My dear, get your sketchbook!"

It was Lucy who pointed out that while the procession was headed and filled with women, their skin was painted pale white. The men were represented in a deep red brown. Some of the figures in kilts were marked dressed as men but represented as women. These were mixed in with the other fellows in kilts and armbands, leading a bull with gilded horns. Eulalie touched the fresco. "It is as fresh as if it were painted yesterday. I recognize her, this one, this priestess. She has a monkey on a leash. How magnificent is her hair caught up in that crown! She walks with the bull dancer, the woman. Perhaps this is her tomb?"

"It might be. Read this as a story. It begins here, left of the door. The procession begins; all walk and carry offerings. The bull is led. Here, the corner is turned. The women dance, spinning, hair flying. I am not sure, but that may be a goddess, winged, on a temple roof." Lucy narrated as she walked. "Then, we turn again, and it is the bull dance! The women watch, the dancers before and after the bull, head tossed back. One holds the horns, red, so he is male. There, leaping, white. Female. Same arm bands as before."

"Astounding. Women bull leapers? But the iconography is clear."

"Now we turn. The bull leaper stands with the priestess, who has the monkey on the leash. They clasp right hands, walking. Part of the ritual?"

Eulalie shook her head. "No, the procession is gone. They are alone. The fresco wends here, at the doorway again, and is finished. I think this is their tomb."

"Both?"

"That handclasp, the right hands? I have seen it in Etruscan burials. Man and wife."

"Both figures are painted white."

Eulalie smiled. "Such things are known to happen. Do you have it all?"

Lucy held up her sketchbook. "I have it. Let us gather their bones, set the larnax back up. They deserve the right to rest together, again."

It took the rest of the daylight, until the sun sank away into the West. They left the tomb in silence. Lucy clutched her sketchbook. "No one will ever believe it."

"Women cannot publish."

"And Cecil is dead."

Eulalie looked out over the rise, past the crown of fennel, toward the ocean. "I always liked the name Augustus better."

"A man who never existed can't be unmasked," Lucy took Eulalie's hand.

"You know we stand outside the law. Outside custom."

"To achieve greatly one must dare greatly. We keep our faith, we keep our work, and we wait for the world to catch up," Lucy said.

In the next season, an expatriate Englishman named Augustus and his beloved wife went looking on the coast of Turkey for the plains of Ilium. Their work was foundational for the eventual discovery of Troy. An earthquake shook the island of Crete, dropping a certain crag into the sea. The palace at Knossos and the Cretan civilization would wait for decades to be uncovered again. The man who did so was convinced that he was the first to do so.

We know better.

Propriety

Cara Patterson

Vienna was falling away behind them.

Lise peeked around the edge of the window. It was so strange to see the city from a distance.

The coachman cracked his whip, giving the horses a freer rein. The carriage leapt forward. Lise clung to the handle by the door, laughing in delight as the wind tugged at her bonnet and dragged her hair free to whip against her cheeks.

"You should sit," Marie-Augusta said from behind her. "The road may be uneven. I would hate for you to fall."

Lise reluctantly drew back from the window, and sat on the bench opposite the other woman. "I've never been so far from Vienna before," she confessed. "It's exciting."

Marie-Augusta smiled. "I know," she said, "but you ought to save a little excitement for Bad-Vöslau." She glanced at the window, then back to Lise. "Come." She patted the leather-cushioned bench beside her. "You would see much better if you sat here."

Lise always felt flustered when the Archduchess drew her near, even after months of closeness. She knew her

89

cheeks were flushing, but she obeyed. The floor swayed beneath her feet, and she stumbled. Marie-Augusta caught her arms, laughing.

"You see. The road can be treacherous."

Lise blushed more deeply, sitting down beside her quickly. If she was a little closer than she needed to be, what of it? "I'll be more careful," she promised.

Marie-Augusta's broad smile softened into the more familiar, secret one they often shared. "Good." She patiently loosened the tangled knot in the ribbon of Lise's bonnet. "You should not be bruised."

Lise gazed at her as Marie-Augusta removed her bonnet, as serious as a Priest giving Mass. "Your Highness..." she began.

Dark eyes met hers reproachfully. "Lise, please."

Lise lowered her eyes. It still made her heart skip a beat. "Augusta," she said softly.

Marie-Augusta sighed with pleasure. "Not so difficult, is it?" she teased, setting to work, putting Lise's disordered hair back in order. Her fingertips brushed Lise's cheeks, curling behind her ears. "God in Heaven, you look as if you tumbled backwards through a hedge."

Lise put out her tongue. "As you look each morning before I get a brush?"

Marie-Augusta's lips twitched. "Why do I tolerate your insolence?"

Lise shrugged, then shivered as Marie-Augusta's nails trailed down the side of her neck, light as a breath of wind.

"I don't know." Her voice was catching. She saw the pleasure and the colour rise in Marie-Augusta's round cheeks. She loved to set Lise to trembling with only the lightest of touches. Lise swallowed hard, her heart drumming. "I think you like it."

The fingertips drew back up, the nails tracing lightly. "You may be right."

Lise's tongue darted out to wet her lips. Sometimes, when Marie-Augusta looked at her, she wanted nothing more than to lean in and kiss her, but now, she knew she could not. As always, they had to act with care.

It was difficult when Marie-Augusta's fingers ran across the back of her neck. They were alone, unattended, for the first time in days.

"Augusta..."

"Mm?"

"My bonnet." She was proud that she managed to speak clearly.

Marie-Augusta sighed sadly. "Ah. Propriety." She retrieved the abandoned bonnet, setting it back in place, and tied the ribbon neatly.

Lise offered an apologetic smile. "Windows," she clarified. Still, she settled closer to Marie-Augusta, as close as possible with their travelling skirts between them. She drew Marie-Augusta's hand over to her lap and held it there, warm and resting high upon her thighs. "Tonight, there will be curtains."

She heard the way Marie-Augusta's breath caught, and did not need to look to know her mistress was smiling like a cat. "Fine curtains," she agreed. "And a door too, I expect. With a lock."

Lise's face felt warm. She pressed her cheek to Marie-Augusta's shoulder. Marie-Augusta's fingers threaded between hers, and Lise gazed down at them. Gloves separated them, fine, rich fabric for the Archduchess, and plainer cloth for her maid.

Lise drew her thumb along her lady's.

She had no idea why Marie-Augusta liked her, but the

Archduchess did, and Lise sometimes wondered if it was sinful to consider herself blessed that such a woman, of the line of Habsburgs and the descendent of Emperors, had even noticed her. Marie-Augusta was not just beautiful, but kind and playful too. Anyone would fall in love with a woman like that.

"Is it a long way from here?" she asked.

Marie-Augusta's fingers pressed lightly to hers. "Long enough." She was silent for a moment, then asked, "Tell me another tale."

"What kind of tale?"

"Of the opera?" Marie-Augusta's voice brightened. "You must know so many."

Lise smiled. The City Opera was where they had found one another, when Marie-Augusta had demanded to meet the dresser of the leading lady's hair. All at once, Lise found herself swept from backstage into a palace, and raised from tending actresses to tending royalty.

"Do you remember the production of *Die Fledermaus*, two years ago?"

Marie-Augusta gave an unladylike snort. "Yes."

Lise giggled. It had been a memorable production for the worst of reasons. "I can tell you some of the trouble that was had."

Marie-Augusta settled back against the seat. "Do."

By the time they reached their destination, Lise knew she was repeating stories Marie-Augusta had already heard, but Marie-Augusta never seemed to mind. She loved to hear tales from a world so different, yet so similar to her own: everyone had their roles, their costumes, their positions. Everyone had to do what they were told, and behave just so.

It was no wonder that the theatre was an escape for

her.

They arrived at the palace of Bad-Vöslau in the afternoon. It was warm, the sky clear except for a scatter of clouds. The palace was not as grand as the palace that Marie-Augusta's family lived in, close to the Hofburg in Vienna, but it was still far grander than the rest of Bad-Vöslau.

Lise helped Marie-Augusta down from the carriage, then fell back into the more appropriate position, several paces behind her, as Marie-Augusta moved forward to greet the Count and Countess von Fries who would be hosting them.

The manners were stiff and formal. Lise knew she would be ignored by everyone except servants until she was needed. She watched as Marie-Augusta was swept off to be reunited with her mother and sister, then looked about nervously.

Several servants were already moving forward to unload the luggage, and one of them smiled and said she could go with them to the room to await her lady. She nodded gratefully, picking up Marie-Augusta's book, and followed.

The lobby of the building was as grand as any Lise had seen, and she hurried after the servants, her boots tapping on the floor. They were halfway up the main stairs when she heard some of the servants' voices drifting up from below.

"They say she didn't bring a single one of her companions."

"Not one? I thought her mother said she would bring the Countess Mistelbach?"

Lise stopped short on the stairs, her heart thumping.

Mistelbach was one of the group of women who

surrounded Marie-Augusta, yapping like annoying little dogs. They were always there, put in place by Marie-Augusta's mother, the Archduchess Ludovika. Mistelbach was older than Marie-Augusta, and from an ancient family, which she never got tired of reminding everyone about. If she was expected to attend, Archduchess Ludovika would not be happy to find her absent.

"There was a room prepared..." The voices below faded as the servants moved out of range.

Lise was holding Marie-Augusta's book so tightly that her palms ached.

Questions would be asked—if Marie-Augusta was defying her mother.

Lise gathered up her skirts, hurrying after the train of cases, trying not to think on it. She was here as Marie-Augusta's dresser and nothing more. She had no right to question Marie-Augusta's decisions, no matter how much she might agree with them.

The room she was shown into was beautifully furnished, with thick drapes and carpets on the polished marble floor. The scent of flowers filled the room, drifting from a bowl thick with colourful blooms. She crossed the floor, flinging one of the windows wide. It was so very unlike the closed in streets of the city, the air fresh and fragrant.

Despite herself, she smiled.

Once the household servants departed, she closed the door behind them—and there was indeed a heavy lock and key—and removed her travelling clothes, then set about putting Marie-Augusta's possessions in order. They were only to stay for a week, but there were sufficient clothes and jewellery for all occasions.

She was arranging the dresser, with its ornate gilded mirror, when the door was flung open. Lise almost dropped the brush in alarm at the look on Marie-Augusta's face. She was white with rage, and turned, closing the door, locking it. She remained there, rigid as a statue, her hands on the polished knobs.

Lise rushed to her side. "What is it? What has happened?"

"I am to write to Mistelbach." Marie-Augusta's voice was level. She was staring at the door. "She is to attend upon me while I am here."

Lise stepped closer, putting her arms about Marie-Augusta's waist. "Surely it is your decision."

One of Marie-Augusta's hands moved to cover Lise's. "My decision was to bring you in her stead. It is...I am to be grateful that the Count's household does not have an available dresser, else they might return you to Vienna."

Lise's legs shook beneath her. "She *is* a more suitable companion."

"She is nothing but my mother's eyes and ears," Maria-Augusta growled.

It was never good when she was angry. More than once, there had been broken dishes and overturned furniture. It had never been turned against Lise, not once in fourteen months, but she had seen it too many times to let it get worse.

"She's not here yet," Lise said softly.

"She will be, soon enough."

Lise pressed against her mistress' back, sliding one arm up and the other down. She felt Marie-Augusta's ribs rise and fall as she sighed. "But not yet," Lise said again. She spread one hand on Marie-Augusta's chest, feeling the flutter of her heart against her palm.

Some of the tension left Marie-Augusta's body. "I told them I wished to rest and refresh myself from the journey," she murmured.

Lise hid a smile in the ruffles of Marie-Augusta's sleeve. "Oh?"

"Mm." Her hand covered Lise's again, squeezing. "I must be out of these travelling clothes."

Lise rose on her toes and pressed a quick kiss to her neck. "I can help."

When Marie-Augusta turned to face her, colour was returning to her face, and she was smiling warmly once more. "I know you can," she said, drawing Lise into her arms.

The sun was lower in the sky when Marie-Augusta rose from the bed and went to the window, looking out over the grounds. She drew her shawl around her shoulders, and bowed her head, her hair unravelled in dark waves.

Lise sat on the edge of the bed, fastening her buttons. "Do you want me to fetch your paper and pen?" She kept her voice gentle. It was true Marie-Augusta was calmer now, but she was still unhappy.

"I must do as mother wishes."

Lise knew she could not dispute the fact. She rose and padded across the floor, the marble cool through her stockings. Marie-Augusta's writing set was on top of the drawers. She carried it over to the desk. It only took her a moment to lay it all out, but when she straightened up, her mistress was by her side.

"I would rather have had you to myself," Marie-Augusta confessed, lifting her hand to cradle Lise's cheek. "They flock around me like hungry sparrows, never giving me a moment's peace." Her thumb ran along Lise's cheek, and Marie-Augusta tried to smile, but it faltered. "I had hoped..." She shook her head, then brushed Lise's loose blonde hair back over her shoulder. "Forgive me, Lise. I grow maudlin."

Lise hesitated, then leaned up and kissed her mistress softly on the cheek, then again on the lips.

It earned a smile. A small one, but still a smile.

"You are so very lovely." Marie-Augusta drew back reluctantly, her fingertips skimming Lise's jaw as she pulled her hand back. She glanced at the clock on the mantle. "You should go and eat. You must be famished."

"Only a little," Lise replied. "Would you like anything?"

Marie-Augusta shook her head. "I will attend dinner with my family and our hosts." She sounded so exhausted by the idea that Lise reached out and squeeze her hand in silent reassurance. Marie-Augusta returned the touch. "No need to worry, darling. I will be well." The smile was like frost on glass: beautiful but fading quickly. "Now, run along. I could not bear to see you get skinny."

"I'll be back in half an hour," Lise promised.

"No need to rush."

Lise looked at her. "Your hair, your Highness."

Marie-Augusta raised a hand to her hair, then winced. "God above, did you need to tangle it so?"

Lise felt herself blush. "I'm the one to untangle it, so you needn't complain."

That earned a laugh. "Off with you, then! And hurry! I must look respectable for dinner, not half-savaged."

Lise pulled a face and darted out of the door, smiling.

Sadly, such moments of private pleasure only lasted until Countess Mistelbach arrived at the palace. Lise sat on her small cot in an alcove of Marie-Augusta's room, trying to go unnoticed, as Marie-Augusta and her mother argued that she and Mistelbach ought to share one of the larger chambers on the upper level, as good companions should.

"I hardly think so!" Marie-Augusta protested. "I am quite settled here. I see no reason why I should have all my things packed and moved simply because your guest came late."

"It's hardly fitting that you should share a room with a servant! And that...theatre-girl no less!"

Lise's fingers curled into the blankets and she bit her lip to keep from crying.

"Get out." Marie-Augusta's voice was ice-cold.

"I beg your pardon?"

"I would like you to leave my chamber, Mother," she said. "I have come this far. I have invited your precious Countess. I will entertain and be entertaining. But I will not change my rooms, and I will not tolerate you insulting my maid."

The Archduchess was silent for so long that Lise almost thought she had left. When she spoke, her voice was as cool and hard as Marie-Augusta's. "We have allowed you too many indulgences." Her footsteps tapped on the floor, her skirts whispering, echoed by her daughter's. When she spoke next, her voice was so low that Lise could barely hear her. "Consider your position, Augusta. You are not your own to do with as you please. You are a Habsburg. You must behave accordingly."

"Yes, mother."

The door closed. It was not slammed, but the quiet click had the same effect.

Lise dared not move, her fingers still clenched tightly in the blankets. She felt ill. She had never been present when Marie-Augusta and her mother argued before. It felt like she was intruding on something she had no right to hear.

Marie-Augusta's footsteps approached her alcove. "Lise?"

"I'm here." Her voice sounded so small, even in her own ears. She blinked hard, fighting back tears, then looked up at her mistress. Marie-Augusta looked as drawn as she felt. Lise lifted her hands, holding them out, and Marie-Augusta fell into her embrace, holding her tightly. Lise's fingers curled against Marie-Augusta's back. "I'm sorry," she breathed. "I'm sorry."

"For what, darling?" Marie-Augusta's words were warm against her neck.

Lise couldn't contain the quiet sob that shook her. "She makes you so upset, and all because I am here. I should have stayed in Vienna. I make things worse for you."

Marie-Augusta drew back enough that she could look at Lise, her dark eyes wide. "No, no, no, my little darling," she said, her voice breaking as much as Lise's. She lifted her hand to cup Lise's cheek, pressing her brow to Lise's. "If you were not here, it would be worse. It would be unbearable."

Lise's heart lurched. There were tears on Marie-Augusta's face, rolling down her cheeks. She lifted her hand to brush them away, and Marie-Augusta pressed her cheek to Lise's palm.

"Don't cry," Lise whispered. "Please don't."

Marie-Augusta nodded. She blinked hard, to clear her eyes, but that only set fresh tears down her cheeks. "Forgive me." She swept them away with a fingertip, and her fragile smile returned. "I have so few people who truly care for me."

"You are loved..." Lise started to protest.

"They only see the Archduchess and the Princess. Blood and titles are not who I am, Lise. You know that."

"Yes," Lise agreed quietly. "You are bad poetry."

Marie-Augusta's lips twitched. "None would believe that."

"And awful dancing."

There was almost a smile. "You are treading a fine line, darling."

Lise looked at her as seriously as she could. "And you have breath like a mule in the morning."

Marie-Augusta's eyes widened in genuine astonishment, then she caught Lise round the middle, pinning her down on the narrow bed she had not yet slept in. Lise squirmed, laughing, which only made Marie-Augusta smile more. "You, little cat, have large claws."

Lise lifted her hand to touch Marie-Augusta's cheek. "They gave you some colour again."

Marie-Augusta tilted her head and let her lips graze Lise's fingertips. With regret in her eyes, she sat up. "You know I must attend on mother and her lapdogs during the day now."

"I know," Lise murmured, sitting up. "But the nights will be ours."

To her surprise and pleasure, Marie-Augusta's cheeks reddened, and her eyes shone. "I thank God every day that I asked after your name at the Opera." She clasped Lise's hands. "You have made this cage so much brighter."

Lise lifted their joined hands to her lips, kissing her knuckles. "You should go to play your part," she said, "or your mother might come back."

Marie-Augusta shuddered. "Yes. We would not want

that." She rose from the bed, smoothing her skirts down. "Do I look suitable?"

"To me? Always."

Marie-Augusta's expression softened. "Flatterer."

"Honest." Lise smiled. "Why waste time pretending?"

Marie-Augusta cupped Lise's cheek once more. "My lovely darling," she murmured, as if she could hardly believe it. She smiled quickly. "I shall see you this evening. Until then, do as you please, and if any asks why, say you have my leave."

Lise took her at her word.

She donned her bonnet and coat and set out to explore the gardens of the palace. She heard a few of the servants whispering as she passed, but she paid them no mind. Her mistress had given her leave to explore, and the beautifully tended gardens were such a change from the bustle of Vienna.

When she and Marie-Augusta reunited after supper, Lise presented her with a flower she had stolen from the garden. It was a rose, but instead of one plain colour, it had golden petals tipped in red.

Marie-Augusta fingered the petals as Lise unravelled her hair. "Thank you," she murmured.

Lise, her mouth full of hairpins, made a sound of acknowledgement. She dragged the brush through her mistress' hair, twisting it into a braid for sleeping. "You're lucky I managed to get it with no one noticing," she said, once she set aside the pins.

"Oh?"

"Mm." Lise wrapped a ribbon around the end of the braid. "I found an axe in the gardener's toolbox. One of the houseboys chased me up the garden. He thought I had stolen it and was about to climb over the wall."

Marie-Augusta stared at Lise's reflection in the mirror. "You jest."

Lise widened her eyes innocently. Her mother always said she could have persuaded the Saints to sin with that expression. "Do I?"

Marie-Augusta turned on the stool, looking up at her, eyes narrowed thoughtfully. One arm leapt out and pulled Lise closer. "Yes, you wicked tease."

Lise laughed, bracing her hands on Marie-Augusta's shoulders. "Part truth," she corrected. "I did find an axe, and I did attack a rose bush with it."

Marie-Augusta started laughing in earnest. "Lord in Heaven, the Count and Countess will demand that we are sent away!"

Let them, Lise wanted to cry out. *Let them send us away somewhere without your mother or Mistelbach or the watchful servants.*

It was not her place, though. She knew that. Marie-Augusta had obligations, and as much as she—as they both—hated them, the Habsburg lineage brought conditions. One could not be an Archduchess of the house of Habsburg and imagine that she was free to do as she pleased.

Though Lise didn't say anything, something in her expression must have given her away. Marie-Augusta set down the rose in the small glass of water on the dresser, and rose.

"Come, darling," she said, taking Lise's hands. "I am very tired, and I imagine you must be too."

"I am," Lise confessed in a whisper.

With the curtains drawn and the candle snuffed, they could have done all manner of sinful things, but instead, in the quiet darkness, Marie-Augusta only held her.

Marie-Augusta's body was warm and soft against hers, and Lise fell asleep to the rhythm of her mistress' breathing.

With the morning, Lise rose before Marie-Augusta, intending to go and eat quickly with some of the other household servants before waking her mistress. She was tying the stays of her gown when she heard the bedding shift.

"Where are you off to?"

Lise glanced over with a small smile. Marie-Augusta's braid had come undone in the night, and her hair was a mess of wild curls around her face. "Some of the servants break their fast before the Master and Mistress wake. I thought I would join them."

Marie-Augusta blinked at her like a sleepy cat. "Nonsense," she said, patting the bed beside her. "I told the servants to bring me breakfast here. You shall stay with me and share it with me."

Lise stared at her. "That...Augusta, they expect you downstairs, the Count and Countess."

Marie-Augusta snorted and pushing her fingers through her hair. "The Count and his lady wife will be so preoccupied licking my mother's shoes, I doubt they would even notice my absence." She yawned widely. "Anyway, it is too late. My breakfast will arrive at nine o'clock, and you shall share it."

It felt like the world had shifted beneath Lise's feet.

Servants were not permitted to eat at the tables of their betters.

"I shouldn't," she said weakly.

Marie-Augusta smiled, sleepy and warm. "You shall. I insist."

Looking back, days later, Lise realised that agreeing to sit down to breakfast with her mistress was the death knell.

No one said anything at once, but Lise heard the whispers, the sniggers among the servants. Marie-Augusta must have fared no better because she was grim and stony-faced each night when she returned to their shared chamber. Still, she always had a smile for Lise, and each night, they curled together.

Lise couldn't help noticing that Marie-Augusta was holding her a little tighter, breathing a little harder, but she never said what had happened during the day. Lise didn't dare to ask. She only tried to keep Marie-Augusta's spirits up, though it became harder by the day.

When they finally returned to Vienna, Lise hoped the strange tension in the air would ease.

They had a day to themselves, when Archduchess Ludovika was elsewhere, and for a moment, all seemed well. Marie-Augusta doted on her. They walked together around the Ring. They visited the Prater and played skittles, though Marie-Augusta seemed distracted and even more melancholy than usual.

When she undid Marie-Augusta's hair that night, Lise couldn't hold her tongue any longer. "Has something happened?"

Her mistress looked up at her reflection. "My dear?"

"You have been so unhappy since our return," Lise blurted out. "I don't want you to be unhappy."

Marie-Augusta lifted her hand to touch Lise's, where it rested on her shoulder. "I know." She sighed, brief and low. "I fear my mother has taken her grievances to my father." Her fingers tightened on Lise's. "Perhaps even my uncle."

Lise trembled. The Emperor.

"What grievances?" she asked in a whisper, though she knew. She had known from the day Marie-Augusta started showing her favour. More so since the first day Marie-Augusta had smuggled her into a darkened alcove and kissed her, all soft lips and quickening breath.

Marie-Augusta only lowered her head. She looked so very tired.

Lise dropped the brush, and wrapped her arms tight around her mistress. "I don't care if they're angry," she whispered fiercely. "They can be angry, but that won't change anything. I am your maid...your woman. You chose me and I chose you and they can..." The treason almost stuck in her throat. "They can go hang!"

Marie-Augusta shook in her arms, and at first, Lise thought she was laughing, but when she looked at their reflections, Marie-Augusta wasn't laughing. She was weeping, shaking with the ferocity of it. "Oh, my little darling," she gasped out, her voice breaking. "They can do as they wish, and they shall." She clung to Lise's arms. "I dare not think what may happen."

Lise held her tightly, pressing her face to Marie-Augusta's hair. They would be parted. That was what Marie-Augusta feared. "They would have to drag me away," she promised. "I don't want to leave you. I don't want to."

Hot tears were soaking through Lise's sleeve. "Nor I you." Marie-Augusta's voice was trembling. "But my life is not my own."

It felt like they were standing on two sides of a breaking bridge.

All Marie-Augusta had to do was jump from her side of the bridge, where only bad things happened to her. Yes, the bridge was shiny and golden and rich, but what was that really worth? Why couldn't she be brave enough to do that? She was clever, and quick, and could easily get a post of a governess or even a teacher for young ladies. Why couldn't she see she only had to jump?

Lise wanted to ask, but she didn't know how, not when Marie-Augusta was already spent with tears and miserable.

The final toll of the bell came two days later.

The Archduchess Ludovika found Marie-Augusta in the library, where she had been helping Lise improve her letters. Lise scrambled up, curtseying to the Archduchess.

"Leave us."

Lise wished she had the courage to refuse, to stay at Marie-Augusta's side, but the Archduchess looked at her so coldly that she fled from the room, closing the door behind her. The hall was deserted. She looked around nervously, before pressing her ear to the door, straining to hear.

"...this shameless perversion."

"Mother..."

"Enough, Augusta!" The Archduchess's voice was like the crack of a whip. "You have disgraced us before, but at least then you toyed within your own class. Must you go and roll about with the filth now?"

Lise felt ill, pressing one hand to her mouth.

There was a crash from within the room, a chair knocked over. "How dare you!"

"How dare I?" Marie-Augusta's mother's voice rose in fury. "You brought a theatre-girl into our household, and I overlooked it. You had been discreet enough before, but this? Walking with her? Eating with her? Treating that little slut as your equ..."

The sharp sound of flesh meeting flesh was followed by absolute silence.

"I love her, Mother."

106

Outside the door, Lise had to lean against the panel of wood for support, her legs shaking.

The Archduchess laughed sharply. "Love? What does that have to do with anything? You are a Habsburg!" For a long moment, there was silence. "We have found you a match. He is...somewhat lower in rank, but in exchange for elevation, he is willing to overlook your...indiscretions."

"No."

"This is not a choice, Augusta."

"I will not have him."

"And what will you have? Your little trollop's name plastered across the news sheets? Her reputation dragged through the dirt? The Archduchess Marie-Augusta's little whore, the one who pleasures women as well as men?"

"You would not dare." Marie-Augusta sounded horrified. "Mother, please."

Lise's legs almost gave way beneath her. *No,* she wanted to sob. *No. Don't. Not because of me.*

"I would not need to." The Archduchess's tone had softened, but it was the purr of a tiger. "Don't you know how the servants gossip? I wouldn't have to say anything. The longer you shame her and yourself, the more soiled a rag she becomes. For her sake, if you...care as you say, be rid of her and make yourself respectable. Send her back where she came from."

Lise had to pull back from the door. She couldn't listen anymore. Her hands were shaking and her cheeks were wet with tears. She sat down in the window seat opposite the door, fighting the hot sick feeling in her stomach.

When the Archduchess emerged, she smiled at Lise, a victor's smile.

Lise stood numbly where she was. Through the open doorway, she could see Marie-Augusta seated in the chair by the mantle, her head buried in her hands.

On legs that felt like they were made of stone, Lise walked forward.

"You're to marry?"

Marie-Augusta raised her face from her hands. "A fine man, I am told." In half an hour, she looked like she had aged ten years. "How much did you hear?"

Lise's throat burned. "Enough." She took a quivering breath. "You didn't need to...not for me..."

Marie-Augusta's eyes were bright. "Of course I did, my silly darling," she whispered.

Lise had to look away. Her tears fell, shining spots on the marble.

Marie-Augusta was at her side in a heartbeat. "Oh, no, sweet one, please don't cry." She gathered Lise in her arms. "You will be safe and well. You have your old position to return to after all."

Lise blinked hard, trying to fight back the tears. "But what about you? You will be married to some strange man."

Marie-Augusta cupped Lise's cheek, and when Lise looked up at her, there was a flicker of a smile on her lips. "Then I will simply have to find a reason to go out." She met Lise's eyes. "Perhaps to the Opera."

Lise's heart felt like it flipped in her chest. Of course. Marie-Augusta was a patron of the City Opera. She had been for years. No one would question it. "You still have your private box?"

"Mm." Marie-Augusta drew her closer, embracing her chastely. "I do." Her lips were close to Lise's ear, and her breath was warm. "It has a lock."

Her face buried in Marie-Augusta's shoulder, Lise could almost smile.

A Year of Silent Promise

Doreen Perrine

April

Whatever I did in or around the house, this sea called to me, and I garnered my strength before its force. The endless flow of tides. As sure as waves, marriage, and motherhood had passed me by, yet I took on the cycle of life beside the beach. The blood and breath of what I have become. I even dabbled in paint.

The European tour Mother had embarked upon with me on had been no more than ladylike polish to refine me. Her hopes that I'd dazzle suitors with parlor talk to win a husband had been dashed. A virginal sacrifice to the unnamed passion for which I pined. That wealth of art had grown a seed, which, a year—this year—after her death began to blossom. Watercolors didn't pervade the house with the smell of the oil paint that seemed to be the hallmark of a serious artist. What my grandmother had yearned to be.

Now the palette of my paint box filled with tints of Polly's auburn hair. A fiery dawn crowned her portrait with its washy tones of flesh. Her face, a mask of shadows below her floppy hat, shifted with the pulse of light.

⁂

May

Whenever Polly left, I wandered like a lost girl with the dog padding behind. I didn't stop the way she did to pluck Mitzy, the black stray she'd rescued from below the bridge, out of soppy sand. The damned creature lacked sense to skirt puddles, rocks, or clumps of cattails. If only to hush her yippy bark, I would backtrack to wrench her free, a ball of sandy fur. Then I'd let her wander off again. Like my grandmother before me, I had never been maternal.

Yet I was more feminine at forty than Polly, twenty-six, could ever hope to be. A bonnet veiled the golden, silver-tinged twirls of my braids. With my lacy gown and parasol, she'd teased: I looked as though I had stepped out of a Monet. Polly, who'd secretly don Papa's smoking jacket, might easily pass for a man. Her angled cheeks and hair, styled off her forehead, were more handsome than pretty.

Every time I walked this beach, my thoughts were haunted by her absence. I basked in spectacles of backlit clouds, wings, and stars that infused a solace with their light. Breakers, spilling in a foamy necklace across the shore, lulled me to embrace the silence of our secret love. Our bond, deeper than this mask of sexless friendship, didn't need to be spoken. Not while we were so close—together and apart.

⁂

June

Polly dismissed Jill, who had stormed off with her paisley bag, the one she'd arrived with in my childhood.

"Why?" I'd asked, timid as a child.

She'd already coaxed me to let my gardener go.

"An unattached foreigner won't pry into our...intimacy."

One less secret for us to keep.

For some vague reason, the new housemaid had been let go from her position in New York.

"She'll come cheap with nothing but the clothes on her back." Polly winked. "No doubt she'll bite her tongue to keep her place."

The crisp blueness of Polly's eyes burned into my very soul. She might have gulled me into anything.

I trembled with panic and wonder as the housemaid stomped across my porch. We stared at each other as though through a looking glass. We were nothing alike. I was pale, small-boned and tall, and the woman was short and ruddy, more stout than plump. But we were close enough in age, childless old maids the world had all but erased.

"Good morning."

She returned my greeting with a curt nod as she circled me to enter the hall. She ran a finger down the dusty mirror and draped her coat on a tree bench meant for guests. Then she chucked her chin at the parlor door. "Show me into there." Her gravelly accent struck the air.

I led her, our skirts brushing the floor, and Hilda stepped inside as though she—and not the mask of Polly's and my silence—commanded the space. As we settled the details of her duties, Hilda interjected with more curt nods.

I lit a candle to guide her down the twisty steps into the kitchen. I pointed out the pantry, and then we wended our way upstairs to the two bedrooms. I shrugged with a devil-may-care gesture each time she clucked her tongue at the clutter. The unpeeled layers of forgotten years.

I left her to inspect every nook and niche from the attic to the cellar. Then she stomped off to entrench herself in the cottage for the night.

"Small wonder her city lady let her go," I said after Polly had come upstairs.

"Perchance she'll grow on us." She chuckled lightly as she wrapped me in a snug embrace.

I shuddered at the idea of growth as a parasitic outcome.

"Lucky to get a servant where I hail from. Hardworking to boot."

Polly, the youngest of twelve siblings, had been raised on a sprawling farm.

She unbuttoned our skirts, which crumpled in a silky trail across the floor. Her nimble fingers unlaced and unhooked our bodices, corsets, and garters. We slipped out of our frilly underskirts, petticoats, and stockings. She stretched across my bed, stripped off her chemise, and drew me down to nestle on her bosom.

Silence and shadows flooded the room. Our bodies, freed from the weighty garments, floated under and over each other like waves crashing to the shore below.

<hr />

The housemaid wore an apron with a hint of frills that belied her gruff manners. There was nothing frilly about Hilda, whose hair was knotted in a bun that appeared to yank her mouth into a frown. Her thick lips folded along her face as though she held an inner monologue. A behind-the-scenes drama the rest of the world could not be privy to.

"She's crusty," I said. Hilda complained too much and never said thank you or please.

"Yet she bakes like a dream." Polly ran her finger across a plate, spread chocolate on my mouth, and kissed my lips.

I melted like the chocolate with her kiss. Could I deny my Polly anything, even her sweet tooth for Hilda's cakes?

July

We read, half dressed, on the rockers before my fireplace, unlit on sultry nights. We savored *Sense and Sensibility*, our favorite book, until our eyes blinked in sleepy surrender.

Then we quickly unlaced corsets and petticoats, which we tossed into a ruffled heap below my bed. We flung chemises at the brass headboard and I rocked, laughing, in the chair. I curled my toes against the floor as Polly knelt, naked at my feet. Heat fused with our strokes and kisses until I fell back, panting for air. I spread my legs like wings in flight as she climbed on top of me.

My sole wish during those enchanted moments was that Hilda would tiptoe away at dusk. We couldn't afford a courteous maid, so I checked my tongue. Each night after supper, her heavy footfall faded outside as though she couldn't wait to take her leave of us. We could barely wait for her to leave, and then we gathered our skirts to trot upstairs.

113

We dropped onto the bearskin rug before the hearth and the house answered our writhing with creaks across the floor. The sweep of waves across the twilit shore voiced a promise—over and over—of our secret love.

⁓

August

My favorite way to swim is at high tide, flat back and face up to the sky. I flipped my arms like fleshy oars behind my head as currents whisked the world into a tranquil space. Silence mingled with the in-out breath of sea and the endless blue of sky.

The bathing suit, Nana's without the bloomers, stirred a girlhood memory. I had confused blood rushing in my ears with the lap of waves, and she'd explained in her lilting brogue, another comfort to my ears. "It's the flow of blood, Jane, telling us the heart is pumping. Steady on, like waves." I supposed my Nana would have known.

She'd left Granddad to live in this summer home, which appeared offshore as though it might topple into the sea. Grandad had given up the ghost of her after my mother and aunts had begged Nana not to live alone. *Why on earth not?* She had squandered most of her life on every other need except her own.

"Heartbeat," she'd told me, "the very first thing we hear, answers child to mother inside the womb." That made sense even after thirty years—even to a motherless spinster like me.

⁓

The world seemed to close its eyes to twilight, the hour

of bewitching magic. I imagined twinkling lights across the harbor, from lanterns or electric bulbs, to be faeries at play. Then it struck me how witches had burned, not a league from these shores, for less than our sacred bond. A decade into this new century, a lapse from secrecy would plunge Polly and me into poverty. A punishment of our freedoms—my home, painting, our girlish daydreams beside the sea—sucked dry by our breach from society. *No!* Voicing our love had never been a choice.

We let silence weave itself between our panting and the crash of waves. Washed away in pleasure or the heartache of our days apart, silence languished from dusk into night.

September

Hilda unearthed a painting from the musty cellar and stomped with it into the parlor. I squinted at the self-portrait, a profile, of my grandmother, a free spirit who'd studied art before her marriage. Brushstrokes feathered her cheek with a rosy tint that faded into gray. Varnish drowned the impressionistic hues she had gushed over in Boston.

Polly thought we might sell the painting and wanted it appraised. "It was collecting dust in the cellar," she said with an offhand shrug.

"My grandmother fought like the Devil to paint after bearing eight children," I said coolly.

Hilda, who waited in the silence, held the frameless canvas with a firm but tender grasp. Polly pursed her lips and I crossed my arms as though to dam the rage from spilling out of my gut onto the rug.

115

Without a word, Hilda mounted a stool to hang the portrait above the mantel. The framed daguerreotype of my parents on the mantel shrank below the painting's shadow. Nana's visage, if only in her lively eye, seemed to rouse my memories of a freer time. Of girlhood hopes.

October

The golden fabric of autumn unraveled itself to a thread of early winter. Dusk engulfed our bodies in shimmering red as we kissed, naked before the fire. We stumbled, breathless, into bed where the harvest sunset swathed our bodies, glistening with light and sweat.

Afterwards we bathed, taking turns to sponge each other in the tub Hilda had filled between our rooms. We dried off and then slipped into our separate beds, me in mine and her in my parents' bed—into the silence of our different dreams.

I awakened to spy Hilda filling the basin and taking the chamber pot away. She tiptoed back with the cleansed pot and to place lilac in a vase atop my dresser. The lap of waves stirred a hint of brine that mingled with the scent of freshly washed garments. One sensation lacking, I yearned to greet the day wrapped up in my lover's arms.

Hilda was an early riser and Polly feared the risk of her finding us together in my bed. The woman's English was keener than we'd realized, sharp enough to grasp and to gossip: Polly and I were so much more than friends.

Polly left again and I quibbled with Hilda about nitpicky things. She ought to use less oil and hang fewer lanterns above the stairways—inside and out. She countered with quibbles of her own. There was never enough money to spare for butter or eggs to bake her rich desserts.

The last straw, she grumbled about how the cabinets hung "too crooked" off their hinges. I plunked my paintbrush into a ginger jar of water and marched with her downstairs. Just as I'd secretly rebelled against my mother, I stuck my tongue at Hilda's back.

"Hallo? Fix them if they trouble you so much," I snapped and then tilted my head to squint. The cabinets, peeling with grayish paint, were noticeably off-kilter.

"Do I look a Jesus Christ to you?" She gaped as though horrified by the suggestion. "I am not any miracle maker."

"Yet you're loud enough to be a carpenter." I thrust my hands against my hips to defy her stony gaze. "You stomp like a hammer up and down the steps."

Her eyes softened with a grin on her lips, which she began to draw into the usual frown. A sulky pout formed instead and "Humph" was all she said before slapping open the cellar door. She squeezed her bulk and, with quieter footsteps, vanished down the stairs.

I gathered my skirts and scurried to retreat into the parlor. At length, the bang—a hammer, no doubt—reverberated throughout the house. Unable to concentrate on painting, I rubbed my throbbing temples and waited out the noise. No matter.

I bit my tongue as Hilda fixed all ten of my too-crooked cabinets.

November

I veiled my love for Polly in painting the way Jane Austen had hidden words behind needlework. She'd masked her extraordinary gift, frowned upon in women, from off-and-on guests; my paintings, nowhere near extraordinary, engaged the prying eyes of neighbors and my distant kin.

Polly left after the first of the month to pass the holidays—Thanksgiving through New Year—with her farmer folks.

"Why so soon?" I asked the darkness as I tossed alone in bed. "When cold is setting in and I need you here most?" *Why this wanton abandonment?*

A lonely month stretched like the barren beach ahead of me. I wrapped up in Nana's woolen cloak and must have appeared theatrical as I haunted the shore. The dog shivered in my arms but somehow the biting wind had no effect on me.

I walked the beach at different times: beneath a muted or a fiery dawn or dusk; in misty or radiant moonlight, fanned out across waves and shore. Snow settled around dunes, dips, and my boot steps, and stippled the sand like lace on golden flesh. A scarlet sunrise, crisp midday blue, or deep purple of encroaching night painted the sky. Water swirled and frothed with myriad reflections and my mind's eye awakened to the play of light.

December
I cannot shame my kinfolk with the terrible secret we

keep.

I shredded her *Seasons Greeting* card, imprinted with a scene of skating children, and tossed it to the waves. *...shame...secret...keep.* I searched through moist eyes for other words—*love...promise...forever*—that had graced Polly's lips, if not her script. But they didn't float up inside some bottled message from across the sea. Perchance they never would.

Instead of weeping, I hollered at Hilda over specks of ash on the parlor hearth.

"I did not cross this ocean for you to punish with your heartbreak!" She brusquely swept the ashes into a pail and then stomped down to the kitchen.

Polly had been wrong about another thing: Hilda was far from one to bite her tongue.

Soon, the aroma of chocolate wafted upstairs, tantalizing my senses to summon buried memories. Hadn't Mother and I baked, puttered in the garden, or combed for shells and pebbles on the beach? "Gifts from the sea," she'd called them.

Like a greedy child, I relished every morsel of that scrumptious cake. Then, out of sheer delight for Hilda's treat, I swallowed my pride and apologized.

January

What Nana called Women's Christmas was, for us, what spouses call anniversary, that Sunday of our first year together. Polly and I celebrated alone. A third class ticket—the best gift I could afford—had taken Hilda by Pullman, the white ghost train, to visit her sister.

We basked in the quiet and, after a supper of my pasty

soup, we stepped onto the veranda. The swing jerked under us as waves whipped into a blackened fury that spit out splashes. We lingered long enough to hurl strained laughter at the sea.

Her skirts whipped up as Polly spun around. "Pray tell me, how can you bear this cold and lonely place?"

Startled into anger, I wanted to spit like the sea. Didn't she see how I missed the lively theaters, cafes, and the museum where we'd met? "We could never live as secret lovers in the warm city."

"Nor in a warm country village." She nodded at the beach and my sigh was swallowed by the bracing wind.

Icy snow began to pelt across the railings and we scurried into the parlor. After bolting the veranda doors, I raced to latch shutters around the house. Upstairs, we stripped out of our wet garments down to our chemises. Then we burrowed with the dog beneath the quilt my mother had stitched by hand. Its matching curtains had been sold to pay for wood.

Neither of us stirred to rekindle the fire after its embers had died. Wind shrieked like the banshee of my grandmother's folktales as Polly wriggled out of our clothed embrace. Her shadow shrank across the floor planks until she disappeared behind the door.

My watercolors, like our love, fell flat, and I needed to embrace the failure of what I'd never be—not mother, not artist, not lover. The unbroken span of sand and sea had always felt too wide, too open. I couldn't bring such bigness to life, so I confined myself to still life, household portraits I squinted through spectacles to capture.

Polly, whose allowance had dwindled, crumpled a letter to toss it over the fire screen. "Pa wants me to marry."

I glanced up from my painting. "Who?" It came as no surprise that her father had chosen a husband.

"A boy, well, a man now, who owns nigh a hundred acres behind our farm."

She spoke as though my house had never been her home.

"Are you a head of cattle your father needs to auction off?" I sunk into the dip on my end of the faded chaise.

She pursed her lips, and I shivered below the rattling dormer window. The attic was our last retreat where she insisted we hide to make love. She didn't say what, in this godforsaken place, we were hiding from.

⚜

An automobile clattered across the bridge and down the marshy road to whisk her away. What could be so special that her father's horse and buggy wouldn't do? Had a meeting to strike up a match with the farmer neighbor been arranged?

Heartache bubbled with outrage in my chest and I glared at her belly. "Act quickly before your childbearing years crash to an end."

She slapped me, planted a sloppy kiss on my mouth, and then clambered toward the stairs. Her footsteps wound down and down until I heard the front door slam. I clutched my cheek. Like countless slaps I had borne from my mother's hand—every time I'd jilted another suitor—Polly's hand numbed my face and heart.

Unsure which I hated more—her slap or kiss—I flung

121

open the trunk Nana had brought from outside Dublin. What she'd called beyond the pale. I tugged out her wedding dress—the one Mother had saved for me to marry in—and its sleeves enfolded me with lace as I drew them around my back.

I pried caps off paints, miraculously, not fully dried, and rubbed brushes with linseed oil, bending them into pliant tips. Cradling paints and brushes in the folded dress, I stomped down to the parlor. Then I hitched my skirts to run upstairs to drag the easel, its back leg bumping along the steps.

Somehow I needed to voice in paint what I had never dared to speak. I faced Nana's profile like a talisman and, spellbound, gazed into her painted eye—green like mine. A glimmer of the hope that had been snuffed out with her haunted life still sparkled there.

February

I rummaged through Mother's sewing kit for scissors to deftly cut a heart-shaped card. I wouldn't risk the postal service and meant to hand the card to Polly if ever she returned. I penned *Our twain hearts seal this promise, strongholds in a world that mocks our love* between the doubled hearts. Then I signed *Forever yours! J. D.* in my best flowing cursive.

After the ink had dried, I laced the card snugly between my left breast and my corset.

My brush dropped, splattering paint around the

Turkish rug, as I darted toward a shriek. Hilda had slid across the veranda and crashed onto the snowy beach. I found her, doubled up with a shard of glass from the shattered lantern stuck into her thigh.

She shrieked again as I jiggled the shard free. I padded her apron to staunch the gush of blood and then bounded, losing my slippers in snow, across the yard. I yanked the barn doors, startling the cow and chickens I'd bought to stop Hilda's nagging me for dairy. I tugged shaggy Ol' Nel, who curled her lip with a cranky neigh, over to the sleigh. There was no time to blanket the mare or dust the crackled seat, and I fumbled with shaky fingers to hitch the horse onto the sleigh.

Then I gripped the reins to lead Nel, whinnying all the way, down a loopy path of snow and sand. I hoisted Hilda, twice my size, who pushed upward with a brawny arm, into the sleigh.

"Keep still." The runners jerked as we climbed the road and I braced Hilda's shoulder against my hip.

"Something inside of my leg is cracked," she said through bluish lips.

"Doc Cherby'll set that fracture," I said to console her and to ease my guilt. Perchance she'd have found her footing if I had spared more oil for the lanterns.

Cattails bowed with winter stiffness beside the road and mists billowed before the sleigh, which jingled with its strap of bells. I wrapped my bare feet in a rag below the seat and my gloveless fingers chilled around the reins. I squinted at the road. Hazy lights appeared to flit in mist as I strained to steer in their direction.

Why am I doing this? Hilda was neither kin, nor friend, nor lover to me. Struck by my own heartlessness, I shook my head as though to fling the thought onto the icy

123

road.

The horse clomped over the bridge, bumpy with snow, and Hilda's groans rang out with her frosty breath. The road grew smoother where neighbors had plowed and she began to mutter sharply in her native tongue. Cursing herself and me, no doubt. I half smiled, bemused to think of how—this once—I held the reins over my gritty housemaid.

Dawn, a rising beacon to guide us home, wove its light between the branches. Hilda's curses had given way to rhythmic moans as she rocked across the seat. I rapped her hand each time she rubbed the cast, which hadn't fully set, and, spurring the horse onward, I steeled myself against fear. Although Doc had used antiseptic, it was too soon to tell if she'd recover from the gash beside her vein.

I rounded a bend to swerve the sleigh around a sunken dip in the road. The circular plot of my family's gravestones jutted, white against white, out of snow. Moonlight spiraled across the field, a last fetal stage before night was birthed into the day.

"Jane?" Hilda raised her sweaty head.

She only called me ma'am or Miss Devine in Polly's or a guest's presence now. Her Christian name, she'd told me, was Clothilda, which meant battle maid. Small wonder.

She squeezed my elbow with a feebleness that belied her stoic nature, and then she recounted her story in a fragile voice. "The blame was all mine, this...lady tossed us into the night."

I assumed she meant the lady who'd dismissed her in New York. "How so?"

"My sister, just little at that time, got sick on the streets." Her brow creased with folds that rippled on her forehead. "We became two beggars, almost starved to death."

A stranger's voice, like that of a lost orphan's, seemed to speak out of the mist.

"That crass woman was no lady." I flinched. *What do I know of ladies?* The scrape must have taken place in Germany when they had both been girls. "How was that your fault?"

"I spoke too...brash, refused to shut my tongue with her."

"You don't shut your tongue with me," I said.

She bowed her head and a muted chuckle sounded from beneath her scarf. "Here it is me alone. There I had my dead mother's only other child to think of." Raven hair streamed through her fingers as she clutched her face. "It was not alone...me."

"Only." I slowed the horse to a canter as we neared the slanted bridge.

"Hmm?" She arched a brow above the scarlet threads the lined the scarf.

"You meant to say *only* me." I eyed her with a sideways glance as I pulled the reins to slow Nel. Then I abruptly turned to study Hilda's face. Her profile, softened in dreamy moonlight, appeared comely. Almost sweet.

"You saved your sister in the midst of all that...hardship."

"Yes. At long last." She bobbed her head emphatically. "I slaved in a laundry to pay her medicine and a ship to bring us here. But can you not see?" Her knuckles whitened as she gripped my arm. "I...*we* must have another to care of but ourselves."

The reins drooped, slung from my numbed fingers to the arc of the sleigh. As the horse clomped across the moonlit bridge, I was struck by the notion that I'd crossed a gap between our worlds. Hilda's and mine.

March

Polly, who'd returned in a crusty mood, accused Hilda of having been tipsy.

"I gave her a sip of whiskey to ease the pain," I said. "No more. Other than that, I've never seen her touch a drop."

Unlike Polly, who quaffed my father's store of cellar wine. She had polished off a cask and was drunk more often than not these days. What Granddad would have called pretty well over the bay.

"She may walk again." I lightened my tone but narrowed my eyes at Polly, who'd lost the gumption even to cower in the attic to make love.

She smirked and then curled her lip to sip more wine.

Something shifted in the deepening silence of those chilly days. We wore the masks of our pretense but she no longer stole kisses nor entered my room to embrace me at night. Our footsteps dragged to a less than brisk pace to greet each other at dawn. My Valentine card, which I offered without the flutter of my former passion, sparked no warmth on her behalf.

Without Hilda's unflagging energy, the house grew cluttered and I could barely paint amidst the chaos. My sigh dwindled to more silence as I watched Polly pack her bag to leave again. Unlike the thawing beach, our bliss remained frozen with unspoken memories.

Doc sawed off Hilda's cast and I kept a watchful eye on the tender wound. She could just about take the stairs on crutches to crawl into Polly's bed. Each morning and night, I washed and dressed the gash she strained to lift her leg for me to reach. I rolled her onto and off of the chamber pot, which I rinsed between our rooms. She struggled to sit up for me to spoon my bland soup into her mouth. She cringed, wrinkling her face with a look of disgust, but sipped without complaint.

Her smiles became less rare and the odd grin flickered on her lips. Guilt ridden and torn, I'd look away. *Should I send her to her sister's in New York?* If only to appease Polly enough to bring her home?

I plodded down to the parlor to stare at a blank canvas but nothing answered there. I didn't bother to lift my brushes out of the mucky can of oil. A numbness crept over me as I let my gaze wander from where I knocked back Granddad's whiskey on the sofa. *How pointless.* I plunked down the glass and the amber liquid splashed brushes, palette, and squeezed-out paints across the table.

Although neighbors offered to pay for portraits, without Polly, my muse, how could I create? Wasn't she the breath of my brush? Ordinary objects—the teapot, the curve of a spoon, sugar stacked in a pyramid of white—had always caught my eye. Their flair could only be captured with her, if not in the parlor, then somewhere inside the house.

Like an aimless ghost, I passed through the rooms that had become my tomb. A chasm of aloneness I hadn't felt since my mother's death filled me like the earth they'd pitched into her grave. I pictured Mother, thrashing on her deathbed, and was overcome by the sheer agony of losing Polly.

I trudged outside to glare from the veranda at the sea, unnerving in its calmness. Why paint? *Why breathe?*

I trained my eyes on the sea, which seemed to swallow itself in a crush of black waves. I stumbled over the rocks that had reminded my grandmother of her homeland. *Boireann.* I reached the outmost algae-laced rock and faced the waves until they slapped me to my knees. My hair and clothes dripped like the paint of my body, blending into a canvas of sea.

"Come back from there...please!"

The orphan voice from the night I'd driven the sleigh to town struck out of the fog. The sky answered with a shout of thunder that sent the dog, who sprang on her haunches, scrambling toward the beach.

"I'm going to swim." I scanned the water to fix on a cresting wave. Then I stripped out of Nana's wedding dress and flung it from the rocks. Wind tossed the dress in a swirl of white that rode the air until it vanished into fog.

"A storm is about to come." Hilda picked her way, shifting her bum leg between the rocks, to meet me on the edge. Her nightdress fluttered with frills and her unpinned hair twirled with wisps against the wind. "Will you die to swim today?"

Lightning unveiled a horizon of clouds that feathered the sky like graceful fingers. *An artist's hand?* Another roar of thunder, wind, and waves fused with the immense silence in my head. My braids clung to my cheek as I glanced across my shoulder. "My life is worthless without love."

"Your life is worth better than the love she hid from you." Hilda's eyes, moist with seawater or tears, were creased with a look of deep concern. She chucked her chin at me with a soft smile, softer than I'd ever seen, that lit her countenance. "Come home, Jane."

I turned slowly as though some force behind the raging sky guided my motion—an invisible force that wanted me to live. Then I reached for the stout lifeline of Hilda's outstretched hand.

April

"When in April the sweet showers fall/That pierce March's drought to the root and all." Nana's leather bound Chaucer, albeit thumbed and yellowed with age, pacified me into a newborn spring. And the last thing I'd imagined, imagination being my strongest suit, Hilda whipped me into shape. A lifeless lump of paint, I felt myself being brushed with her strokes across the canvas of my soul.

Polly mailed my Valentine with a last harsh note and I watched the papers burn to crumbles in the fireplace. I gathered ashes of the heart along with her scribbly writing—*God and man...disgrace of our bond...a sham*—and flung them to the waves. A sacrificial offering of what she could never have been to me. Not in any genuine way.

It was all I could do to keep up the prim appearance of the parlor to sell my portraits. Not everyone cottoned to this modern clamor for photography and neighbors, especially mothers with children, paid calls for sittings.

Hilda ignored my demands to leave the housework

until she had fully recovered.

"I scrubbed floors for a lifetime on my knees." She wagged a stern finger at me.

I rolled up my sleeves, tucked in my skirts, and dropped to the floor by her side. Why should Hilda, the most genuine soul I knew, grovel alone in crippled servitude? She could just about limp with a cane, yet we scrubbed, swept, buffed, and dusted.

Now we only quibbled over fiery things like where more lanterns ought to hang and when the fireplaces should be lit. I said early. She said late.

"You become extravagant with fire." She thrust a hand to her hip and, with the other, rattled her cane.

I had to laugh at her obstinate vigor.

In between our quibbles, the house metamorphosed into a spotless state. Renewed and all-forgiven.

***

I rented it to a troupe of actors who spilled with their children across the beach. The noisy chaos was just the challenge my Hilda needed to get back on her feet.

We'd carted my easel, paints, books, and quilt, if not my comfy bed, over to the cottage. Its two rooms were enough for us along with one yippy little dog. My brush, flowing with viscous paint, was infused by the fragrance of oils and by my lightened spirit. I promised myself to create a summertime of seascapes—not for money. Harking back to my girlhood days, I painted for myself again.

And again, I fell in love.

"Did you not think I knew?"

She stroked my naked body. Her work-worn fingers were rough yet their tenderness shot tingles of pleasure through my flesh. Her lips, surprisingly supple, sucked my breasts in turn and I rose with moans to meet her hungry mouth.

I was too lost in sheer delight to ask what she knew. Something about my history with Polly, no doubt; something I no longer felt the need to voice. Not now. Not within the hush of our tiny bedroom, white with the blankness of my cleansed soul. The view from the small window straggled out of marsh into the harbor. I snuggled on the pillow of Hilda's chest and closed my eyes. The crash of breakers, the blend of salty air with pine, and the caw of gulls seemed to fade along with memories.

Did I barter one mask for another? More than likely, yes. Unlike Polly, who'd succumbed to the sham of marriage and an acceptable home, this secret life with Hilda was a mask I freely chose. Ours was a promise I embraced with outspread arms and legs—wide and opened like the sea.

The Bridge

Connie Wilkins

Upstream the river riffled over stony outcroppings, but under the bridge it ran deep and clear. Reggie leaned over the wooden railing and stared down into those amber-green depths, willing herself to see only a great speckled trout balanced in perfect stillness against the current. An ordinary Midlands English stream, all green shadow and shimmering sunlight and blue reflected sky. An ordinary fish. Yet she could not block out visions of bodies submerged in other streams throughout the ravaged countryside of France, flowing ever redder with blood until they reached the Somme. Even the songs of birds in flight, spilling over with rapture, warped in her mind into cries for help, help that could never be enough.

"Shell-shock," the doctors might say, but it scarcely mattered what one called it. Pure, searing grief, not war itself—though war would have been enough—had breached her defenses. Grief for Vic. For herself without Vic.

By what right did England bask in such a May morning, calm and lovely, while over there artillery's thunder still shook the fields, and men rotted in muddy trenches? How could she bear to stand idle in the midst of such peace when her place was over there, even...even with Vic gone? All the more with Vic gone.

But she *must* adjust, must let the peace of home heal her—not that anywhere felt like home now. Or ever could again, without Vic. If Reggie could prove herself recovered, not only from her physical injuries but those of the spirit—capable once more, clear-minded—they just might send her back to the war. An experienced ambulance driver, strong as most men, skilled at repairing motorcars and field-dressing wounded men; here in pastoral England she was of no use, but over there she was desperately needed.

Reggie straightened abruptly, trying to focus on the tender green of new leaves, the glint of sunlight on the flitting gold and peacock blue of dragonflies. She shook herself like a retriever emerging from deep water.

"*Don't move!*"

The low, terse command froze her in mid shake.

"There's a nest..." The voice came from below, less peremptory now, but Reggie's mind raced. A machine gun nest? She fought the impulse to drop to the wooden planks of the bridge. Surely not gunners, not here! A nest of wasps?

"Sorry, I didn't mean to startle you." The speaker was almost whispering. "It's just that swallows are nesting below you on the supports of the bridge, and I've been sketching them, but they get uneasy when you move so suddenly and might leave the eggs."

A flush of fury heated Reggie's face. Forced to the

verge of panic by some silly schoolgirl! She bent over the wooden railing, an angry shout surging into her throat, and saw, first, a head of tousled light brown hair cut short about the ears. A schoolboy, then! All the worse! "WHAT do you bloody mean by—"

The artist looked up. The remainder of Reggie's words, stifled, burned like mustard gas in her mouth.

Not a boy. Not a child at all, though she might have been taken for one if it weren't for tiny lines at the corners of mouth and eyes, and a certain look in those eyes that spoke of a share of pain in her life; rather like what Reggie saw in her own when she was careless enough to look in a mirror. Her hair was really no shorter than Vic's pale curls had been in France, and Reggie's own dark thatch had been cropped a good deal shorter back then, a necessity in the filth and chaos of battlefields. She realized uneasily that it was about time she cut it again. Eight months in hospital had left it just long enough to tie back in a straggly knot, which she would have hated if she had cared in the least about appearance these days.

"I really am terribly sorry," the woman said. "I shouldn't have startled you like that. I get too engrossed in what I'm working on; it's my besetting sin. One of them, at any rate." A flashing smile turned her rather ordinary face into something quite different, almost enchanting, in the elven manner of an illustration from a fairy tale. "You must be Lady Margaret's cousin, and this is her bridge, so really you've much more right here than I. We'd heard you were spending the summer with her. I'm Emma Greening from downstream at Foxbanks." She stood from her perch on a mossy rock and made as if to extend a hand, then realized that she couldn't possibly reach up to where Reggie stood and withdrew it in some confusion. "Just a second and I'll climb out of here with my gear."

Reggie found her voice, or at least some version of it just barely suitable for the occasion. The hoarseness couldn't be helped. Vic had claimed to quite like what being a little too slow to get her gas mask on once had done to her tone.

"No, you can go on sketching. I was about to move along at any rate." Emma Greening...what had Margaret said about her? Something, in all that chatter about the local population, something about being an artist, but Reggie had paid no attention to any of it. No one in this dull, placid, countryside mattered to her.

Now she wondered just how much Margaret had told the local population about her. Or how much Margaret herself understood.

"I should be going myself," Emma said. "I can sketch swallows in my sleep—it was the bridge itself I wanted to catch in a certain light, and I think I have enough now to be going on with." She packed her sketchbook and paint box into a satchel slung over her shoulder, and stepped from the rock onto the steep riverbank.

"Here, I can give you a hand with that." Reggie heard the brusqueness in her own voice, and couldn't quite erase the remnants of her angry frown, but found herself reaching down from the top of the riverbank without remembering how she'd got there. Emma's sun-browned hand met hers in a firm grip, and she was up the slope so quickly and easily that it was clear she hadn't needed any help at all.

"Thanks. I'll be getting along now, and I do apologize for disturbing you." Her smile now was merely polite.

This would be as good a time as ever to practice behaving normally, Reggie thought. Best to scotch any gossip about her being a bit odd. "Don't leave on my account, Miss...Greening, is it? I'm Regina Lennox. Make that Reggie. Sketch here all you like. I'm the one who should apologize for being such a troll when you startled me."

Emma's smile flashed brilliantly again. "A troll? How funny that you'd say that! This is indeed a perfect troll bridge, which is why I was sketching it, for a book I'm illustrating. A children's story, the one with the three goats."

"Trip, trap, trip, trap over the bridge?"

"That's the one," Emma confirmed. "For now I wanted to get the bridge itself, rustic and charming, with the swallows, and that wren darting in and out of the bittersweet vines on the other side—she must have a nest there—and the clump of purple orchis just where the bridge meets the bank. All lovely and peaceful before the goats or troll appear. A lull before the storm sort of thing."

"So the troll got here prematurely." There was something comfortably familiar about this sort of conversation.

Emma tilted her head, surveying Reggie with mock seriousness. "No, I wouldn't cast you as the troll, exactly. In any case, I was the one under the bridge, or nearly so. I'm a better candidate for trolldom." She leaned her head the other way with a frown of concentration belied by a twitching at the corners of her mouth. "I see you more as the biggest Billy Goat Gruff—stern, shaggy, putting up with no nonsense from any troll."

"Certainly shaggy..." Reggie stopped short. Memory hit her like an icy blast. Vic used to tease her, rumpling her hair when it got shaggy and needed cutting, calling her a troll—often followed by, 'Well, get on with it, you slouch.

137

Kiss me if you're going to!' She felt her face freeze into grim stillness, bracing against the familiar onslaught of grief.

Emma stepped back. "Sorry again," she said, sounding embarrassed. "I have a bad habit of blurting outrageous things without thinking."

"It's not you," Reggie got out, but no more words would come.

"I really should be going now, anyhow," Emma said quickly. "I'll just leave you in peace. I expect we'll run across each other in the village from time to time."

Reggie watched in frozen silence as Emma picked up the bicycle lying beside the lane, settled her art supplies in the canvas panniers at the back, mounted, and rode away. Her divided skirt revealed a brief glimpse of quite nice lisle-stockinged calves above sturdy boots—and a smudge of moss stain where she'd been sitting on the rock.

So much for behaving normally! Reggie's spasm of grief was subsiding, and she wished she could call Emma back, but the bicycle had disappeared around a bend edged with dense shrubbery. And what could she have said? "I froze up because you reminded me of someone." Which wasn't even true. Emma didn't particularly resemble Vic. It was more the light, pleasant conversation, the brief exchange of banter...

Ah. That was it. Just as the rehabilitation counselor had said, but Reggie had resisted. Guilt. Survivor's guilt, they called it. Why should she be the one to survive? How could she deserve, or accept, even the least pleasure?

Well, she *had* enjoyed herself, if only for a few minutes. Maybe that was a sign of healing. She rubbed her hands across her eyes, then turned back to the bridge. A swallow darted under the arch, and a second bird took flight from the nest on the wooden underpinnings while the first took over hatching duty. On the far side a wren darted in and out between clusters of tiny white flowers on a trailing tangle of vines—bittersweet, Emma had called it. A small butterfly speckled like polished tortoiseshell flitted between masses of ferns on the upper bank. Emma would probably know what it was called.

It occurred to Reggie that this side of the bridge was the farthest she'd been from Margaret's house since she'd come here, and also that it must be close to time for lunch. A quick sound in the water and a spreading ring of ripples showed that the trout concurred and had snatched a mayfly from the surface.

She went back across the bridge, pausing to look down into the water. Only when she was well along the lane did she realize that her mind had played no tricks this time. She'd seen only the river, and the fish, and the reflection of a swallow in flight.

Margaret met Reggie at the edge of the garden, clearly relieved at her return.

"Elsie told me that you'd walked down toward the river, so I was just coming to tell you that lunch will be ready on the table in a very few minutes."

Margaret was kind, but closer to a middle-aged aunt than a cousin, and she worried far too much. The river at the bridge was nothing like deep enough for anyone to drown themselves in. Someone with Reggie's height would need to lie prone in the water like some pre-Raphaelite vision of Ophelia in order to manage it, and she was certainly not the Ophelia sort. Nor the Hamlet sort, when it came to that. Back in their Somerville College days at Oxford, she had played Othello to Vic's Desdemona in the all-women dramatic society, Vic teasing her into laughter so often during rehearsals that the actual performance startled them both with a fierce tension that went well beyond the dramatic...and well beyond the performance.

The thought brought a stab of pain, but also a wave of relief. She had not been sure that her mind still held such happy memories, that the tragic ones had not destroyed them. Margaret need not fear that she would destroy herself, with such memories to preserve.

She supposed she should make some effort to appear less submerged in despair, whether she were or not. "Very pleasant down by the bridge," she said casually as they walked back to the house. "That artist woman you spoke of was there, sketching birds' nests or something of the sort."

"Oh, you've met Emma! How nice! We must have her over for tea one of these days."

Tea. Over there, tea had been at best a brief pause, or no pause at all, to swig a bitter brew from a thermos bottle; tea or coffee, no milk or sugar. Still hot only if you were lucky. And when any of the lads you transported in the ambulance were in good enough shape to sit up and drink, you willingly gave your share to them.

"She didn't strike me as a tea party sort." Which was a plus in Reggie's opinion, or would have been if she'd cared. She did care a bit, in fact. Emma seemed like someone she could enjoy chatting with, bantering, in a casual friendship uncomplicated by passion or drama.

"Well, she keeps quite busy with teaching drawing at the Midbury School for Girls, and does the most charming illustrations for children's books, and is active in village affairs and war relief as well, so she might not have much time for tea. But she's really quite nice, and from a good family."

How genteel, Reggie thought. Although the split skirt

and the slim strong calves that clambered up a steep riverbank as easily as they propelled a bicycle had not struck her as particularly ladylike.

It occurred to her that Margaret was sounding suspiciously like a matchmaker. Of course she couldn't be blamed for wishing Reggie to make friends, or to at least do something besides mope about the house, but could there possibly be more to it? Surely not. Hard to be certain whether her cousin had guessed how much more Vic was to her than a chum from student days, or a teammate in the grim work of bearing stretchers and driving ambulances on the battlefield...where an exceptionally long ranging shell could hit vehicles, patients, drivers...

Trying desperately to distract herself from that last image, she played along with the casual conversation. "Yes, she introduced herself. Said something about wanting to catch the bridge in a certain light."

"Artists can be rather odd like that," Margaret prattled on. "But they say she's very good. I've only seen her sweet watercolors of birds and flowers and local scenes, but her work is shown in galleries in Birmingham, and even a few times in London at the Royal Academy of Arts, which is quite grand, I believe."

Reggie was relieved to be stepping through the French doors from the garden into the morning room, where the housekeeper Elsie had lunch laid ready. For once she even had an appetite.

"Is there a competent seamstress in the village?" she asked Margaret when the meal was nearly over. For an instant her cousin's mouth hung open in astonishment before she could answer.

"Oh! Well, yes, there's that Miss Ogilvie who used to be a governess until she retired here to live in Bramble

Cottage after her great-aunt died and bequeathed it to her. You know, that charming little thatch-roofed house just where the Mosely road branches off from the High Street? Thatched roofs are dreadfully susceptible to vermin, of course, but so picturesque, and Miss Ogilvie has had her roof rebuilt and sealed off from the interior, and then re-thatched, and—"

"An admirable woman, I'm sure," Reggie broke in. "But can she do a decent job of altering clothing?"

"Oh yes. Of course no one is having new frocks made these days, with everything so scarce and so dear, so she does a great deal of mending and taking in and letting out and restructuring, until one would scarcely believe that the garments weren't new. She even...well, I took her that immense paisley silk shawl my great grandfather brought from India, the one that used to be spread across the grand piano, and she sewed folds and tucks and fashioned it into a quite stylish evening wrap without making a single cut in the fabric! I'm so glad you're thinking of having some clothing altered. You've lost so much weight during your illness!"

There was some truth to that, although Reggie knew quite well that Margaret also wished she would dress more conventionally. The tunic and trousers and trench coat that had been the accepted uniform for ambulance drivers in the war zone were fairly close to what the Women's Land Army girls wore as they farmed here in England, and thus not exactly unconventional, but there were times and situations where they were out of place. Not that Reggie gave a damn for such times and situations.

The next morning Reggie packed up such clothing as she'd brought, mostly those tunics and trousers, but also two severely styled black gabardine dresses and a long skirt of brown twill. She drove an old cart pulled by grey Molly, a pony elderly enough not to have been requisitioned by the army with most of the other horses in the area. The Daimler that had been the pride and joy of Margaret's late husband still stood forlornly in the stable, only saved from being requisitioned by being in poor repair, and likely to be taken soon for parts in spite of it. Margaret went along into the village to do some shopping.

"I do think you'll like Miss Ogilvie," Margaret said cheerily as she went off to browse the meager wares of the baker and greengrocer and have a look-in at the tea room in case any close friends were there.

Reggie did like Miss Ogilvie. They recognized each other as two of a kind almost immediately. Reggie in her trousers was, of course, easier to spot, but Miss Ogilvie in her tailored suit had a way of moving, of holding her head, meeting Reggie's eyes with a certain subtle smile in her own that was unmistakable if one spoke the unspoken language.

When Reggie held up the brown twill and asked whether it could be refashioned into a split skirt, the seamstress cast a professional eye over it, then over Reggie's hips and thighs, and nodded with just a touch more than professional approval. "Quite enough fabric for that. Styles are shorter now, so I can take a good deal off at the bottom and use it for paneling to insert along the inseam." She knelt to take the required measurements with no hint of impropriety, to Reggie's slight regret and great relief. No complications, just an acknowledged fellowship.

Miss Ogilvie looked up. "Do you ride a bicycle? A split skirt is just the thing for riding."

"I might take it up for the exercise. And the

convenience, of course."

"Excellent exercise, especially when one has been in hospital for some time."

Reggie stiffened. "Yes. I suppose Margaret has spoken of it." How much else had she told her backward, countrified world about Reggie's affairs?

Miss Oglivie rose, jotted down numbers in a journal on her desk, and turned with a companionable smile. "Just that you'd been injured driving an ambulance in the war, and in hospital for several months, and had come to recover in the fresh country air. Nothing more, I assure you. No gossip gets spread around town without making its way here, but no gossip originates here, or ever will."

Reggie relaxed just a notch or two. "Well, that's all true. I'm a bit scarred on the back and shoulders, but nothing to interfere with bicycling." It occurred to her that a little innocent gossip about Emma Greening might not be out of line. "I thought of the split skirt when I chatted with a lady artist yesterday who wears one when she cycles."

"Oh, I'm so glad you've met Emma!" Miss Ogilvie's words spilled out in a manner quite startling after her professional coolness. "She could use the company of someone from beyond this rural backwater. It's been stifling for the poor girl this last year, taking care of her elderly parents. They went quite to pieces after her brother was killed. Of course this is her home, and the basis for most of her art, and she keeps busy with her teaching and volunteering for war causes, but other than the art she has precious little joy in her life. She can't even get away now and then to London as she used to, visiting artist friends in Bloomsbury and Chelsea and, you know, all that lot."

Reggie did know "all that lot." And she understood what Miss Ogilvie, despite her claim of initiating no gossip, wanted her to know.

After a few more measurements pertaining to taking in the waists of the trousers and dresses, and advice as to a barber who might do a decent trim of her hair, she left Miss Ogilvie's establishment with her mind in turmoil. So Emma Greening was indeed a country girl, but one with a decidedly worldly side and artistic tastes that went well beyond sketching birds and flowers. If both Margaret and Miss Ogilvie were bent on pushing them together...well, Reggie had clearly been underestimating Margaret's powers of perception.

Perhaps it would be better not to think of friendship with Emma Greening after all if Reggie meant to avoid complications, and drama, and...and passion. She thought again of that slim, strong hand, those calves below the split skirt, that sudden, brilliant smile. Definitely some danger there.

Once she'd been out and around and visible in the village, Reggie thought it best to keep up the effort to avoid appearing any odder than she could help. There were some fittings with Miss Ogilvie—"Lydia" by then—and a single appearance at church wearing one of the altered gabardine dresses (which were then hung at the back of her closet and ignored.) She found that passing the gravestones on the way through the churchyard was so disturbing that only the exquisite organ music got her through the service. So much death in war...so many denied a peaceful rest in a country churchyard...

Reggie also accompanied Margaret by bus to the nearest good-sized town. While her cousin shopped, she found a fix-it shop that sold repaired bicycles, chose one to be delivered once suitable adjustments had been made, and struck up a companionable conversation with the

145

owner. He'd been invalided home early in the war, but swore that operating from a wheeled chair or on crutches just made him better at understanding the mechanics of vehicles in general. They swapped stories of jury-rigging repairs to ambulance lorries and the horse-drawn caissons that bore the great guns, using whatever unlikely bits of metal or binding could be scrounged, from bent metal stirrups to leather bootstraps.

What Reggie did not manage, in all this whirl of sociability, was to see any trace of Emma Greening. Could the artist be avoiding her? She could scarcely be blamed after Reggie had been such a...well, such a troll. Strange that the absence of someone she'd barely met could feel like a hollow place inside her. Just as well to leave it at that.

Still, she mentioned Emma's absence to Lydia Ogilvie, who was not deceived by the attempt at an off-hand tone. "Yes, she's away doing volunteer work at least one week out of each month. If you want to know more than that, you must ask her yourself."

Three days later Reggie saw a bicycle with familiar canvas panniers leaning against the low wrought iron fence surrounding the churchyard. In a far corner of the enclosure, someone with unruly light brown hair sat in the grass by a gravestone, bent over what might be a sketchbook. Not a suitable time at all for a casual greeting. Still, Reggie leaned her own second-hand bicycle against the fence and stood watching against her better judgment.

The bent head lifted. Emma gazed at the stone for a long minute, then raised a hand to rub an eye. To rub a tear from an eye, Reggie was certain. Quite definitely not a time to invade someone's privacy.

Yet there Reggie was, setting one hand on the top rail

and vaulting easily over the fence, striding between the ancient and not-so-ancient headstones, and dropping to the grass beside Emma.

Emma looked up, face drawn, eyes bright with tears. She didn't seem surprised at all to see Reggie. "Mother can't bear to come here," she said in a low voice. "But if I draw the stone, with flowers that bloom here or some I've picked, and leave my sketchbook open on the hall table, she'll pick it up and look. That's the closest she can come to acceptance."

The open sketchbook showed a watercolor scene, still damp, portraying the grey stone with softly muted edges and an inscription that could just barely be read, although the one on the actual stone was sharp and all too recent: "Lieutenant Edward Greening." In front of the pictured stone, small bright buttercups danced on delicate stems, minutely detailed mirror images of the actual flowers before them, just as an oak branch in full leaf at the top of the page matched the very one arching above them

"Your brother?" was all Reggie could think of to say. Something about sitting on the grass together made any formality absurd.

Emma looked back at the stone and went on as though they were longstanding friends, the sort with whom one could share deep thoughts when one desperately needed to speak them. "At least Eddie came home. So many others never will. Who knows—you might even have carried him in your ambulance. But he was too broken to live long, in too many ways. And he'd lost someone he loved over there. I think he would rather have been buried there too, in 'some corner of a foreign field...'"

"'...that is forever England.'" Reggie continued the quotation without conscious thought. "So you know

Rupert Brooke's poetry." Vic had loved Brooke's poetry. Reggie braced for the pain the thought must bring, her face tightening.

"Oh yes. Rupert was from this district, a distant cousin in fact, and Eddie knew him at Cambridge. He was given his book when it came out. Eddie thought him rather too sentimental, but his words were sadly prophetic and do stick with one in times like these." Emma turned, saw Reggie's expression, and reached out to touch her arm. "You lost someone there?"

The pain came, but now she could speak of it, which made all the difference. "Vic only went to the war because I did...and now she's dead, when it should be me." She drew a gulping breath. "I want to go back, I must do the work again, but with her gone..." She groped in a pocket for a handkerchief. She'd thought all her tears had been spent long ago, but one was making its way down her cheek.

Emma passed her a paint-stained square of cotton cloth. "Work is the only thing that helps, no matter how hard it is to do, but there's more than enough of it on this side of the Channel. I go to Oxford once a month because I'm needed, but also because I need to do the work."

Reggie stared at her blankly. "Oxford?"

"Somerville College has been converted to a hospital for the duration," Emma explained. "I was in training there to go to France as a nurse, but then Eddie...then I had to care for my parents. Now I go one week a month as a nurse's assistant, filling in when others need time off, helping with cleaning, changing dressings, lifting, sitting with cases who can't be left alone. Sometimes the lads like me to make sketches of them to send home to their families and sweethearts, pictures showing them less...less harshly than a photograph would..." She snatched the cloth back and used it on her own cheek.

The flush on Reggie's face this time was of shame, not anger. What a thick-headed jackass she'd been, assuming that folks in the peaceful countryside knew nothing of the horrors of war. And giving no thought to what became of the wounded she carried to the field hospitals, or from those to the ships, once they got back to England.

"I could be of help there," she said slowly. "I could go with you."

"Yes. You could."

A long, considering silence. Then: "We were at Somerville together, Vic and I. Victoria and Regina. We got ragged about the names, of course, but eventually everyone just took it for granted that we did everything together."

Emma smiled at that, not her brilliant, flashing smile, but one of understanding.

"I should go there," Reggie went on. "There are people in Oxford I must see, a tutor who was a mentor to me, and to Vic, and wrote to us when we went to the war, as did some others as well. But I've been putting it off. To be there, when Vic never will be again...to tell them how it was, how she died... It's a bridge I must cross, but I don't know how I can bear it!"

Emma wrapped her fingers around Reggie's as though they had a perfect right to be there. To Reggie it felt as though they did.

"I can give you a hand with that," Emma said, echoing Reggie's words by the wooden bridge where they'd met. "Over any number of bridges."

Reggie tightened her grip, leaned forward, paused, and thought briefly of looking about to see whether any passerby could see them. But Emma had leaned forward as well, so that their faces all but touched, and a breeze through the oak leaves above them sounded uncannily like Vic's voice saying, 'Get on with it, you slouch!'

So Reggie did. And the salt of spent tears had never tasted so sweet.

Captain My Captain

Lexy Wealleans

"So this is famous Duncliff, is it?"

The house was only visible in snatches through the trees—a leaded window here, a glimpse of Tudor brickwork there—as the car made its way up the drive. It seemed larger than Sylvie remembered it, alone on the grassy clifftop, easy prey to high seas and crumbling chalk.

As they rounded the corner and the house came into full view, it seemed shabbier too, the paint on the windowsills peeling under the sandpaper winds, ivy growing unchecked between the bricks. Even so, Laurence craned his neck forward, looking up at the brickwork, the complicated chimneys, all that old English splendour, and let out a low whistle.

"Nice spot," he said. "Bit out of the way, but still..."

She understood: it was the kind of place he wished his people came from, rather than suburban Richmond with its villas and communal tennis courts, its socially aspirant families and new money. The car crunched through the gravel, Laurence easing it to a halt in front of the steps.

151

Sylvie moved to open the door, unfold her legs from their travelling position, but Laurence stopped her.

"Wait," he said, a restraining hand on her arm. "What do you call him, your godfather?"

Sylvie stared at him blankly for a moment, confused.

"Uncle Charles, generally."

"Yes, but what do I call him?"

"Oh, well. He'll tell you, I'm sure. But you could start with Lord Wingfield."

"Lord Wingfield," Laurence repeated to himself. She hadn't realised he was so nervous. They were virtually her family, after all—they were who she was, a long time before she knew him. "Lord Wingfield, pleased to meet you. Pleased to meet you, Lord Wingfield, Lady Wingfield. Alright, Laurence, alright." Then he paused, doubted himself. "Do I bow?"

But Sylvie was already out of the car, heading toward the open door.

"Aunt Maud, Uncle Charles," she said, letting herself be caught up in a hug. "It's so good to see you, it's been far too long."

Her godfather was fatter and redder than she remembered, his wife more pinched and drawn. They had same haunted look about them that you saw on many people these days, that civilian sort of shell shock that showed no sign of wearing off.

"Shame your father can't come, Sylvie," he said as he let her go.

"He sends his apologies, but business keeps him in town."

"Of course, of course. Oh well, eh Laurence, just you and me on the links tomorrow then."

"Yes, sir."

"Did you bring any clubs?" It was almost an accusation.

"I didn't, no." Laurence's head bobbed in some form of apologetic nod, twitching a smile onto his face.

"Never mind, never mind. Come in here, I think I've got spares that should suit you admirably." The older man clasped his arm around Laurence's shoulder, marching them off into an adjoining room. His wife watched them go, twisting her hands together as though they were cold.

"Oh dear—you've started him off now. Your young man will never get away." She smiled at Sylvie, motioned ahead of her up the stairs. "Let me show you to your room."

Unlike its owners, the house hadn't changed between visits, eight years a mere instant to architecture. The same wallpaper, the same carpet, the same long-dead ancestors staring down solemnly from the walls. The only difference was the quiet—no running children, no bustle of servants. Even the dog, lying in front of the fire, barely raised its newly grey muzzle to watch them, a few thumps of the tail their only greeting.

"Here we are, Sylvie. Next to Harriet, the same as last time. I've put Laurence down the hall, in William's old room." She smiled down at her shoes, and swallowed. "I'll leave you to get unpacked. Just going to check on Cook and dinner."

Sylvie stood in the room, drinking in the changes. The silence, the thin patina of dust on all the side tables and lamp shades—these, Sylvie supposed, were the hallmarks of the new world order, servants up and left for the city, for office jobs or the factory floor.

"There you are," Laurence said, peering round the door and moving forward. "Thought I'd never escape—I

153

wasn't quite prepared for just how posh it all is, you know? How old money."

He hadn't seemed to notice the dust, the silence.

He caught Sylvie's waist and pulled her closer. The thin, sandy moustache above his lip quivered.

"Now we're on our own, how about you come here and give me a kiss."

"Not here, Laurence," she hissed, batting him away. "She could be back any minute."

Laurence stepped forward again, insistent.

"She won't—I heard her go down the stairs." He leant in, hands against the wall on either side of Sylvie's head. "Come on—we never have time in town. Just one."

The door of the wardrobe opened, and a girl fell out.

"You were taking forever," she said irritably. "Weren't you going to unpack? I've stood in there grimacing so long that I think my whole face has seized."

It took a moment for Sylvie to recognise her, this friend of childhoods past.

"Harriet!"

She'd been stuck in Sylvie's mind as a fourteen-year-old—long plaits and girly dresses, a crop of sun-ripened freckles across her nose and cheeks. The freckles were still there, of course, but just about everything else had gone. Her hair had been cut to a cheek-length bob, not the sleek lines of London coiffure but curling and untamed, and the fancy dresses had morphed into shirts and jodhpurs.

Harriet's mouth twitched into a half-grin, and Sylvie remembered she was staring.

"I was starting to think you were avoiding us."

"Never." The woman with Harriet's name and voice pressed a kiss to Sylvie's cheek, then turned to Laurence, looked him up and down appraisingly. "Hullo."

She held out her hand for an efficient, practiced handshake. Next to Sylvie, still in her long tweed skirt with its pre-war cut—high at the waist and down to her ankles, she seemed very confident, very modern.

"You must be the fiancé. Laurence, isn't it?"

"Yes, that's right."

Harriet turned victoriously to Sylvie.

"See? You can tell Mother I do listen."

"I hear you've got a brother, Lady Harriet," Laurence said, bending as if to look under the valence. Sylvie took a step forward, hand outstretched, marshalling her mouth into some kind of sensible movement—there was no stopping him. "Is he under the bed?"

Harriet's mouth opened soundlessly for a moment, before her hands found her trouser pockets.

"He died, in seventeen. Of wounds. Shrapnel everywhere, apparently." She paused briefly, rocked back on her heels, sniffed. "The parentals never talk about him—at all—but I am surprised no one's told you that."

Sylvie stepped forward, her hand reaching for Harriet's arm. The flesh beneath the shirt felt solid, strong, warm, the muscles bred of hard work rather than tennis strokes.

"I'm sorry, Hattie."

"Oh, it's alright." She was embarrassed, Sylvie could tell, hiding it behind breezy affectation. "Been a whole four years in October, and we're getting used to it. Me to being the sole focus of familial ambition, and Père to the idea that a girl will have the estate next and run it without her head exploding."

There was a long, awkward moment of silence.

"So," Harriet said, jovial again, "you're engaged."

"Yes." Sylvie forced herself to smile in return, catching Laurence's hand. "I'm very happy."

"No ring?"

"It needs resizing—it's a bit big for me at the moment."

Harriet smiled, nodded, then—to Sylvie's relief—somewhere downstairs the bell rang for dinner.

—❦—

"What do you think, Laurence?"

Laurence swallowed, patted his mouth with his napkin, chose his words carefully.

"I think they have about as much chance, Lord Wingfield, as the State Medical Service Association do with their dream of a nationalised health service."

Uncle Charles harrumphed into his dinner.

"Quite right, my boy. Quite right. Can't go giving these damn micks their independence. Then what? We just give away India? Australia? For God's sake, Scotland?" He took another draught of wine, ran his tongue along his front teeth. "You mark my words, Laurence, Lloyd-George won't let this go any further, not if we've got anything to do with it."

Harriet leaned close, her mouth almost touching Sylvie's ear.

"He means the House of Lords, of course. Which really is nothing more than a retirement home for grouchy old men."

As though aware of her daughter's seditious line of thought, Harriet's mother leaned forward, catching Sylvie's attention with a soft touch to the wrist.

"It's all rather above me, I'm afraid." She smiled, wanly, while her husband and Laurence continued unimpeded. "I know we have lady members of Parliament now, Sylvie, but I confess I think politics is much better left to our men. After all, they're the ones out in the world. Don't you agree?"

"Well," Sylvie started. Laurence would agree, and want her to agree as well, and so would her father. But in the war she'd seen female tram drivers, lady doctors, women manning factories and farms. And look at Harriet, so clever, so confident, as put together and completely herself as any man. "Not exactly...I think that, in some cases..."

She stumbled over the words, the influence of finishing school—be polite, be discreet, remember your manners, your duty to please—still too strong to let her get her own opinion out.

Harriet rolled her eyes, motioned for Sylvie to pass the wine.

"Oh, Mother," she said, filling up both her and Sylvie's glasses. "Sylvie doesn't agree with you—she's a modern woman, like me. We're young, you know, ready for change. I think you'll find the war's quite done away with all that stuff."

It was clearly a common argument, for her mother sighed, and bent her head to her fish again.

"Harriet, please..."

"No—by the time I'm gone we'll have the vote, you bet, and equal rights. And at the same age of majority as men. We'll have jobs, and proper careers, and no one will think less of us for doing so." It was a standard spiel—you could read it on the lips of any number of pamphleteers in Trafalgar Square—and yet, in this setting, with the portraits of long-dead bastions of the establishment staring down at them, it felt brave.

"Votes for Women!" Harriet banged her cutlery on the

157

table, startling Laurence and her father from their conversation. "Right, Sylvie?"

Flushed with wine, Sylvie smiled, huffed a laugh despite Laurence's brow-heavy stare.

"Right! Votes for Women!"

———

The next morning Sylvie woke with her head full of cotton wool. She rolled over, swung her legs out of the bed, and her stomach twisted in protest.

By the time she got downstairs the breakfast room was empty, the food eaten and cleared away. Sylvie sunk into a chair and rested her head in the hands.

How awful, to have completely missed a meal because she'd been too drunk to get up. Laurence would certainly have a lecture saved up for the car journey home—if, that was, her headache didn't kill before then.

"Sorry," Harriet said over her shoulder, "I thought you'd want to sleep, after last night."

"Was I very embarrassing?"

"No, not at all." Harriet was very convincing, earnest and sure, until she caught Sylvie's eye and couldn't stop a lopsided smile spreading across her face. "No worse than Père, anyway."

She smiled, rubbed Sylvie's arm.

"Everyone else has gone out already," she said, "which means you get to come treasure hunting with me instead."

The walk through the grounds was gentle enough even for Sylvie's head. Harriet chatted easily, called out hellos to the ground staff, to people passing in the lane. Sylvie was starting to feel better, feel more alive, her fingers tucked into the crook of Harriet's arm, until they came to the cliff edge.

The ground dropped away in front of them, white chalk exposed beneath the grass. It was a long way down, and the steps looked small and steep to Sylvie's half-focused vision.

"I don't really feel..." she started. "I mean, aren't we a little old for treasure hunting these days?"

"Look," Harriet said, perched on the edge of the cliff, "I told you before—you're never too old for treasure hunting."

She grinned, the wind catching her hair and pulling it across her eyes. If Sylvie didn't give in she'd only start pouting, kicking at grass tufts despondently, and Sylvie had never been able to resist Harriet's pleading.

"Alright," Sylvie said, scrunching up her eyes against the reflected sparkle of the sea, "but only because it's you, Hattie."

After all that, the cliff path wasn't too bad in the sunshine, Harriet talking the whole way down. Every so often she'd stop and gesture expansively to the cliffs or the beach, to the black-backed gull circling overhead, and Sylvie would stop and catch her breath, her heart slowing to a normal pace.

Sylvie remembered this stretch of beach, the gentle incline, the rocky jagged cliffs. They'd played down here all summer, it seemed, and the only wet day had turned them into cave-dwellers, pressing themselves through cracks in the rock, drawn in by Harriet's story-telling and the gleam of gold in the darkness.

They walked along the shoreline for a minute or two, Harriet skimming stones in the surf, until they reached a boulder the height of two men.

"Go on then," Harriet said, cocking her head at the

rock. "Up you go."

Sylvie laughed, shook her head. Cliff paths and skimming stones was fine, but rock climbing was too much for her delicate, Harriet-and-wine induced condition.

"No, Harriet, I don't think so. I'm not dressed for..."

"Oh go on." Harriet laced her hands into a stirrup. "You remember the way up, don't you?"

The cave was smaller than Sylvie remembered, the ceiling lower. Harriet's head appeared at the ledge, shortly followed by the rest of her.

"You made that look easy," she said, pulling a torch from her pocket. "Don't know what you were complaining about."

All the nooks and crannies were empty now, stripped of the treasure they'd found. Even the old barrels and chests had disappeared, small patches of rusted rock the only indication they'd ever been there.

"Where's it all gone?"

Harriet shrugged, directing the beam along the wall.

"Sold, mostly. Turned into new ploughs and window casings. Nothing exciting, I'm afraid."

"And you've brought me here again, to this cold and empty cave, because...?"

"Not here, dummy," Harriet said. She lifted the torch into the corner of the cave, to a dark hole not four feet across. "In there."

Sylvie let herself be lead through the gap, Harriet's hand warm and firm in her own. The space was very narrow, just wide enough for them to shuffle down sideways, face and back pressed against the rocks.

Sylvie was starting to feel uncomfortable, trapped, when Harriet let go of her hand.

"Nearly there," said her voice from the darkness ahead. "It gets wider here."

The torch beam was turned upward, bouncing off the walls, off the dripping stalactites. And, just as before, off glinting gold.

Sylvie took a step forward, reached for Harriet's arm for balance.

"Oh," she said. "Gosh, Harriet." There was far more stacked up here than there had been in the outer cave, coins and trinkets spilling out onto the ground. "I didn't expect..."

"No, I know," Harriet said, "and best of all, look at this!"

A sword flashed through the torch light, Harriet lunging and feinting into the empty cave.

"Well, you've got a pirate's treasure," Sylvie said. "Seems only fair you get his sword as well."

"Perhaps I am the pirate, have you thought of that?" Harriet lowered her voice, rolling it into a bad imitation of the local burry drawl. "And you're in my cave, lady, with all my treasures. You here to steal 'em?"

They'd played the same game the summer they found the treasure—the pirate and the ingénue—and had gone over the scenes again and again, until the story fit them just right. They'd drawn maps of the Caribbean, wanted posters with terrifying beards and scars, schematic outlines of frigates and galleons bristling with cannons. They'd written warrants for Harriet's arrest, offering ten thousand doubloons for her capture.

Despite the intervening years Sylvie fell easily back into that well-rehearsed role.

"Of course not, Captain."

She didn't have to pretend nervousness—even after lying mouldering in a cave the sword was surprisingly sharp against the skin of her neck. She swallowed, feeling the steel restrict the movement of her throat.

"Hmmm." With her free hand, the pirate scratched her cheek in thought. "Perhaps you is one of the treasures yourself, then. You're certainly pretty enough."

"And you're very gallant." Sylvie could feel herself blushing, warmth spreading along her neck. "A gallant scourge of the seas."

"That I am." The accent was getting worse with every sentence. Sylvie had to laugh, just a breath and a smile, but enough to offend her captor. "What? I am! I'm the gallantest pirate on all the seven seas. And I'll prove it to you."

"Oh yes? And how will you do that?"

Harriet stepped in, backing Sylvie against the damp cave wall.

"With a kiss."

Oh.

Their games had always been dangerous like this, even back before Sylvie was old enough to recognise the danger, to see past the make-believe and eye patches and stuffed parrots.

"Very well." Sylvie reached up, lightly fingering the collar of Harriet's shirt, feeling the starch stiffened points. "But Captain, remember I am just a nervous maid. Be gentle with me."

Harriet's mouth against Sylvie's was cool, soft. Sylvie couldn't help herself, letting one hand flutter away from Harriet's shirt, tangle itself in the weight of Harriet's hair, thumb brushing against the curve of her jaw. There was no scratch of stubble, no irritating tickle of a moustache. Just the press of their lips, the warmth of the other woman under her palms, the thunder of her heartbeat in her ears. The kiss itself meant nothing, of course—like kisses meant nothing to Romeo and Juliet, who might make love to each other, night after night, up on the National's stage, meet and love and pine and die and then go home to her husband, his wife, their real selves resumed—but it flustered Sylvie anyway.

She stepped back, hands feeling for the support of the rocky cave wall, and Harriet followed, her free hand reaching for Sylvie's hip, nestling over the waistband of her skirt. She would have leant in again, but Sylvie turned her head, raised a hand in defence.

"I think you've made your point, Captain."

Laurence's ring on its chain fell loose from her dress, flashing as it passed through the torchlight. Harriet caught it on the flat blade, letting it dangle and spin.

"What's this then? Not mine—mine was rubies, I remember."

That had been the end of the game, a few days before she went home. The customs men were coming for the Captain and he had to sail for warmer waters—Jamaica, Barbados, somewhere the fat hulks of the Spanish fleet floated, ripe for the plunder—but not before he'd sworn his love and sealed it with a ring.

Harriet had actually found her a ring, thick gold and a ruby the size of a fingernail, buried amongst the cave's empty rum barrels, and pressed it onto her finger. Sylvie had treasured it: worn it when no one was looking, polished it late at night in the darkness of her school dorm, kept in her pocket and turned it over and over in her fingers during Maths and French and interminable Home

Ec lessons. Mashing on another girl was fine, was normal—everyone did it, were perfectly open about it—but Sylvie kept her ring hidden, special, a secret just between the two of them.

Then the war came, and she grew up and her fingers got too fat for the pirate's rubies and she met Laurence and realised how queer it was to still think so much of another girl's ring.

"Nice, isn't it? Old fashioned a bit, but they're very good stones. It was Laurence's mother's."

Harriet frowned, turning the sword back and forth, making the ring shine.

"Us pirates don't like other men taking our treasures. Who is he, this Laurence? Local lad? Some lily-livered customs man? Bring him here—I'll run him right through."

"That's not funny, Harriet."

"No," she said, abruptly dropping the accent and the point of the sword, "I don't suppose it is. Still, here we are." She turned and sat on a chest, wood creaking under her weight, idly poking the sword into the stone floor. "And is he a hero?"

"A hero?" That wasn't exactly the word she'd choose to describe Laurence. He was more dependable than heroic—steady and reliable, definitely, but hardly swashbuckling.

"That's what you wanted, remember? You wouldn't marry Captain Bluebeard, or Blond- or No-beard or whoever I was, because he was a villain, not a hero. Even though I had a parrot."

Sylvie did remember. But the man you dream of at fourteen and the man you marry at twenty-two, war weary and only getting older, are bound to be different people. Fourteen-year-old girls get caught up in romance and adventure, they expect a grand passion, love against the odds, and give no thought to the benefits of respectability, of a stable job and a government pension scheme.

"Your parrot was stuffed, and his feathers were falling out."

"Well," said Harriet, checking her watch, "I suppose even suburban GPs can be heroes if you love them. Come on, we'll be late for dinner if we don't get a move on."

The climb up from the beach was significantly more dreary than the scramble down, the sky clouded over and threatening. This time, Harriet didn't stop to point out interesting plants or admire the view, just puffed and sighed her way up the cliff path.

Just as they reached the top Sylvie stopped, leaning on a stile to catch her breath.

"Harriet," she said, "wait a second, I just..."

There was a crack of thunder, and the world flashed bright with lightning.

"Here!" Harriet caught her by the wrist and ran for the cover of a nearby oak. The rain was no less fierce for its suddenness, swept in heavy sheets from the sea, salted and stinging.

The tree was large and old enough to shelter them from the worst of it, but even so Sylvie's hair was wet round her face, sticking in tendrils across her forehead and cheeks. Harriet brushed them away, tucked them behind her ear. Her own hair was slick against her head, a tiny rivulet running down her temple.

"I'm sorry," she said. "About, you know, just now. In the cave. I shouldn't have..."

Sylvie shook her head.

"Harriet—"

"No, really. You're engaged and I..."

"Harriet. Listen." Sylvie reached out, hands gabbing tight around Harriet's shoulders, shaking, forcing her attention. "There's nothing to apologise for."

"No?"

"No." Sylvie swallowed, moved closer, hiding from the blank staring windows of the house. She lifted her hand to Harriet's cheek, ran her thumb across her eyebrows, across the line of her jaw, wiping away the rain. "Not at all."

There was no Captain, this time, no maid, no play-acting to hide behind when the show was over. Her hand shook against the line of Harriet's jaw, her fingers twitching against soft skin. Just screw your courage to the sticking place, Sylvie, she thought, and you'll not fail.

Harriet came easily, moving forward under the lightest pressure of Sylvie's hand against her neck, her hands bunching in the heavy tweed of Sylvie's skirt, her lips warm despite the rain.

"So," Sylvie said as she pulled away, "what comes next?"

"Next?"

Harriet was still flushed, the pulse at the base of her throat fluttering wildly, her hands still clenched in Sylvie's skirt. Any second now she'd say something stupid, something impulsive, something Sylvie couldn't ignore.

"What about, you know... What about Laurence?"

Harriet stepped back, her hands falling to her sides. "Ah. Right. Laurence."

"What do I tell him?"

"You don't have to tell him anything, if you don't

want."

"No, Hattie, I mean... What do I do?"

"I'd tell you not to go through with it, but I can't offer you a good alternative." Harriet sighed, running her hand through her fringe, shaking the rain onto the grass. "Just me, and this place, and probably scandal. So if what you want is marriage, kids, society standing, you know, then Laurence seems a good enough kind of man, as they go."

She knew it was daft to take it as insult, but Sylvie felt the brush-off like a punch.

"Is that what you'll do? Marry?"

Harriet waved her away.

"Oh, it's different for me. Doesn't matter what I do. Now Will's gone, well, even if I marry the title belongs to my cousin, and Duncliff will too, in time. So I'm set for life and I might as well live how I want, you know, love who I want."

"And you want...me?"

"Don't sound so surprised. Always have." Harriet laughed, leant her back against the tree trunk. "I was the most woefully smitten fourteen year-old ever. It's never gone away, and now, after all that, I don't suppose it's going to."

"Harriet..."

"I know—don't answer me right away. Think about it." Harriet smiled, stepped out of the shelter of the tree trunk. "If, as Bathsheba Everdene herself says, you can think outdoors." She held her hand out, testing the rain. "Come on—we really will be late for dinner now."

⁂

The next morning the goodbyes with her godparents

were easy, affectionate, all hugs and kisses and promises not to leave it so long. But, stood by the door, Harriet was a different story.

"It was nice to see you, Harriet."

"Yes. And congratulations, again," Harriet said, directing her words down to the floor, "on your engagement."

"Thank you."

"We ought not to leave it so long, next time. See each other sooner."

"Yes, quite."

Their hug was as short as politeness allowed, Harriet awkward and tense, Sylvie aware of the tightness of her hand around Harriet's collar. Laurence was right behind her, shifting awkwardly on the spot, his own perfunctory handshakes long finished.

"Sorry, darling," he said once they were cocooned in the relative silence of the car, "we didn't spend much time together, did we? For a weekend dedicated to our engagement, that is."

"It's alright," Sylvie said, craning to watch the retreating figures in the wing mirror. "It was nice to catch up with Harriet, get to know her again, you know?"

"She's a funny one, if you ask me." Laurence changed gear, finishing the move with his hand resting lightly on Sylvie's knee. "Was she like it when you knew her before?"

"Like what?"

"Oh—suffrage and trousers and all that."

"Yes, always."

"Hmmm." His voice had gone cold, clinical again. He wasn't on shift until tomorrow but there he was, already reverting to his professional self—that's Dr rather than Mr, if you don't mind—falling so easily into diagnosis. "There's a touch of the BD about her, I'd say. Saw it all the time with ambulance drivers in France. They like adventure, you know, those girls, all adrenaline and danger and that kind of thing."

"She did always want to be a hero, or a pirate."

"There you are then. Shame I put my foot in it about the brother like that—I did feel awful, but I didn't know. Do you remember him much?"

"Not really." She remembered flopping boyish hair, a dog at his heels. Not enough, really–not even a face, or a voice. "My memories of that summer are all...faded."

Of Harriet, she'd meant to say. My memories are all of Harriet, of games run round chairs in the library, of climbing the cliffs and a cave full with pirate gold. But Laurence seemed to disapprove of her, and so Sylvie kept her thoughts to herself, passing the drive in a daydream haze.

The city seemed smoky and crowded, after the countryside. Sylvie pressed her head to the window and watched the busy streets slide by, watched the people go about their business in darting shoals.

Coming out of Kensington tube station was a group of girls. They were Sylvie's age or thereabouts, laughing and hanging on each other's arms. Between them they were wearing just about every shade of blue Sylvie could imagine, but they looked like they were having fun and she turned to watch them as the car pulled away.

After all, London should be fun, she thought. Harriet would make London fun. With her there'd be bars and dancing, picnics in the park.

Instead the week ahead stretched out interminably: Laurence's mother and sister dragging her round seamstresses and hosiers, haberdashers and milliners, demanding she decided on colour schemes and patterns. She'd have to let them pose her and dress her, moving her arms and legs as they directed, even while her thoughts drifted back to Harriet and her new hoard of pirate treasure.

It'd help keep the estate going, at least. Sell a ring for a new ploughshare, a gold necklace for a housemaid. She had no doubt Harriet would make a fine job of it when her father finally gave her a chance.

"When we get back," she thought as the London streets blurred past, "I'll talk to Laurence and then to Father." The fuss she was going to cause didn't bear thinking about; there were invites to rescind, her trousseau to cancel, and tradesmen still to pay. It'd be in all the papers, no doubt, in the mouths of society gossips up and down the city. *"Have you heard?"* they'd say, *"throwing her chap over like that, and you'll never guess why..."*

"And then I'll speak to the jewellers, see about getting the pirate ring resized."

The Rum Runner and the Showgirl

R.G. Emanuelle

Fanny looked into the spotlight. A deep breath filled her lungs with cigarette smoke, then she belted out the last line of her song until her voice reached the soaring final note.

A wave of applause and whistles filled the club and she absorbed every clap and hoot. She'd nailed her solo on New Year's Eve!

The Grand Chameleon Ballroom was a burst of silver and gold, curlicues of glittery ribbon hanging from the ceiling, garland-framed mirrors on the walls. The dance floor was packed and every table in the house occupied.

Fanny left the stage and ran to the table where Luella sat drinking a Manhattan.

"Fan, you were the bee's knees up there!"

"Yeah, now if only Mr. DeMille would find out, I'd be set." She sat down, pulled the cherry out of Luella's glass, hung it above her face, and lowered it into her mouth. The stem joined others on the tablecloth, like a collection of tiny firewood.

"Oh, he will. Mary Pickford, eat your heart out!" Luella raised her glass, took a swallow, then put it down with a thud, her feathers drooping further.

"What's wrong?"

"It's almost midnight and I have no one to kiss," Luella replied, pouting.

"So what? Neither do I."

"I guess we can always kiss each other." Luella, the master of ceremonies, grabbed the microphone. "Okay, ladies and gents, it's almost that time. Twelve, eleven..." At ten, the entire club began counting down, the collective voice growing louder and louder. Fanny and Luella stood up and joined in the chorus.

"Five! Four! Three! Two! One! Happy New Year!"

A cacophony of cheering rose to the ceiling as the band began playing *Auld Lang Syne*. A few stray balloons fell and long paper ribbons streamed across the room.

"Happy New Year, doll!" Luella threw her arms around Fanny.

"Happy New Year." Fanny gave her a hug. "I have to get ready for the next number. You're done for the night, right?"

"Yes," Luella said, pouting again. "I was only in the two numbers."

"Okay. I'll see you later. Have fun." Fanny waved and went backstage. She wrinkled her nose. The back corridor reeked of gin and smelled vaguely of sex. It was starting to look like the filthy alley that harbored the secret door to the speakeasy. The repulsive activities that went on in that alley only served to drive Fanny harder toward her dream.

In the dressing room, she grabbed another costume off the rack. As she fixed her skirt, her ring caught her stocking. "Damn." She twisted the silk until it came free of the ring.

"That looks bad," a chorus girl said as she walked by.

"I know. And I go on in ten minutes." She glared at the stocking.

"Go beg Marty for that pair he's been holding onto for that trampy girlfriend of his." The girl pointed her thumb in the general direction of the manager's office.

With a sigh, Fanny went down the corridor to Marty's office, steeling herself for the overtures. She raised a hand to knock but stopped when she heard voices. Marty and Joe, the assistant manager. She leaned her ear to the door.

"I'm telling you, Marty. You gotta nip this in the bud. They can't get away with this."

"I know that," came Marty's reply. "Right now, I need you to stop twisting my nuts and go keep an eye on things. Think you can do that?"

"Sure, boss."

Fanny pulled back quickly when the door swung open. Joe headed down the corridor and she peeked into the office. Marty picked up the phone. "Yeah, it's Marty. Send Nick over. Yeah, I know it's New Year's Eve. But I wanna settle this tonight."

Fanny drew back slightly. Marty was poking the desk with his finger. Freddy, the stage manager, flew by. "You're on in five," he said as he passed.

Fanny looked into the office and waited until Marty had replaced the receiver to knock.

Marty looked up. "Whaddaya want? I'm busy."

"Marty." Fanny used her sweetest voice. "Would you consider lending me those silk stockings you've got?"

Marty studied her a moment, picked up his cigarette, took a drag, and let out a long, slow stream of smoke.

"What's in it for me?" He languorously raked his eyes up and down her form.

She put her hands on her hips and steeled her eyes. "Nothing. Except my gratitude."

To Fanny's surprise, he acquiesced quickly. "Okay, okay. I don't have time for this. Here." He took out a red box out of a desk drawer, placed it on the desk and took another drag of his cigarette. "Just remember I did that for you."

"Yeah. Thanks."

Stockings in hand, she ran back to the dressing room. She'd just fastened the last garter hook when Freddy opened the door. "Okay, let's go. Café number's up *now*."

The band began playing "Five Foot Two, Eyes of Blue," and the chorus line danced their way onto the stage. When the number was over, Fanny stepped down from the stage and scanned the audience to find Luella. Among the sea of faces, she noticed a man who appeared to be weaving his way toward her. He broke through the crowd, caught her eye, and slowed down a bit. Did she know him?

Now only inches away, his eyes seared into hers, and just when she thought he was going to stop in front of her, he kept walking and went through the door leading to the back area.

Fanny felt as if she'd been kicked in the stomach. There was something about this guy, like she knew him from somewhere, though she was sure she'd never seen him before.

Luella waved at her. Fanny pointed her index finger in the air. *One minute.*

She walked through the door to the back area. The man turned into Marty's office. Was this the Nick that Marty had wanted to see, then? When Marty had closed

174

the door, she went to it and put her ear to the wood.

"I don't know what's happening," Marty said, "but I want you to get it straightened out." Fanny heard something slam against Marty's desk. "Here, try it."

A moment of silence, then "I see." The young man's voice was softer and calmer than Marty's and more difficult to hear.

"Fix it."

"Yessir."

The door opened. She pretended she was walking to the dressing room, then followed the young man back to the ballroom. Luella was seated at the table, talking to a man. She looked up. "Fanny! This is Leon. Leon, Fanny."

Leon nodded. "Hiya."

"Thanks. Pleasure to meet you." She turned to Luella. "I don't want to interrupt.

"Sit down and join us," Leon said. "We were just talking about the things we like." He leered at Luella. Luella giggled, and Fanny looked around for someplace else to go, but the room was crowded. Reluctantly, she sat down.

"Here, have a drink." Leon pushed a full glass toward her. Fanny took the glass, sipped, and turned her head away from the conversation. At the bar was the man who'd just been in Marty's office. The bartender was leaning in. When their conversation ended, the man straightened up, fixed his tie and jacket, and pushed his hat slightly back so that it was perched on his head at an angle.

On his way out he again caught her eye. His eyes bore into hers, harder than before.

"What are you looking at?" Luella asked after he'd passed.

Without taking her eyes off him, Fanny responded,

"That fella, there." She jutted her chin in his direction.

Luella leaned in close to her ear. "That's Nick. He's one of Marty's guys—a rum runner."

Fanny faced her. "You've seen him before?"

"Oh, sure." Luella pulled back and smiled. "Cute, huh? Kinda looks like Rudolph Valentino."

"Yeah. Cute." She continued to watch him as he disappeared. "I'm gonna call it a night."

"Already? It's only two."

"Happy New Year, huh?"

"Happy New Year, doll. Get home safe."

"Yeah. You, too." She hugged Luella and waved to Leon.

Fanny got her coat and went out the back exit. The night was cold but filled with the sounds of revelers from nearby homes. This wasn't her first New Year's Eve alone and she was sure it wouldn't be her last, but remembering special New Year's Eves with a few of the women she'd loved over the years made her chest hurt. She got in a cab and went home.

By January 2nd, Fanny was ready to jump right into the new routines Freddy had choreographed.

She stepped to center stage and waited for her cue, muscles aching from the intense rehearsals they'd had the past couple of weeks for Freddy's ambitious new act. It was exciting but exhausting, and she hoped her legs wouldn't buckle in the middle of her number.

When the band played the right chord, Fanny began her song. A few lines in, she took some steps to the side and turned with a flourish, and when the music picked up tempo, she launched into the Shimmy, her new favorite dance because it was so naughty. If you had anything at all to jiggle, this dance saw to it that it did. The fringes of her dress swung back and forth, emphasizing the swaying of her breasts.

After the last notes of the song, her chest was heaving and sweat coated her face and neck. She released the tension in her legs and arms, then waited for Freddy's response.

"Okay, that's better," Freddy said. "The turn toward the end is still a little sloppy. Let's clean it up."

Fanny nodded and walked off the stage. In the wings, she wiped her face with a towel while the ensemble began the next number. She watched as they kicked and spun. She was going to miss these girls when she was a big star.

As she looked on, she saw a figure walking into the ballroom followed by two men pushing a crate. It was Nick. The big block letters across the side said "COFFEE." They pushed the crate behind the bar and quickly exited the building. Nick spoke a moment to Freddy, then sat down at a table in the back and lit a cigarette. The bartender placed a shot glass in front of him. Nick held the glass up to the light and turned it, as if inspecting the contents, glided the glass beneath his nose and sipped, then leaned back and proceeded to watch the rehearsals.

There was something about him that set off sparks in Fanny's brain. And, to her dismay, elsewhere. He was clean-cut and refined looking, unlike most of the mooks who worked for the Torrenti family.

Freddy approached her. "Fanny, someone wants to talk to you." He nodded at Nick. Fanny felt her limbs go numb and the sweat on her brow turned cold. Had she done something wrong?

She went to the Nick's table and stood in front of it, silent. Nick's gaze slowly traveled up her body until it reached her eyes.

Her spine tingled. Something in his eyes stirred familiarity deep in her stomach.

"Please sit down." Nick pushed a chair with his foot.

Fanny sat, but said nothing. Nick made her nervous in a lot of different ways. With her butt perched on the edge of the seat and her back pin-straight, she waited for him to speak.

"Nick." He extended his hand.

She took it. "Fanny."

"Pleased to meet you."

"Likewise."

He waved at the bartender, who evidently read minds because he brought over two more glasses filled with an amber liquid.

Nick picked up his glass and held it aloft. Fanny realized that he was waiting for her to respond. She picked up the glass with no idea what they were toasting or why.

"Have we met?" she asked.

"No."

Unlike his previous glass, he downed this one in its entirety, then placed it on the table and looked at her expectantly. Fanny sipped hers. The harsh liquid seared her throat before settling in her chest with a radiating warmth.

"Whoopee. That's amazing. I've never had anything like it."

He smiled, and it softened his features. Fanny's heart sped up. "No, I'm sure you haven't. This," he said, turning the glass in his hand, "is real Irish whiskey. No one's seen this stuff in years. Not like the hooch you get in most places."

"So, how come you have it?"

Nick didn't respond, but his smile spread into a grin.

Fanny took another sip. The guy was a rum-runner! After a moment of silence, she looked at him. His face was thin but not angular. The curves of his cheeks were soft, and his dark, almond-shaped eyes were clear and sharp with just a hint of mirth. Rudy Valentino.

The whiskey heat began to spread to her extremities. Her muscles felt as if they were letting out air, and her fear of Nick was subsiding.

Nick sat back and looked at her with amusement. She looked into his eyes and, in her mind, traced the lines of his lips.

Then Fanny realized that she did know this person. Not *who* he was, but *what* he was. She berated herself for not recognizing it sooner. She had known so many like him, yet he'd managed to fool her—briefly.

There was something else, too, but for the moment, she pushed that thought aside.

"So, why did you want to see me?"

"I just thought I'd share this with you." He tapped the side of his glass.

"Why?"

Nick suddenly seemed unsure and shifted in his seat, looking down into his glass.

Fanny leaned in very close and whispered, "I know who you are."

Nick sat back and stared at her, the amusement leaving his face.

"I know this is all a put-on. Not that I care. I'm actually impressed."

"What are you talking about?"

Without really intending to, Fanny ran her eyes down to Nick's torso, his pinstriped vest neatly fastened beneath his unbuttoned jacket. But she quickly brought her eyes back up. Nick's face turned a pinkish hue; Fanny didn't know if it was embarrassment or just the booze. "It took me a bit, but I finally realized what it was."

"Well?"

Fanny leaned in closer, narrowed her eyes seductively, and whispered, "You're not a fella at all, are you?"

Momentary panic registered in Nick's eyes, but then he grinned again. "Very good. You figured it out right out of the gate. It usually takes people a while, if they figure it out at all."

"So, it doesn't bother you that I know?"

"A better question is, does it bother *you* that you know?"

She smiled. "No." For a second or two, she couldn't stop her mind from wandering, thinking about what Nick's skin felt like. Not all women looked that dapper in men's attire. Nick was damned handsome, a real cool cat.

Nick pursed her lips. "So, whaddaya say? Want to have dinner with me?"

Fanny let her smile linger for another second, as she finished her naughty thoughts. She dropped her smile and sat up. "No, thanks."

"Why not? I thought—"

"Well, you thought wrong." Fanny got up and strode toward the stage, not looking back, and went directly to the dressing room. The space was empty, everyone being either onstage or in the wings. She sat on a chair and closed her eyes. Until now, it had been easy to say no to an attractive woman, even if she was passing as a man. Fanny had been strong, focused on her goals. But just now, with

Nick, she'd had a moment of weakness. She could feel her shell crack and the word "yes" rise up in her throat.

That couldn't happen. Never again.

Fanny woke up, groggy. The week's performances had knocked her out. As she did every morning, she reminded herself that this was the work before the reward. Everything she was doing was going to make her the next Tallulah Bankhead, Mary Pickford, Clara Bow, or Lillian Gish. Maybe she'd even get a part in one of those new talkies.

She slid out of bed and washed up. There wasn't much in the ice box, so she grabbed an apple and ate it while she sat and absentmindedly stared at the wall. A photo of new starlet Greta Garbo stared at her with sultry, demanding eyes. She'd give anything to be next to her in the movie magazines. She stopped chewing a moment and thought *or to be next to her at all.*

Her mind went briefly to Nick. Or whatever her name was. She was really attractive but there was no way Fanny would go down that road again. She finished her apple, dressed, and headed out to the club.

In the dressing room, the other girls greeted her with strange looks and mysterious little smiles.

"Hi, Fanny. How's your night? Do anything *special?*" Luella asked. The others snickered.

"What does *that* mean?" Fanny looked around.

"Oh, nothing."

Fanny went to her table and stopped abruptly. A huge vase of roses sat there. "Hey, whose flowers?"

"Yours."

181

"Mine?" She sniffed one, then looked for a card. There was none.

The ladies finished preparing themselves, then filed out. Fanny was about to follow when Freddy stuck his head in the door. "This is for you." He handed her an envelope and walked away.

Fanny stared at it and wondered if this was her pink slip. She opened it slowly. Inside was a white notecard. On it was written, "Have dinner with me tonight. Please?"

It had to be Nick. Who else would it be? Fanny went out to the ballroom and there was Nick, sitting at the same table as last time, with a cigarette and a shot.

Fanny approached the table. Nick started to speak but Fanny cut her off. "Look, you seem nice, but I told you, I'm not interested."

"Why?"

She glared and sat down. "I don't have to explain anything to you."

"Why don't you anyway? I get the feeling you probably want to."

"Oh, yeah? And just who do you think you are?"

"Someone who knows your type."

"My type. And what would that be?"

Nick raised an eyebrow.

Fanny clenched her jaw. "You think you're so smart."

"Am I wrong?"

'Yes."

"Then tell me."

"Geez, you don't take no for an answer, do you?"

"No."

Fanny didn't want to reveal anything about herself, but as she looked into Nick's dark eyes, her resolve ebbed. "I'm trying to make it into the moving pictures."

"I see. And what does that have to do with the price of tea in China?"

She gave him another glare. "If certain...facts about me were discovered, I'd be drummed out of the business."

Nick laughed. "Haven't you heard the rumors about Greta Garbo or Marlene Dietrich?"

"They've been lucky. I haven't."

Nick frowned. "What do you mean?"

She'd already said too much. "I don't want to talk about it." And with more bravado than she felt, "It's none of your business, anyway." She stood up, began to walk away, then remembered the roses and felt her entire body ripple with warmth. She turned back. "Thanks for the roses."

"My pleasure."

Fanny knew this wasn't the last she'd see of Nick.

<hr />

Nick waited until all the performers had finished their numbers. Freddy stood up, threw a towel over his shoulders, and clapped twice. "Okay, girls. Better. But tomorrow I want to see you tighten that Lindy. Okay, see ya later."

Nick stepped up to Freddy, whispered in his ear, and discreetly pointed to the woman Fanny had been drinking with on New Year's Eve. Freddy nodded and went to her. Nick sat down at a table.

The woman, panting and sweaty, approached the table. "Hi," she said, somewhat timidly. "Freddy said you wanted to speak to me."

"What's your name?"

She looked at Nick warily. "Who wants to know?"

"Name's Nick. I work for Dominic." Nick knew she was just being careful. Everyone who worked at this club knew the score.

"Luella."

"Luella. Have a seat." She pushed the chair out with her foot.

Luella sat, unease in her eyes.

"Relax. I just want some information."

"About what?"

"What do you know about Fanny?"

"Our Fanny? She's a great gal. One of my best friends." Fear returned to her eyes. "Why?"

"I just want to help her."

"Is she in trouble?"

"No, not at all. I just want to help her."

"How?"

"I know she wants to be in the moving pictures."

Luella looked over at Fanny, who picked up a piece of costume she'd shed and was about to walk backstage.

"What do you want to know?"

"I know she likes women."

Luella raised an eyebrow. "Yeah, so? A few of the girls like other girls. It's no big deal."

"Yes, but something happened, didn't it?"

Luella stared at her.

"I know about it. I just want more details."

Luella seemed to relax a bit. "It was awful. She was about to audition for a part in a talkie. Some crazy religious kook found out that she was seeing a girl and had her pulled. She didn't even get to show them what she can do. And she can do it all—sing, dance, act. Poor thing. Had to start over. Even changed her name." Luella's eyes widened as if she'd just made a grievous error.

184

Nick pulled out a wad of money, peeled off a couple of bills, placed them on the table, and pushed them toward Luella. "Thanks for your time."

Luella looked at the money a moment, then took it, closing her hand tightly. Without a word, she stood, gave a last puzzled glance, then walked away.

Nick went home, shed the suit and tie, and ran a bath. As she sat in the water, she thought about Fanny. It hurt a little that Fanny hadn't recognized her. She'd fallen for Fanny three years ago, but Fanny had moved away before she could pursue it further. She'd fallen in love almost instantly, and it had taken a long time to get over it. Maybe now, she could start from scratch.

Fanny put on her jacket and hat and grabbed her gloves. When she opened the door, her path was blocked by a large box of chocolates. She pulled out a card tucked inside the ribbon. It said one word: "Please."

Her phone rang. "Hello?"

"Did you get the chocolates?"

Fanny recognized Nick's low, lush voice. It sent a shiver up her arms.

"Yes, I got them."

"Well?"

"I told you, I'm not interested."

"What if I told you I could help you?"

"How?"

"Have dinner with me and find out."

Fanny huffed. "Boy, you just don't quit." She could practically hear Nick smile.

"No, I don't."

Every logical streak in her head told her to say no, but in the battle between mind and desire, desire was winning. Even the curly, neat script of Nick's hand seemed to come off the card, wrap around her fingers and hands, and wind up her arms to caress her shoulders.

"Look, I'm late for voice class. I'll think about it." She hung up.

She pulled a rose out of the basket and pinned it to her lapel, then shut the door and locked it.

On her way home after class, she was startled by a voice.

"Would you like a ride?"

Fanny's heart pounded. "Are you following me?"

"No," Nick said. "I just knew you'd be here."

"How?"

"You'd be surprised at what I can find out."

"Actually, I wouldn't." She began walking again.

"Well," Nick said, "do you want a ride or don't you?"

Fanny stopped. Getting a ride home in a car seemed infinitely more attractive than taking the trolley. "What's the catch?"

"No catch. The ride is free. But I *will* take the opportunity to convince you to have dinner with me."

Fanny quirked her mouth into exaggerated annoyance.

"Whaddayasay?"

With a dispassion she didn't feel, she said, "I'll take the ride. You can talk all you want. Doesn't mean I'll have dinner with you."

"I'll take it." Nick guided Fanny to a gleaming new Chrysler.

Fanny whistled. "Holy smokes, what a beaut."

"Hop in." Nick opened the passenger door and Fanny

slid into the leather-upholstered seat.

"A girl could get used to this." Fanny bit her lip. What was she doing? She had resolved to stay away from women. *This is just a ride. Nothing more.*

"How was class?" Nick asked as he started the car.

"Fine. My instructor says that I have a strong, pleasing voice. All I need is a little practice to sound more cultured and refined." Fanny, jaw tight, looked straight ahead at the road. Nick's intrusion into her life was getting too close. She'd spent too much energy remaining private to have this one unravel it all.

An old Model T sputtered and bounced past them, releasing a cloud of smoke. When it cleared, Fanny took a deep breath. "What do you want from me?"

Nick seemed to ponder. "Dinner."

"Why don't you stop being so pushy?"

"Why don't you stop being so hard-headed?" Nick grinned, accentuating her profile. The gnawing feeling that Fanny had seen her somewhere before returned.

Through the wind hitting her face and the rumble of the car's engine, Fanny could hear her own heart beating. *Damn her.*

"Okay, fine. Dinner. *Just* dinner."

Nick kept driving. Fanny kept her eyes straight ahead but stole a peek at Nick. She had a smug expression and Fanny wished she'd refused.

"Where are we going?"

"Dinner."

"Now?"

"Sure, why not? I'll have you at the club in time for your show."

"Well, it's just that I don't like to eat a big meal right before a show. It makes me feel heavy and sluggish. And if you're going to take me to dinner, then you're going to take me to dinner."

Nick seemed to enjoy this comment immensely. She smirked and her eyes lit up, as if she'd just been invited to a party.

"Tuesday, then. You don't have a show on Tuesdays."

"Fine. You can take me to the club now. It's early, but that's okay."

Nick headed in the direction of the club.

The Chrysler relaxed into a low growl when Nick pulled into the alley and stopped by the staff entrance. She jumped out, went around to the passenger side, and opened the door for Fanny.

Fanny got out and turned to face Nick. "Well, thanks."

"Sure. I'll see you on Tuesday."

"Yep."

Fanny went in, closed the door, and watched Nick through the peephole. Nick lit a cigarette and looked up at the door. Fanny shrank back, as if Nick could see through the steel. Then Nick got in the car and drove away.

Fanny was left with the feeling that things were about to change, and she wasn't sure whether for the better.

Tuesday held promise of a sunshine-filled day. Fanny went to the beauty parlor and got her hair trimmed, and now, with her hair properly shaped and curving in the right places, she took on the task of choosing an outfit for dinner. The problem was, she had no idea where Nick was taking her.

She pulled out a few dresses, finally settling on a long-sleeved black number with black embroidery. She looped a long strand of fake pearls around her neck twice and slipped a matching pearl bracelet over her wrist. A spritz of lavender cologne and she was ready.

She paced back and forth in her small one-bedroom apartment. She'd dated plenty of men and women and even a few who, like Nick, were both. Nothing new.

Nothing new. Since that day she'd first sat across Nick at the club, she'd had the growing sensation that she knew her from somewhere.

Fanny adjusted her hat in the mirror. At a knock, she nearly jumped. "Just a minute." She made a few last adjustments to her hair, grabbed her gloves, and opened the door.

Nick, hair neatly slicked back, stood in a finely tailored gray suit, hat in one hand, a bouquet of chrysanthemums in the other. "Good evening," she said with a flourish.

"More flowers?"

"A beautiful woman can never have too many flowers." She held them out and Fanny took them, grudgingly admitting to herself that they were pretty.

"I'll put these in a vase." She left the door open but didn't invite Nick in. She needed to keep a boundary between them. Her home was her only bastion of privacy.

"Okay, let's go." Fanny pulled her door shut and walked ahead of Nick. They drove in silence.

Nick pulled up in front of Armando's restaurant, a place she'd always wanted to go but could never afford. When they entered, the maître d' immediately approached them. "Mr. Nick. So good to see you," he said in a thick Italian accent. "Your table is ready. This way, please." He led the way to a corner booth. The high backs, done in deep-red leather upholstery, provided them with privacy.

A waiter placed glasses in front of them, as if he'd

189

already taken their order. "Two apple ciders."

Fanny sipped hers. The familiar dryness of champagne hit her palate, sharp bubbles crackling on her tongue and lips. "Some apple cider."

"Yep. The best." Nick licked her lips.

"*Mister* Nick?" Fanny said.

"Some know, some don't. Those that do extend me the courtesy of pretending they don't."

"Okay, let's get this over with. What do you want?"

"I like you."

"You could have any girl in the chorus. Well, almost. A few could be persuaded—"

"I don't want them. I want you. If you're looking for some kind of deep reason, there isn't one."

The waiter came back with two plates. "Oysters Rockefeller."

Fanny's pulse quickened and she quickly dug into a mollusk covered in spinach and cheese. A procession of plates followed. As they were enjoying their prime rib, the maître d' approached and whispered in Nick's ear. Nick wiped her mouth and put her napkin beside her plate. "Excuse me. I'll be right back."

Nick followed the maître d' to an area out of sight. After only a couple of minutes, she returned and replaced the napkin on her lap.

"Sorry about that. Where were we? Oh. How you ended up here. From Topeka, right?"

The escargot Fanny'd swallowed felt like it was trying to crawl back up her throat. "I don't think I like you knowing so much about me."

"I also know that Fanny's not your real name. How'd you pick it? After Fanny Brice?"

Fanny stabbed a little potato on her plate with her fork.

"Yes." That came out more emphatically than she'd intended. "Okay, smarty pants. Your turn. How'd you end up...?" She didn't have to finish her sentence.

"Well, my parents died and my little sister and I were left alone. My father knew one of Dominic's gang so I went to him for a job. He needed someone to...uh...purchase goods and make deliveries."

"I'm sorry. I mean, about your parents." Fanny poked at her asparagus. "Why do you—"

"Dress like a man? I figured I'd have an easier time."

"Is this what you plan on doing the rest of your life?"

"I don't know about the rest of my life, but for now, the pay is good."

Nick pulled out a cigarette case, opened it, and held it out. Fanny plucked one out and positioned it between her lips. Nick lit it with a match, then lit one for herself.

"What's your name?" Fanny asked.

Nick let out a long stream of smoke. "What?"

"What's your name? I mean, it isn't Nick."

"Well, it is, sort of. It's short for Nicolette."

"Nicolette. That's nice. I knew a Nicolette once—" And then it hit her. "Oh, my god. I *do* know you. I thought you seemed familiar."

The look on Nick's face told her she was right. Nicolette had been the last woman she'd seen in Topeka. A striking dark-eyed beauty Fanny had dated a few times and quickly forgotten when her life went to crap.

"I wondered if you'd remember," Nick said, voice soft.

"Geez, I'm sorry."

Nick tapped the table with her spoon. "You disappeared. What happened?"

Fanny decided there was no point in holding back any more. "I went to Chicago for an audition. The producer

191

pegged me for an invert—I never found out how—and not only threw me out but splashed it all over town. I couldn't get a job anywhere. I don't think anybody really cared. There are lots of us in the business. It was just the bad publicity they didn't want. I came to LA and changed my name and basically started over."

As Nick sipped her espresso, Fanny watched her face and thought she saw something there, something deeper.

Nick put down the coffee cup and reached into her pocket. She pulled out a small card, put it on the table, then pushed it closer to Fanny with two fingers.

Fanny looked at the card. "Joseph Kasowicz." She slowly sounded out the last name. Below that: "Talent Agent."

"So?" Even as she said it, she couldn't help but feel a ball of excitement in her stomach.

"He's looking for the right girl to cast in a talkie. I've arranged an audition for you."

Fanny leaned back on the leather banquette. "Are you kidding me?"

"Friday at one. Address is on the card."

Fanny glanced down at it. "I don't know what to say."

Nick looked down into her coffee and scratched at the tablecloth with her forefinger. Her face flushed. Fanny could see it even in the dimly lit restaurant.

Nick had fallen for her.

"You know, we only went out a couple of times," Fanny said cautiously. "You don't owe me anything." It sounded worse when she said it. The hurt expression on Nick's face confirmed her suspicions but she seemed to recover.

"I happen to think you're talented. It's not fair, what they did to you."

Fanny smiled. Nick definitely wasn't like the other

gangsters she knew. Well, of course she wasn't. In fact, she wasn't like most people. Generous and selfless. Maybe some indiscretion would be worth it.

———

At Fanny's door, Nick waited for her to unlock it. She didn't dare attempt a kiss—it had taken so much just to get Fanny to have dinner.

"Would you like to come in?" Fanny asked.

Nick had wanted nothing more since she spotted Fanny on New Year's Eve. But she pulled herself back. "I'll take a rain check."

Fanny's eyebrows went up slightly. "Oh, okay. Thanks again for dinner, and thanks so much for the audition."

"My pleasure."

"See you around, then?"

"Yeah. I'll call you."

"Goodnight."

"Goodnight."

Fanny shut the door quietly.

On the drive home, Nick let the night breeze caress her face. She'd dreamed of seeing Fanny again so many times, and now that she had, she didn't think it could go any further.

She could give Fanny the kind of life she deserved. But for how long? Things were changing and not the way she wanted. Soon, she would have to make a decision that could mean the end of her career with the Torrenti family. She'd have to leave everything behind. Including Fanny. Her initial hope of picking up where they'd left off in Topeka hadn't lasted long.

She pulled into Domenic Torrenti's driveway. This was

the moment of reckoning.

～ ⚮ ～

A week later, Fanny still hadn't heard from Nick. How could someone go from hot to cold so quickly? She got Nick's number from Marty, with an odd warning not to get "mixed up with that one." Later, she picked up the phone and asked the operator to connect her to the number.

"Hello?"

"Hi, Nick. It's Fanny."

"Oh. Hi. How did you get my number?"

"Marty."

Nick was silent.

"I was wondering—"

"I'm sorry I didn't call." Nick said. "I felt it was better this way."

Fanny's stomach dropped. "I thought we got along swell."

Nick cleared her throat. "Yes, we did. But things have changed."

What could possibly have changed in a week? "Look, I know we only went out once—" Was that it? Was Nick trying to give Fanny a taste of her own medicine? "—um, but I felt like something clicked between us."

Nick cleared her throat again. "It did. I can't explain why, but I can't see you again." She hung up.

Three weeks later Nick made one of his deliveries.

Fanny was sitting at a table, watching one of the other numbers during rehearsal. Nick came in with his two cohorts, dragging a crate. This time, the crate was labeled "BANANAS." Fanny watched as Nick passed and went through the staff door. She got up, hurried down the hall to

Marty's office, and leaned in to listen, sure the door would end up with an imprint of her ear.

"Are you sure you want to do this, Nick?"

"Yes, it's time I did what's right."

"Okay, then. We're gonna miss you."

Fanny heard Nick walking toward the door, so she ran to the dressing room. When she saw Nick leave, she ran after her.

Outside, Nick was getting into a black Ford Model A, where the other two thugs were already waiting.

"Nick," she called out.

Nick stopped, remorse coloring her face. "Hi, Fanny."

"Can we please talk?"

"There's nothing to talk about."

"Yes, there is."

Nick sighed and glanced at the setting sun. "Okay. I'll come to your place tomorrow night."

Shivering, Fanny watched the car drive out of sight.

Fanny opened her door and was surprised at what she saw.

Nick wore a straight-line lavender dress down to her knees, a decorative flap on her right shoulder.

"Come in." Fanny was unable to reconcile this vision of Nick with the one she had come to know. It was clear that Nick had gotten used to her role as a male mobster, judging from the way she stood tall, feet apart, hands in her pockets. She'd almost forgotten what a beautiful woman Nick was.

"Sit down." Fanny gestured to her sofa.

Nick sat down with her legs spread apart, but quickly

closed them.

"How about a drink?" On a side table one decanter sat on a mirrored tray with four tumblers. Fanny poured liquid into two glasses, then poured tonic into each. "Sorry, this is bathtub gin."

"How'd you get it?"

"Someone gave it to me."

Nick looked down into the glass and sniffed it. "Well, bottom's up." She took a sip and grimaced. "This isn't booze, it's turpentine."

Fanny chuckled. "I know. But beggars can't be choosers."

Fanny watched Nick—should she call her Nicolette now?—take another swig with a look of resignation on her face. "So?"

"There's talk of repealing Prohibition. It could come any day now. Could be tomorrow, next year, or five years. But it's coming."

Fanny waited for her to continue.

"My bosses started looking into a new business." Nick drained the rest of her drink, then took a deep breath. "They want me to do something that I just can't do."

"What?"

Nick hesitated. "They want me to distribute drugs."

"You mean like opium?"

"Morphine, heroin, and cocaine."

Fanny sat back.

"I just can't do it. I had a good friend who got hooked on heroin. She died."

"I'm sorry."

"I'll do many things, but I can't do that."

"Okay, so what does this have to do with us?"

Biting her thumbnail, Nick regarded her for a

moment.

"Fanny, no one leaves the family business."

"But it's not *your* family."

"Doesn't matter. Once you're in, you're in for life. The only way I could get out was to tell them I want to have a normal life and get married. I mean, how could they say no to that, right?"

Fanny smiled.

Nick smiled too, briefly. "I've made enough money to last a while, but I can't stay here. I have to find work somewhere where they don't know me, so I can pass. Men make more money."

Fanny didn't know what to say, so she remained silent.

Abruptly, Nick changed the subject. "How did the audition go?"

"I got the part."

"Hey! That's terrific. Congratulations."

"Thanks. Thank you for doing that for me."

"My pleasure."

"Can you stay?"

"Well, I have some packing to do."

"No, I mean here in LA."

Nick sighed. "No."

"As long as you stay dressed as a woman, you can continue the pretext. If anyone questions you, you can just say you're shopping for a husband."

Nick laughed.

"What's so funny?"

"I already got a proposal."

"From who?"

"One of my runners. He said he wondered why he was attracted to me. Personally, I think he's a swishy boy."

Fanny laughed. "After Chicago, I didn't want to take

the chance of my career being ruined again. But if you leave, I'll miss you." She put her hand on Nick's thigh.

Nick smiled and Fanny saw a hint of hope in her eyes. Nick leaned over and caressed Fanny's cheek, then drew her close and kissed her, and it was soft and deep and took her back to Topeka, when she'd wondered if maybe Nicolette could be something special. Before things got crazy.

Nick nuzzled Fanny's throat with her lips and sparks shot down Fanny's spine. "Maybe we can make this work," Nick whispered.

Fanny wanted it to. She'd been right—things were going to change. And no matter what happened, she'd be ready.

Nightingale

Jean Copeland

Sid smoothed the sides of her greased back hair as she paced in front of her Uncle Ray's desk. She was buckling under the pressure to find a replacement singer for The High Notes, an all-girl band she managed and had booked at her uncle's supper club every Saturday night through the summer tourist season.

She sighed. "How many more of these damned auditions, anyway?"

"One more," Ray said, chewing an unlit cigar as he sifted through a pile of invoices. "Florence something. She could be the one."

"Ahhh." Sid waved off Ray's optimism and stuffed her hands in her trouser pockets. "Amateurs. They don't have what Marjory has. Nobody does. This is all her fault. What difference would a few more months have made?"

"Listen, kid, Marjory is out. Her fiancé is back from his tour in the South Pacific, and they're getting hitched. That's that. Now we gotta get The High Notes a replacement so we can start packing 'em in again. We've lost a lot of lettuce these last two weekends. We need our Saturday night draw back."

Sid grunted. "Fine, Ray, whatever you say. Let's just pick this Florence dame and be done with it."

Ray pulled out a bottle of Johnny Walker from the desk drawer. "She'll be here at six. In the meantime, see if this won't get Marjory off your mind." He poured a shot into a filmy glass and handed it to Sid.

"Yeah, yeah," she said taking the glass. "She's off all right. She was off the minute she ditched the other girls."

"Yeah, sure." Ray smirked. "The *other* girls."

"Ah shut up," Sid said and clicked her glass against Ray's.

"Excuse me." A husky voice harmonized with a soft rap on the open office door. "Sorry to interrupt, but it looked like the place was closed." She took out a cigarette from a tin case and packed the butt against it.

"You must be Florence," Sid said, regarding her with a begrudging glare. "You're early."

Ray jumped out of his chair to light Florence's cigarette. "Where's your manners," he said to Sid and nudged her out of the way.

"Thanks," Florence said, exhaling a stream of smoke.

"Why don't you have a seat right out there, dear, and we'll be with you in a minute," Ray said, a boyish charm brightening his leathery face.

"Put your eyes back in your head," Sid said. "She ain't your type."

"How do you know she ain't?"

"She's clean and smells sophisticated, that's how I know."

Ray leaned against the edge of the desk, folded his

arms, and studied his niece carefully. "All right, Sid, I'll make you a deal. I'll leave her alone if you do. I can tell this one's a keeper, and I haven't even heard her sing."

"I'm not bothering anyone anymore. Trust me. Who needs the aggravation?"

"You knew Marjory was rationed sugar, but you fell for her anyway."

Sid's cheeks flushed. "You don't know what you're talking about. C'mon. Let's go see if this Florence is some kind of a nightingale or what."

Ray chuckled and then downed his last sip of whiskey. "Florence Nightingale. That's a good one."

***

After Florence's audition, Sid sat at the piano waiting for Ray to stop clapping—and clapping and clapping. She stared into the ceiling rafters wishing Florence hadn't just sent them to the moon. She wasn't ready to forgive Marjory for abandoning them and turning their whole operation upside down. But Ray was right. She knew Marjory was taken. If only the heart cared about such details. Florence sure had it all, though, beauty, killer charisma, and a set of lungs that could the blow the brass off a sax.

"Uh, thank you, Miss Greer," Sid shouted above the smacking of Ray's palms.

"We'll call you," Sid said and "You're hired," Ray said simultaneously. They glared at each other.

"Well, which is it?" Florence asked.

"Uh, since I own this place..."

"Till you die," Sid chimed in.

"Since I'm the owner, I say you're hired. Be here

Monday night for rehearsal, six-thirty sharp."

"Will do," Florence said with a lazy two-finger salute. She grabbed her wrap and her purse and sauntered off.

"I hope you know what you're doing," Sid mumbled to Ray.

Moments later, Sid elbowed open the door to the ladies' room and was startled to see Florence washing her hands. Florence flinched when she saw her.

"Say, what's the big idea? This is the ladies' room."

"Relax, toots. I'm just a lady who don't like dresses," Sid said and made her way to a stall.

Florence smirked. "Oh, I get it. The Marlene Dietrich look. Smart. I should try that sometime. Maybe the wolves will keep their hands to themselves."

"No need to worry here, Miss Greer—it is Miss, isn't it?"

"Yeah, it's Miss. What's it to you? Writing a book?"

Sid couldn't help chuckling at her spunk. "Just making sure you're not planning to take a powder on us the minute your boyfriend, or fiancé, or husband gets his discharge papers."

She looked directly at Sid, giving her the once-over. "Look, I'm here because I want to sing. I may spend all day at the plant drilling rivets into Corsair fighters, but I'm a singer at heart, see? That's what makes me tick."

"Okay, I got it," Sid said, warming to a smile. "Something tells me, dress or slacks, you don't need help keeping the wolves away."

"I guess I do all right," Florence said, easing her defensiveness. She headed for the door and stopped. "See you Monday at six-thirty sharp, if that's okay with you? Your boss kind of strong-armed you into agreeing."

"As much as I hate to admit it, sometimes the son of a

gun is right." Sid closed the stall door still smiling.

The first night of rehearsal, Sid strode into the hall, checking her watch, quietly doing a head count on the girls.

"Hey, big shot," Mary the piano player called out. "So you decided to hire a singer on your own without even running it by us?"

"Mary, don't you trust me, doll?" Sid asked. "I can tell who's got the goods."

"She may have the goods, but does she have a clock?"

"It's six-thirty-one. She'll be here," Sid said, loosening her suddenly constricting tie.

"Well, I hope for your sake we all like her."

"Sorry I'm late," Florence shouted as she trotted into the hall. "The traffic on East Broadway was murder." She blotted sweat from her face with a lace hanky and introduced herself to the girls in the band, saving the scowling Mary for last. "How do you do?" she said, offering Mary her hand.

"Swell." Mary squeezed her fingers like a vice before heading behind the piano.

"You got quite a grip there," Florence drawled as she walked to the microphone stand center stage. "You could crack walnuts," she added in a fully audible mumble.

"I operate a machine press at Sargent. It's tough on the hands," Mary said. "What do you do, bake pies?"

Florence wheeled around on her heels. "I make fighter planes." She arched an eyebrow to mark a first-round victory.

Sid's eyes darted between them. "You two are gonna

be real pals," she said wringing her hands. "I can tell. You both take your music very serious."

"Hey, can we get going here?" Louise asked from behind the drums. "My mother's already threatened that if I don't start getting home at a decent hour, I'll have to find a new babysitter."

"Let's start with 'What'll I Do'," Mary said. "You know that one, cookie?"

"Sure, cookie," Florence said. "Who doesn't?"

Sid leaned against the wall watching carefully, praying the girls would click. Summer in Walnut Beach was the one season businesses made any real money. Tourists came in droves and only stayed and spent until September. The band had to start playing again. She had no doubt Florence had what it took to front the group. Her only concern, as usual, was Mary.

She closed her eyes as Florence's voice carried her off with its dulcet falsettos and dipped her down into a husky lower register. Let Mary grouse all she wanted—the crowd this weekend wasn't going to know what hit them.

After rehearsal ended, Sid found Florence's handkerchief on her music stand. She looked up and saw her last in the line of departing girls.

"Hey, Florence, hang on," she called out. "Your handkerchief."

Florence stopped as the rest of the girls filed out, with the exception of Mary who lingered, rifling through her purse.

"Thanks." Florence grabbed the hanky and turned to leave.

"Wait a minute," Sid said, grasping for something to say.

"Yeah?" Florence said expectantly.

"You sounded great kid, really great. This is gonna work out fine." Sid bestowed a cool wink of approval.

"Thanks," Florence said. "The girls are really keen. Sweet sound."

"You've got the sweet sound," Sid said shyly.

An awkward silence swayed between them.

"Say, how long does it take Mary to defrost?" Florence whispered.

Sid shoved her hands in her pockets and avoided Florence's eyes. "Aw, don't mind her. She's always got a bee in her bonnet."

"What happened? Her old man leave her for some share crop?"

Sid blushed. "Something like that."

"Listen, I have to get going. Uncle Sam wants me reporting for factory duty bright and early."

"Sure," Sid said. "Let me walk you to your car."

"You're talking to the girl who can fight off wolves on her own, remember?" Florence threaded her arm under Sid's, and they headed for the door. "Gee, I hope I'm not being escorted by a wolf in Marlene Dietrich's clothing."

Sid laughed. "You're something else."

___

After the band's final rehearsal before their public debut, Sid hovered by Mary as she stood at the piano organizing her sheet music.

"Great rehearsal, Mar," Sid finally said, realizing Mary had no plan to acknowledge her. "You gals are gonna bring down the house on Saturday. Just when I thought things couldn't get any better than with Marjory," she said, her thoughts drifting off.

Mary looked up. "You're some piece of work, Sid."

"What?" she asked innocently.

"Things couldn't get any better than with Marjory? Did you mean for the band or yourself?"

"For the band. I'm the manager, aren't I?"

"Yeah, you're our manager, all right, and always helping yourself to the merchandise."

Sid looked over her shoulder to make sure everyone else had gone. "Look, you can't still be sore over us. It's been almost a year." She paused, but Mary wasn't budging. "We weren't right for each other, Mary. You know that. We had a good run, but we weren't happy."

"We were until Marjory came into the picture."

"That's not true. You and I were fire and ice, fighting all the time even before Marjory came along. You made her the patsy so you could be angry at something besides me."

Mary grinned like a fat cat. "The joke was on you in the end. Shot down by her handsome ball turret gunner fiancé."

Sid shrugged even though that one smarted. "You got it all wrong. I knew there'd never be anything between us. She was a swell kid and quite the songbird. My interest in her was strictly professional."

Mary scoffed. "You don't just dress like a man, you lie like one, too." She gathered her purse and threw a light sweater over her shoulders before heading out. "Suit yourself, Sid. I'm through looking out for you."

"Mary, come on. At least let me walk you home."

"Thanks, but I learned I can get along without you." Mary walked briskly to the door then stopped. "You wanna know something?"

"What?" Sid asked.

"I'm almost gonna feel sorry for you when this one

blows up in your face." She walked out as Sid tried to shake off the rant.

Mary was just chewing on sour grapes. Sure, Florence was a sight—flowing auburn hair, fire engine red lips and a set of gams that Mussolini would've surrendered for—but Sid wasn't interested in her. Besides, she couldn't even peg whether Florence vacationed on the island of Sapphos or not. And that's one kind of doll she wasn't playing with anymore.

A few nights later, Sid defied all reason and asked Florence if she hadn't wanted to take a stroll along Walnut Beach's boardwalk.

"This was a nice idea," Florence said as the moon trailed them like a chaperone.

"Ah, it was a safe bet," Sid said. "Who doesn't like ice cream and summer nights at the shore?"

"Not me. It's lovely here. After winters in Burlington, this is heaven."

"What brought you down here?"

"My cousin from Stratford. When she wrote me that Vought Aircraft was hiring girls for factory work, I jumped on the first Greyhound out of there."

"And how about a boyfriend? Got one of those?"

"No, I don't got one of those," Florence said teasingly. "You make it sound like a French poodle or something."

"Just making conversation."

"That's right, making sure I won't leave you high and dry."

Sid shrugged as she licked her ice cream cone. "You don't want to talk about your love life, fine with me. What do you want to talk about, your dear old mom? Your job making fighter planes?"

"Either one would be more interesting than my love life—mainly because I don't have one."

"You're kidding, a dish like you? You must be combing them out of your hair."

Florence frowned. "Yeah, like lice. Say, what's your real name, anyway?"

"If you must know, it's Sylvia, Sylvia Grace McGinty.

"Sylvia?" Florence guffawed.

"Yeah, and if you spread it around, I'll slug you one." Sid nudged her playfully in the arm.

"Boy, you sure don't look like a Sylvia. Why do you call yourself Sid?"

"I'm a businesswoman, and guys don't care much for doing business with broads. When I'm making phone calls and talking to suppliers, they hear the name Sid, hear me talk over the phone and we got no problems, understand? When new business is done in person, my uncle Ray handles it."

"What happens when your uncle isn't there anymore?"

Sid stopped at a garbage can to throw out the napkins from her cone. "What do you think, I got a crystal ball?"

Florence smiled and handed Sid her bunched up napkins. "How about you win me a Kewpie doll or something?" She tilted her head toward a bustling wall of chance games lining the boardwalk.

"If I do, will you tell me about your love life?"

"Nothing much to tell," she said with a shrug. "Let's ride the merry-go-round later, and I'll make something up."

Sid grinned as she approached the hawker at the ring toss game. She threw down a few nickels and said,

"Keep 'em coming until I get one of those Kewpie dolls up there."

She took the rings and began tossing them toward the row of milk bottles, missing throw after throw. When Sid reached into her pocket for more change, Florence tapped her on the shoulder.

"Listen, I don't want you going broke over a crummy doll. Let's head over to the carousel. We can catch the last ride before it closes."

"Hold on. Let me give it one more shot." Sid measured the distance with an outstretched arm. "I don't think I was releasing at the right time." She swung her arm up and back a few times for practice. The first ring sailed to the bottle, just bouncing off the lip. Sid glanced at Florence from the corner of her eye. "That one was practice."

"Like the first dozen?" Florence flashed a devilish grin.

"Wise guy," Sid muttered.

She tossed the second, and it bounced off the opening just shy of making a ringer. On the third throw, the ring whirled around the top of the bottle, threatening to bounce off like the others, but landed dead on. Florence shrieked with delight and hugged Sid.

"Lady's choice," Sid said to the hawker, savoring the feel of Florence's arms around her.

"Which one should I pick?" Florence asked, her twinkling eyes lingering on Sid's.

"It's your doll, but if it were me, I'd pick the red head—reminds me of you."

"I'll take the redhead," Florence said to the hawker while still eyeing Sid.

As they continued down the boardwalk to the carousel, Sid checked her watch hoping it wasn't time to leave. She couldn't remember ever having a better time.

"Oh no," Florence cried as they approached the carousel. "Looks like they're shutting it down."

"C'mon." Sid grabbed her hand, and they trotted over to the young man who had just turned out a set of colorful lights around the carousel. "Hey, fella, how about letting us have one last spin before you close up?" Sid gave him a wink to seal the deal.

"I'm sorry, sir, it's midnight. I have to shut it down."

"Say, are you being funny or something?" Florence said over Sid's shoulder.

The boy looked startled. "No ma'am."

"Then what are you calling her 'sir' for? That's an insult," Florence went on dramatically. "Just look at those angelic blue eyes and soft, pouty lips. How do you think your boss like how you treat his customers?"

"I'm awfully sorry, ma'am," the boy stammered. "I didn't mean any disrespect. Here, go ahead, get on. I'll send it around one more time."

"Make it a few more times and we'll forget the whole thing," Sid said, following Florence's lead.

They stifled giggles until they were across the platform and then giggled again as they climbed up and chose their fancifully adorned steel horses. Carnival music blared as they began moving. Sid stared at Florence's auburn locks flowing behind her like a horse's mane. The carousel made so many revolutions under the star-filled sky, they'd lost count.

Nearing one a.m., Sid pulled up in front of Florence's apartment, threw the gearshift into park, and stared at her from the corner of her eye. Florence was examining her fingernails resting in her lap as though suddenly stricken shy. What a moment. By this time, she'd figured she knew which side Florence buttered her bread on and wanted so badly to lean over for a kiss. Until Uncle Ray's voice suddenly taunted her. *Will ya leave this one alone,* it warned. She reminded herself of the last year of hell she went through, between Mary and Marjory and then having to scramble to find her replacement. Things had been working out beautifully the last few weeks. Then again, who ever said Uncle Ray had to find out?

"I sure had a swell time tonight, Flo." She looked straight ahead, her hands gripping the steering wheel.

"Me, too," Florence said, still looking down. After a moment of unbearable silence, she said, "So was this a date?"

"Gee, I don't know. It could be if you wanted it to," Sid said. "Do you—want it to?"

Florence nodded shyly. "If it's a date, then don't we have to kiss goodnight?"

"We don't have to, but it's kinda customary, isn't it?"

"Sometimes," Florence said. "If you really like the person."

"I like you all right." Sid leaned over to kiss Florence on her cheek, but Florence turned her mouth toward Sid's.

"Lovely," Florence purred. She licked her lips and got out of Sid's car. After shutting the door, she poked her head in through the window. "I like you all right, too, Sylvia McGinty."

For weeks Sid had enjoyed getting to know Florence better—skating at the boardwalk, going to the show, dinners and all-nighters spent at her apartment. She hadn't realized how fast they were moving until she sauntered into the office at the club one night, whistling like a sparrow.

"I don't get you," Ray said the minute she walked in. "It's like you go out of your way to foul things up."

"What do you mean?" Sid said.

"Oh, so that's how you want to play it? Fine. Why can't you go for one of the strippers, instead? They're a dime a dozen."

"Let me guess—you've had a chat with Mary."

Ray arched his eyebrow at Sid.

"Boy, it's so easy for you to choose who you fall in love with," Sid said. "Well, I can't. I don't know any girl who can."

Ray shook his head. "You can throw a suit on a dame, slick back her hair like Bugsy Siegel, even give her a Cuban to chew on once in a while, but she's still a dame through and through. Why couldn't you have a brother?"

Sid shrank into herself. Uncle Ray had been like a father to her and her younger sister since their father passed away years earlier. Sid had idolized him—his carefree, exciting nightlife as a popular supper club owner. How she hated herself for disappointing him.

"I'm sorry," Sid finally said. "Look, I'll cool it with Florence. She's a tough cookie, not like Mary. She'll be fine."

"If you ask me, Sid, you're acting like a kid. Almost thirty now and still flipping your wig over puppy love. Didn't anyone ever tell you don't shit where you eat?"

Maybe Uncle Ray was right. She was being childish and unprofessional, allowing her emotions to complicate business. Regardless of how she felt about Florence, ending things before it went too far was the only thing to do.

～•～

She'd been doing a terrific job avoiding Florence in the week since she'd talked with Ray. She hadn't called her or asked her to go out, and didn't show up at the club Saturday until the girls' set was nearly over. Despite the success of The High Notes's new line up, Sid's heart still ached for Florence. After the show, she entered the ladies' room half in a fog.

"Well, well, well," Florence said in disgust. "I'll be seeing you in all the old familiar places, heh?"

"Florence, hi," Sid said, startled. "Great show tonight."

"How would you know?"

"I was here. I caught most of it."

"You know who I had an interesting conversation with over dinner?"

Sid swallowed a lump in her throat. "Who?"

"Mary. She sure had a lot to say about you. I kind of wished I had dinner with her a month ago. Would've spared me a lot of trouble."

For a moment, Florence's tough veneer almost cracked.

Sid was mortified. "I don't know what she told you, but I'm sure most of it was an exaggeration."

Florence stared into the mirror as she applied lipstick. "The details aren't important," she said, cold as ice. "The point is it made a lot of sense. I wish I'd known it all before I fell for you, but those are the breaks, right?"

"Flo, I can explain..."

"Save your breath," she drawled. She blotted her lips,

213

powdered her shiny nose, and headed for the door.

"Wait." Sid gently grabbed her arm. "You fell for me?"

"Yeah, Sid," she said, jerking her arm free. "That's what you wanted, wasn't it? A little roll in the hay with the new girl in town and then back to business."

"Flo, don't listen to Mary. She's got an ax to grind. I mean, I really like you, but it's—well, my uncle says..."

"I got it. Bad for business." She looked deep into Sid's eyes. "Don't look so glum. You won't need to find a new singer again. I'm not leaving this plum set up, no matter how many game-playing jerks work their angles on me. You stay on your side of the road; I'll stay on mine."

She walked out of the bathroom, and Sid sank lower than she'd ever felt.

Honoring her uncle's wishes and Florence's request, Sid stayed on "her side of the road" for the rest of the summer. She traded Saturday nights for Fridays with Ray—he'd keep an eye on The High Notes while she kept the place calm enough to keep out the cops on burlesque Fridays. The club had never had a season like this one, but Sid had never been sadder.

Labor Day Weekend happened out of nowhere it seemed. Sid arrived at the club early Saturday night. She had to see the girls' final show for the season and had to experience Florence in all her stunning glory one last time. She carried six long-stem red roses to the girls' dressing room and tapped a knuckle on the door. "It's me, Sid," she announced through the crack. Someone yanked the door open and sat down before Sid noticed who.

She walked in and looked around at the ladies

applying their face powder and lipstick, unrolling their hair curlers. "Sheesh, I think the Red Army gets a warmer welcome during an invasion," she observed as she handed out the roses.

"Hiya, Sid," Louise called out in a mocking tone.

"If the helmet fits..." Mary glared at Sid through the make-up mirror.

"Aw, now that ain't polite, girls," Florence said as she emerged from the bathroom. "Sid took time from her busy schedule to see our final performance of the summer. Let's show her a little gratitude."

"Here's some gratitude for ya," Charlene, the trumpet player, called out. "Where the hell ya been all summer?"

"You know," Florence said. "She was handling the strippers every Friday night."

The girls laughed in derision.

"Well, I wouldn't put it that way," Sid said sheepishly.

"No?" Florence was suddenly in her face. "Was it only one stripper?"

"Can I speak with you privately, please?" Sid whispered.

"Sorry, boss, we got ten minutes to curtain and I don't even have my face on." Florence grabbed the last rose from Sid's hand, sat beside Mary to finish her make-up, and tossed the rose in the garbage.

Defeated, Sid skulked out. With a fresh high ball, she retreated to the back of the room to catch the show. It wasn't long before she realized why she avoided them all summer. Florence's stage presence and allure were irresistible. And when she sang, "I Got My Love to Keep Me Warm," Sid was ready to surrender. How could she have let her go? To please her uncle? A guy who let his own marriage fail to become a big time nightclub owner. So she could follow in his footsteps and be a lonely big time club owner, too?

After the show, she trailed the girls to the dressing room.

"Not again," one of them grumbled.

"All right, now listen to me," Sid began, strong and resolute. "Look, I know you're all sore at me for not being around and supporting you all summer. I had a problem, and I let it affect my work here and with the band. But I realize I was wrong, and unprofessional, and I let you down. I'm here to apologize to you, but not just with words—with an offer."

Suddenly the girls weren't faking interest. "We're listening," Mary said as Florence and the others looked on.

"I talked with Ray, and we decided, if you girls are interested, we'll keep the band going throughout the year. Not every Saturday, but certainly a few weekend nights a month, with a raise of course."

The girls broke into cheers, all except Florence who seemed to be studying Sid.

"Well, I'll let you gals mull it over. I'll be in my office doing some paperwork." She left with a last, lingering glance at Florence.

Later, Sid looked up from the desk to see Florence posed against the office's door frame, arms folded, eyes boring into her.

"There's no plan to keep us together all year, is there?" Florence accused.

Sid reclined in her chair. "Not true. There's a plan. I just haven't run it by my uncle yet. But I'm as certain as the clap on shore leave he's going to say yes. The crowds will be smaller, mostly beach trash, but just because summer's over doesn't mean this amazing ride has to shut down."

She stood up and gazed at Florence in earnest. "Flo, this band has never sounded better or been more dazzling, and it's because of you."

"So this brainchild of yours is all about business?"

Sid shook her head. "That's the part that'll win Ray over. For me, it's got nothing to do with business. I miss you like crazy, Flo."

"Oh, Sid." Florence sighed. "So you miss me, so what?"

Sid took Florence's hands in hers. "I was crazy to listen to my uncle, to listen to anyone who'd talk me outta you. Whenever I'm with you, that's the kind of happy I've been searching for. But everything was moving so fast."

"I was never just a fling to you?"

"Look, I don't know what Mary told you, but no, never. I fell hard for you, Flo."

"I fell for you, too, Sid. Imagine how I felt when you started avoiding me."

"I'm awful sorry for hurting you. For what it's worth, I've had a lot of time to think over the summer. I know what I want now, and what I want is you."

She lunged at Sid and clutched her.

After a moment, Sid gently pushed her back. "Are you crying?"

"Me? Cry over a wolf in Marlene Dietrich's clothing?" Florence tried wiping away the evidence. "Never."

Sid kissed her last tear. "C'mon. Let's go take that last carousel ride of the season."

My Elizabeth

MJ Williamz

The Japanese had bombed us. It was in all the newspapers, on all the radio channels. We were at war. Men were signing up right and left to go serve. Times were hard on the home front. Families were issued ration stamps to buy a variety of things, from clothes to food to even fuel. People were willing to make the sacrifices, though, so our boys over there could have more. We all worried about the boys fighting for us. We wanted them to have all they needed so they could win the war.

At the time, I lived in Ypsilanti, Michigan. There was a factory there that made airplanes. The men were gone, but planes needed to be made. I was thrilled at the idea of working in the factory. It appealed to me so much more than being a secretary or any other traditional woman's job. I didn't feel like a traditional woman. I was different. I didn't know how or why, but I knew it. I could feel it.

So I went to work building airplanes, doing my part for the boys. When I asked what we were supposed to wear I was told pretty much anything went. We could wear pantsuits or dresses, if we preferred. Or we could wear dungarees. Dungarees! Oh, can you imagine? I was in heaven. I had a job in a factory and I could wear dungarees to work. The world may have been at war, but, at twenty-two, I was the happiest I'd ever been.

I showed up the first day at work and sat in the office waiting area. I was to meet with a Miss DuPont, who was going to have me fill out paperwork and show me around. I was so excited, I could barely sit still.

Finally, the office door opened and out walked the most beautiful woman I had ever seen. She was tall in her heels, but not as tall as I was. Women weren't allowed to wear nylons, but that's okay. She didn't need them to show off her shapely legs. Her auburn hair was in a loose bun at the back of her head and her green eyes spoke of an intelligence that would be welcome to work for.

"Mrs. Josephine Moore?" she said.

"Miss," I said. "I'm a miss. And you can call me Jo."

"Okay, Jo. Well, I have some papers I need you to fill out."

She handed me a clipboard with several forms on it that I needed to complete before I could get started. She walked back into her office while I took care of my paperwork. They were easy to fill out, and in no time, I was knocking on her door.

She came out again and took the clipboard from me. "Thank you. Now let me show you around."

We walked out into a cavernous space. There were several airplanes in various stages of production. There were also stations along the edges where women were busy at work.

Miss DuPont explained to me these stations were

where the wings were built. It was all so beautiful to see. It took me a while to absorb all I was seeing. She warned me it would be loud on the floor, so to expect to have to shout to be heard.

First stop was a wing station. Miss DuPont yelled to me, "This is where you'll be working."

"Why can't I work on the actual plane?"

"Everyone starts on the wings. It's a promotion to work on the plane itself."

"No problem. I understand. Working on the wings is just as exciting for me."

The women wore full face masks and used acetylene torches to weld different parts of the wings together. It was hard to accept that someone was going to pay me to play with tools. I couldn't wait.

"When do I get to get started?"

"You'll start training after lunch," she shouted.

"And when is lunch?"

A horn sounded that shook the whole building. It was followed by a deafening silence.

"Right now," she said.

"Great," I said. "Where do I eat?"

"Most of the girls eat on the picnic tables out back. I'm sure you can find a spot. Find me afterward and I'll issue you your welder's mask and earplugs."

"Sounds good. And thank you so much, Miss DuPont."

"You're welcome." She smiled, and the whole factory lit up.

I made my way out back and found an empty spot at a picnic table.

"May I sit here?"

"Sure," A woman with frizzy red hair said. "I'm Mildred."

"I'm Jo."

"Well, it's nice to meet you, Jo." She went around the table pointing to the others. "This here's Dorothy, this is Patricia, and this is Lillian."

"It's a pleasure to meet all of you."

"Is this your first day?" Lillian said.

"It is. I'm so excited."

"Oh honey," Patricia said, "Pace yourself."

"Oh I will. Don't worry. I'll be careful not to use all my energy right off the bat."

"Good girl. You do that and you'll be fine," Mildred said.

I opened my lunch bucket and ate the measly lunch my mom had packed. I wasn't sure if it would be enough once I started working full time the next day. I thought I might need to keep my energy up. I decided I'd need more than a sandwich and a thermos of milk and made a mental note to ask my mother to add something more.

The buzzer went off again and everyone stood.

"It was nice meeting you again," Mildred said. "We'll see you on the floor."

Unsure of what to do, I walked back to Miss DuPont's office. She greeted me with another warm smile.

"Okay, Jo," she said. "Are you ready to work?"

"Oh, yes."

"Okay, then, follow me."

Miss DuPont led me down a hallway lined with lockers on the other side of her office. She stopped at an empty one and pointed.

"This will be your locker." She handed me a lock. "This is your lock. The combination is on the back. Take it off immediately so no one else knows it, okay?"

"Okay."

We continued down the hall, which ended at a large room full of supplies. Miss DuPont spoke to the woman behind the counter.

"Caroline, this is Jo. She's new and needs wing welder equipment."

The woman handed me a welder's mask and welding torch. The weight felt good in my hand. She tossed me leather coveralls, a turban, and gloves.

"Sign here." She handed me a clipboard. "Change in the locker room."

I signed and turned to Miss DuPont. "Then I can work?"

"Then you can work." She placed a hand on my shoulder, and I felt the warmth flow all through my body. I stutter stepped then regained my footing. I quickly pulled on the gear and rejoined her.

"I'm going to introduce you to a woman named Mildred. She'll show you what to do, okay? Pay close attention. We don't want you or anybody else getting hurt. Safety first. And we also want these planes built correctly. Understand?"

"I think I met Mildred at lunch," I said.

"Oh, good. She's a nice lady and a good worker."

Miss DuPont led me back out to the floor and over to a section of wing workers. She moved so she was standing in the view of one of them who shut down her equipment and lifted her mask.

"Yes, ma'am?" she said.

"This is Jo," Miss DuPont shouted.

"Yes. We met at lunch."

"I'd like you to show her the ropes."

"That would be my pleasure."

"Great. I'll leave you two to it. And, Jo, if you have any

questions or concerns, you know where my office is."

I watched her walk away. I didn't realize I was staring until Mildred called out.

"You ready? We should get started."

"Oh, yeah. Sure."

Mildred showed me how to attach my torch to the TIG line. She tapped her face mask. "Always remember your shield. The light from these things is dangerous and could damage your eyes. Got it?"

I nodded.

"Good. Now watch. This is your filler rod. You hold it here at just this angle. Now you use the torch to create the arc. Now watch." She made it look simple, the smooth line of weld joining the wings together. "Okay, now you give her a go."

She handed me the flux and my torch, then stood at a cautious distance as I went to work. Just as I leaned in to start, she slapped my shield down over my face.

"Always remember your shield."

I made a few mistakes in the beginning, but soon had a handle on the process. I worked hard and stayed focused and about jumped out of my skin when the horn sounded again. I turned off my equipment and looked at Mildred.

"Quittin' time, kid," Mildred said. "Did Miss DuPont show you the timecard system?"

"No."

"Well, you better find her then. She should be in her office."

I smiled. "Thanks for all your help today."

"No problem, Jo. You're a natural."

I felt good about my day, but as I approached Miss DuPont's office, I got butterflies in my stomach. I didn't understand my feelings, but I was still happy I got to see

Miss DuPont again.

I walked into the waiting area of her office and her secretary told me that Miss DuPont would be right with me. I couldn't sit still. I got up and paced the small room.

"Are you okay, Jo?" Miss DuPont said.

I hadn't heard the door open. I blushed. "Yes. I'm fine. I just need to learn about the time card?"

"Oh, yes. I didn't show you that this morning, did I?"

"No, ma'am."

"Well, come on into my office with me and I'll get you a blank card. After this, you'll find one with your name on it by the clock at the start of every pay period."

I followed Miss DuPont into a small but nicely decorated office. I felt like I could barely breathe in the tight quarters. Something was wrong with me, but I didn't know what. I wasn't normally claustrophobic.

Miss DuPont went to the other side of the desk and opened a drawer. I watched her, but quickly looked away when I realized I could see down her blouse. I felt a blush creep over me. What was wrong with me?

Miss DuPont took out a blank timecard and wrote my name across the top of it. Then, in the right column, she wrote the date and in the next column, the time my day had started, eight o'clock.

"Now, every day you clock in when you get here and when you leave. All these boxes will fill out automatically. Understand?"

"Yes ma'am."

"Great. Now follow me and I'll show you where the time clock is."

I did as I was instructed and watched as Miss DuPont inserted and removed the time card.

"That seems easy enough," I said.

"It is. But, as always, any questions or concerns, you come see me."

"Yes ma'am."

I was exhausted when I got home to my mom and dad's house. I ate dinner, but then begged off listening to the news as I really needed sleep. But a good night's sleep escaped me as my dreams were all haunted by Miss DuPont. At one point I woke in a cold sweat. I didn't know what was going on, but decided to avoid Miss DuPont at all costs in the future.

I woke the next morning and ate breakfast with my parents, then showered and tied my long hair up in a bun before donning my dungarees and work shirt. I rode to work with my dad, who dropped me off at precisely eight o'clock.

I found my timecard and punched the clock, then found my locker and got my equipment out. I headed for my place on the floor and went to work. Mildred watched over me again for a while, but then told me I was good to go on my own.

I was focused on my job when I caught movement out of the corner of my eye. It was Miss DuPont. I turned off my equipment and raised my mask.

"Hi," I said, hoping the nerves wouldn't make my voice quiver.

"Hi. I just wanted to check in with you to see how things are going."

"They're going great. Mildred watched me for a while this morning, but now I'm on my own."

The horn sounded then and the place went quiet.

"I won't keep you from your lunch," Miss DuPont said. "I just wanted to check on you."

"Thank you."

I hurried past Miss DuPont to my locker to get my lunch bucket. I sat outside with the same ladies from the day before.

"Is everything okay?" Mildred asked me.

"Sure," I said. "Why do you ask?"

"Miss DuPont never comes down to the floor unless she's showing a new employee around."

"She just came by to make sure I was doing okay."

The other ladies all looked at each other like they knew a secret.

"What?" I said.

"Nothing," Mildred said. "It's just that was nice of her."

"Yes. I thought so."

Something didn't feel right to me. I felt like I was the butt of some joke that I didn't get. The table was quiet the rest of lunch, which only made my unease grow. The horn blew and I was relieved to get back to work. On the way in, I grabbed Mildred's arm.

"What happened at lunch?" I asked. "I feel like a pariah."

"Oh, it was nothing, hon. Just do yourself a favor and stay away from Miss DuPont. She's not like the rest of us."

"What do you mean?"

"I mean, she's *different.*"

"How so?"

"You know, *different.*"

"I don't understand," I said. "But I'll take your word for it."

We worked the rest of the day and, after that, the days fell into an easy routine. I knew my way around the shop by then and was becoming known as an excellent welder. I sat with the same group at lunch every day and nothing more was said about Miss DuPont. And no more visits were made by Miss DuPont. Things were going smoothly for me. I loved my job. I loved helping to make airplanes that would eventually bomb the Nazis. At least, that's how I pictured it.

At the end of the day, several weeks later, I was walking toward the time clock. This meant walking past Miss DuPont's office. Miss DuPont came out of her office this particular evening and grabbed me by the arm.

I felt the heat sear into my arm. I wondered what that meant.

"Jo? Can you come in here for a moment?" Miss DuPont said.

"Sure." I looked around to make sure none of my friends saw me. I didn't want them to think I was *different*.

"Jo, you've been doing a great job," Miss DuPont said.

"Thank you."

"I'm fairly sure you're going to be made a riveter any day now."

"Oh, thank you, Miss DuPont. That would be wonderful."

"And I was thinking, I'd like to have you over to my house for dinner to celebrate."

An alarm went off inside me. Something told me this was a very bad idea. And yet, the butterflies were back. I thought how nice it would be to be with Miss DuPont away from the factory.

"Jo?"

"Oh, I'm sorry. Yes. I'd like that very much."

"Obviously, we'll have to keep it a secret," Miss DuPont said. "We can't have the other workers knowing about it."

"Oh, of course."

"Wonderful. Shall we plan on tomorrow night?"

"Sounds swell."

"Okay. I'll see you then. You can ride home with me and then I'll take you to your house after dinner."

I walked off with a spring in my step. I didn't know why I was so happy and so excited for dinner. Probably because I was about to get a promotion, I reasoned. But, whatever the reason, I couldn't wipe the smile from my face.

That night, I told my parents I was going to be having dinner with a woman from work the next night.

"Oh, dear, that's wonderful," my mother said. "It's great that you're making friends."

"Yes it is. I'm very excited."

"Good for you, Josephine," my father said.

"I don't know what time I'll be home tomorrow night," I said.

"I'll wait up for you, regardless," my father said.

I went to work in an abnormally good mood the next day. I was actually whistling while I waited to punch in. Mildred was in line in front of me.

"You're in a good mood today."

"I am," I said. "It's a beautiful day."

"Yes, I suppose it is."

I worked all day, and, at the end of the day I punched out as usual. Then I went back to Miss DuPont's office. Her secretary had already left for the day, so I knocked on her door.

Miss DuPont opened her door and smiled broadly.

"Hello, Jo. I'm so glad you didn't forget."

"No ma'am."

"Are you ready to go then?"

"Yes ma'am."

"Great. And, Jo?"

"Yes ma'am?"

"You don't need to call me ma'am when it's just the two of us."

"Yes ma'am. I mean, okay."

We both laughed and my nerves began to unwind slightly. She drove me to a small house on Chestnut Street.

"This was my parents' house while they were alive," she told me.

"I'm sorry."

"Oh, don't worry. It's been a while. So now the place is mine. I've made it as homey as I can."

We walked inside and I looked around. The furniture was well kempt and the doilies on all the armrests were clean and tidy.

"Did you make these yourself?" I held up a doily.

"I did. I used to love to make things like that. But things are in short supply these days. So I keep myself busy knitting socks for the soldiers. There's always plenty of wool."

"That's great. I should learn to knit."

"I could teach you," she said.

"That would be swell."

"May I get you something to drink? It won't take long for dinner. Would you like a glass of wine?"

"Wine sounds great." I seldom drank. It just seemed odd to do, living with my parents. And I didn't get out much. So I guessed a glass of wine would be a nice, grown up thing to have.

"Wonderful. Excuse me while I go pour it."

She brought me a glass and pointed to the couch. "Please. Sit."

"But I thought maybe you'd like some help making

dinner."

"No, you relax," she said.

"Please? I'd be more comfortable if I was helping."

It was true. I didn't understand why, but a profound sense of discomfort coursed through me.

"Well, if you'd like, you can make the salad," Miss DuPont said.

"Great."

I walked into the tiny kitchen where she had a variety of vegetables laid out by the sink.

"These are from my victory garden," she said.

"That's great," I said. "It's wonderful that you're doing your part."

She went to work mixing items on the stove for the spaghetti she was making. At one point, we both turned toward the sink at the same time. I stood so close to her, I could smell the faint scent of her perfume. The butterflies in my stomach were back. We stood facing each other, looking into each other's eyes.

I wanted to kiss her. I realized it and almost dropped the big bowl of salad I was holding. Maybe I was *different*. I wondered if that's what the ladies at work meant about Miss DuPont. It took every ounce of self-control I had not to lower my head to taste her lips. Instead I took a step back.

"I'm sorry. I'm in your way."

"Oh no, Jo. You could never be in my way."

She touched my elbow and the fire burned hot. The sound of my name on her lips was different now. I thought about leaving. I was so confused. But I liked the feelings, strange though they were. And, as much as I hated to admit it, I still wanted to kiss her.

We ate dinner in the small cove to the side of her

kitchen.

"Your house is so quaint," I said. "I really like it."

She went on to tell me about the year it was built and the architect who designed it, but I really didn't hear anything. I saw her lips move and could think of nothing else but kissing them. I'd never kissed anyone before, so this was a big step. And she was a woman, but it was still all I could think about.

After dinner, I helped her clear the plates and offered to help clean up.

"No. Let's sit on the couch and talk. I'll clean up later," she said.

"I hardly think that's fair, Miss DuPont."

"It's my house and if I say it's fair, it's fair. By the way, when we're here, please call me Elizabeth."

"Elizabeth." I tried the name on my tongue. "Okay. I can do that."

"You're very cute, Jo," she said.

"Thank you?"

"Yes, it was meant as a compliment. Now, can we move to the couch?"

"Okay, Elizabeth."

I loved that name. I'd never heard a name so lovely. And it fit her.

We sat on the couch and my leg started bouncing. I had no control over it.

"Are you nervous, Jo?" she said.

"Should I be?"

"I don't know." She placed her hand on my leg. "Should you be?"

"I don't know," I said.

She moved closer to me on the couch.

"I really like you, Jo."

"I really like you, too."

"Do you like girls or boys, Jo?"

"I don't know," I said.

"Have you ever kissed a boy?"

"No."

"Have you ever kissed a girl? You can tell me."

"No."

"Well, Jo," she moved closer still. "I want to kiss you."

"I want you to kiss me," I said.

She leaned in to me. I watched her lips get closer and closed my eyes just as our lips met. Hers were so soft and tender. I wanted to kiss her again and again.

"That was nice," I said when the kiss ended.

"Yes it was. I'd like to do it again."

"Yes, please."

That time she pulled me close so we were pressed into each other as we kissed. I felt things I'd never felt before. I felt alive.

"That was wonderful," I said.

"It was. Now, Jo, this needs to be our secret, okay?"

"Oh yes. I understand. No one can know."

"Good girl. Now come on. Let's get you home."

Elizabeth dropped me off in front of my parents' house. I wanted to ask for one last kiss but knew that wouldn't be smart. As a matter of fact, it could be dangerous.

"I'll see you at work tomorrow, Elizabeth."

"Yes. And remember, you'll need to act normal."

"Oh, I will."

I got out of the car and went inside.

The next day at work it was hard not to make up an excuse to go see Elizabeth. Miss DuPont. But I did my best and got through the workday. As I was heading to the time clock, she called me to her office.

"Hello, Jo."

"Miss DuPont."

She closed her door.

"I want to see you again. I need to."

"Yes ma'am."

"Next Wednesday?"

"Sounds good."

"Okay. I'll be waiting for you after work."

We fell into an easy routine. Once a week Elizabeth would take me over to her house after work where we'd have dinner and sit on her couch and kiss. Our kissing turned into more, with some heavy petting happening. It was all so exciting, and I knew I wanted to be with her all the time.

One week she asked me to come back on Friday and spend the night. I was terrified. I knew what that meant and while I wanted it desperately, I didn't know what it was I wanted. But I said okay and told my parents I would be having a sleepover with my new friend from work.

Friday after work, we drove to her house. On the way, she slyly reached out and squeezed my hand.

"Are you okay?" she said.

"Sure."

"Are you nervous?"

"A little. Should I be?"

"I suppose. I'm excited myself," she said.

"So am I."

"Good."

We arrived at her house and there was a tension between us that was palpable. There usually was. It started in the car, then reached a fevered pitch just as we sat on the couch to kiss. That night, kissing on the couch only served to further excite me.

When Elizabeth stood up and reached her hand out toward me, I almost said no. My body said yes, but my mind still wasn't convinced. And then I looked up into her eyes and my resolve melted. It was going to be okay. I was with Elizabeth and that was all that mattered.

Elizabeth took me into the bedroom and made me feel things I'd never dreamed possible. And when she was through and I was exhausted, she held me tight while we slept. It was the most magical night of my life.

The next morning, Elizabeth made breakfast for me and we sat and talked about the night before.

"I don't know what you did, but it was amazing," I said.

"What I did was make love to you. That's all you need to know."

"Well, you made me feel so many things."

"That's how it's supposed to be. Jo, I want you to move in with me."

"What? But what would people think?"

"I have a spare room. We can put your things in it. It'll look like two women sharing a house. Please, Jo. I love you."

My head was spinning. She loved me? Of course. That's what I'd been feeling. It was beginning to make sense.

"I love you, too."

She grabbed my hands and stared into my eyes. "Please, Jo. Tell me you'll move in with me."

"Of course, Elizabeth. I'd love to."

My father had friends with trucks, and we moved all my things into her spare bedroom the next weekend. My parents were thrilled that I was moving out almost on my own, but with a nice roommate we all knew I got along with.

The girls at work treated me like an outcast, but there were always new employees and soon I had a new group of friends who didn't seem to care that I rode to work and home every day with Miss DuPont. They were impressed that I had a room to rent on my own, away from my parents.

Elizabeth was my friend and lover until nineteen-ninety-six when she quietly passed away in her sleep. Nowadays, women are able to marry other women. We didn't have that, but our love was just as real and I'll never stop loving my Elizabeth.

With a Spark

Aliisa Percival

*Defense Industries Limited, Pickering Works (a.k.a.
the Ajax Allied Bomb Factory)
Ontario, Canada
1943*

The day a movie star came to visit the factory, the other girls fell all over themselves to look their best, make the best impression. Watching from the sidelines, I couldn't help but think that for one day it looked more like the rest of them were the ones with unnatural desires, while I was the normal one.

I would never think to so cheerfully throw myself at some women, and risk crossed wires, misunderstandings—while they could never think of a reason not to.

It was amusing, to be sure, to watch the goings-on, even if it was all at too shrill a pitch and too high an energy level for me to truly enjoy it. Leaning my elbows back on the concrete ramp behind me and crossing my ankles, I pretended to watch the clouds float by as girls frantically rubbed lipstick off their teeth on all sides. *You're all beautiful*, I wanted to say, *she almost certainly goes with boys.* That gave me a chuckle, and I let my eyes drop to look for my friend Judy, who was on the far side of the crowd with other, more festive friends.

When I found her, she had her back turned, but just then a car crept through the factory gates and the hubbub escalated. I thought for sure I'd lost my chance, but Judy only proved her mettle by turning in the opposite direction of the others, catching my eye, and making a face with her eyes crossed and her tongue sticking out. I snorted, the unladylike sound beneath the notice of the women around me, and she grinned before looking toward where the car was pulling in.

I glanced over, too; a tall man wearing a chauffeur hat stepped out of the car and turned neatly toward the rear. Before he could reach for it, the back door opened, and a woman climbed to her feet and waved away his grasping hands. She turned to him and said something, her look pointed but her smile warm, and he shifted back a step, clasping his hands at the small of his back.

I recognized the woman from the posters in every hall, as well as the movie they'd played for us last Saturday night in order to pique our excitement. Her name was Lillie Madison, and she'd been born and raised in northern Ontario, though she'd managed somehow to make it all the way to Hollywood. Still standing beside the car, just this side of the gate, she turned now and swept her smile over the assembled women, lifting one suit-clad arm in a wave and raising a flutter of excitement in response.

Her other hand came up to shield her eyes, the uplifted arm slowly lowering, and she was beautiful. I knew she would be, from the posters, from the film, but the as sun glanced off her dark brown curls, shone brightly over the pale skin of her face, I drew an involuntary breath and felt a grip seize my chest.

The next instant, I looked away and took another, more controlled breath, and everything was fine. The girls were buzzing, and nobody had noticed my momentary lapse—no one, that is, except good ol' Judy, who I was beginning to think might be *too* good a friend, time to cut ties and scram. Ha-ha. I certainly would have done it long before now if it had ever really been an option.

Judy popped up at my side, apparently having left the company of her other friends, and leaned one elbow back on my ramp so that she was half-turned to me and half to the crowd. "She's something, don't you think?"

I raised my eyebrows, my attention now very apathetically on the girls just in front of me. "Who?"

The angle wasn't great for Judy to give my arm a good smack, but she made it work before gesturing wildly back toward the gate. "You know who! The big star."

"Yeah?" I said with studied nonchalance, not looking over. "You're impressed."

"*You're* impressed," Judy shot back immediately, and it was something of a performance now as I pretended not to smile, studying the fingernails on one hand.

"I don't know what you mean."

We were still surrounded while the foreman, Marvin, tried to work out where everybody should have been just then, so Judy just sighed and turned back to rest fully against the ramp. She'd get after me once we were in our residence room, she knew it and I knew it and I knew she knew I knew it.

In the meantime, Marvin was walking forward to

introduce himself to Miss Madison, wearing his best suit with his hair carefully slicked across his bald spot in that way that made his scalp shine like a grease slick. I admit I watched this interaction closely. Marvin had a lot of power in the factory, but none of that power involved interacting with the girls on the floor, following them down to the basement when no one else could make that run, waiting outside the ladies room for just one more question. Just the day-to-day running of the factory, he'd say, but I wasn't the only one who got the strange uncomfortable feeling that something wasn't right.

Marvin walked right up to Miss Madison and stuck out his meaty, forever damp hand for a shake, and I felt a sinking in my belly when Madison clasped his hand, took a step forward, and tipped her head back all at the same time, so that instead of a civil greeting, it was more like an open flirt. She knew what she was doing, and she was good at it, too; Marvin was already flushing red and sputtering out the words he meant to say.

"I can't say my reaction would be any different," I said blandly, and got a poke to the side in exchange.

"She's a minx!" Judy replied admiringly. "Got him right around her little finger and they've just met. What are they teaching them down in Hollywood, anyway?"

"You wanna sign up for a class?"

"Yeah," Judy said, standing up straight, "just one." She turned to me and stuck out her hand, so I reluctantly gave her mine and then watched as she stepped forward, laid her other hand on top of mine, and tipped her head back. Then she remembered I was shorter than her without heels and tipped her head forward instead. "Well, I guess you have to practice with actual men."

"I could stand on an apple box."

That earned me my third smack, and just from one conversation! Before she could fire back verbally, the attention of the crowd shifted once more and we turned with them to see that Madison and her driver had vanished and Marvin was addressing the gathered women.

"Ladies," he said grandly, "as you know, the factory has been shut down today to allow us all to join in on the bond drive. Miss Madison will be doing the same, donating her *valuable* time to perform and speak before us."

The level of emphasis he placed on the word *valuable* made me wonder what he thought our time was, if not as *valuable* as Miss Madison's. When I glanced over at Judy, she had a similarly sour expression on her face, so I rolled my eyes to the sky, asked for strength, and shook it off.

"The stage is set up behind the rec centre, as well as a table of refreshments. Please remember that this event is open to the public, so be on your best behaviour."

Again, what was that supposed to mean? As the group of us turned and started to tromp across the grass toward the rec centre, I leaned toward Judy and said, "What a waste we've made of our lives, devoting ourselves to the war effort instead of *acting.*"

"Well," Judy replied glibly as she took my arm, "you know they call us blue collar. She'd be, I imagine, diamond collar. Amatol ain't half as glamorous."

"Yeah, well," I said, my voice dropping as I essentially began grumbling to myself, with Judy patting my hand understandingly. We came around the corner momentarily, and it was indeed quite a nice spectacle to see. Marvin had had the red shift do the decorating; the yellow shift had prepared the food a few days prior, and we lucky blues were on cleanup duty. Everyone who pitched in was welcome to the party, but considering the other girls would have to sacrifice their off hours, their attendance seemed less than likely.

The stage was set up flush against the back of the rec centre—or more accurately, the long side wall that was used for such things, as the true back wall of the large building was home to a loading dock and the main refuse storage area. Bunting, handmade and painted and strung, lined the front and back of the stage; there was a grand piano in one corner; and a radio microphone stood front and centre. The area in front of the stage was set up with folding chairs, and a few ladies were grouped beside the refreshments table, pastel in their finery. Judy gave them a small wave, and I nudged her in that direction and reminded her that I needed to go inside to look for my granny's handkerchief.

I'm sure the other girls would have been surprised to know what a wreck I'd been when I discovered the hankie gone—I wore it under my coveralls every shift, never let it get far from me, and it tore me apart having lost it. Judy had offered to help me—which would have made the most sense, really, having twice as many eyes and half as many places to look—but I didn't want anyone to get suspicious if the two of us disappeared together for too long. Thus far she'd been spared from the "deviant freak" rhetoric, and I didn't want that to change.

Anyhow, I knew that if anyone had found it and turned it in, I would have gotten it back already, so I intended to poke around in the shadowy corners of the factory building—jammed under radiators, caught by loose baseboards, that sort of thing.

I headed in through the side door, which had been left open to allow for the use of the washrooms during the festivities. Starting there, I made my way slowly to the end of that hall, inspecting each inch as I went. At the corner I turned and continued down the next hall.

When I reached the door to the women's change room, I pushed it open and walked in without hesitating, only to pull up short when I saw that someone was already inside. She was sitting up against the opposite bank of lockers, one leg crossed over the other with her heel bouncing rapidly up and down, and an unlit cigarette in her hand. Only after taking note of this did I look at her face, surprised to find that it was Miss Lillie Madison herself.

Before I could catch myself, I blurted out, "There's no smoking in the building." As an afterthought I added, "Miss Madison."

She looked up at me, her eyebrows rising in very mild interest, and then held up the cigarette. "I was under the impression a ciggy had to be lit to be smoked." Tilting the cigarette back toward herself, she stared at the tip and muttered, "But what do I know?" before tugging the front of her dress down slightly with her other hand and pushing the cigarette past her neckline and into her bra.

Embarrassed, I looked away, but when she proceeded to plant her hands on either side of her legs and hunch forward I stepped into the room and let the door fall shut behind me. "Are..." I scratched the back of my neck, looking at her and then away again. "Are you okay? Miss."

"Please call me Lillie," she sighed, and lifted one hand to motion me forward. Even the exasperated wave of her hand held grace.

I took several halting steps forward before deciding to commit to it, striding the rest of the way to her side. Plopping down on the bench with a good few inches between us, I folded my hands in my lap and stared across the room at nothing in particular.

"Do you have a name?" she asked after a moment.

Well, this was off to a stellar beginning. "Of course. It's Evelyn. Evie. I work here, if that isn't obvious." Now that my tongue was loosened up there was no stopping it. "What *is* obvious is that you're Lillie Madison, guest of honour and star of this bond drive, the only draw we've got, and we'll be lucky to get half as many visitors as we have employees considering people only leave the city when they have to, and that's not to say you aren't a *draw*, certainly you are, but to be that you need to be, well, visible. If you catch my meaning."

She laughed, if you could call it that—a dry rattle on a sigh as she slowly straightened her spine and rose to her feet. She checked herself in the mirror, smoothing her skirt, and said to what she could see of me in the reflection, "I'm fine, by the way."

"Yeah," I murmured, "try to sell me that one on a different day."

She spun back with a sudden lightness to her air, her heels rising slightly off the floor. "Is that a proposition?"

I looked at her like she was crazy, I know I did, because I *thought* she might be crazy. "What?"

One of her feet came forward to land flat in front of her, the other tipping the rest of the way up onto her toes, and I wondered if she'd been a dancer—wondered if she still was. But her knee bent in a way that was all *flirt*, no *technique*, and suddenly I was more in the picture. She tilted her head to the side, none of her previous weightiness in the smile she let dance around the edges of her mouth. "You'd like to see me again," she said, confident and pleased, and a protest was on the tip of my tongue, an affronted look on my face, not because it wasn't true, but because she wasn't supposed to *know* that it was true.

She read that instantly, too, before I could wipe the frown from my face, and her expression dropped to neutral as her heels hit the floor and she turned toward the door, poised to leave. Her head was still high, and all she said was, "Well, can you check my nylons? Please."

I did so, starting at the backs of her heels and following that black line up to the hem of her skirt. It wasn't far to travel, and when Miss Madison—*Lillie*—turned back, it might have been slightly obvious that my eyes were quite a few inches higher than that. She raised her eyebrows, and I blushed.

"I didn't *say*—," I began.

"I see," she replied, taking a slow step forward. "I may have jumped to conclusions?" She took another step, and I had to force myself not to back away.

"You may have," I said, sounding strangled, my throat closing as I lost my battle of wills and took a step back as she took another one forward. She backed me right up to the wall, no pretense, and I hit it with some force as one of my hands flew back to smack against the mirrored glass.

Bringing a hand up, she traced my jaw with the lightest brushing of fingertips and murmured, "You don't get out much, do you, Evie?"

My face twisted in consternation and she smiled, but before I could open my mouth to protest, she kissed me, just like that, her hips pressing me back into the wall and her hand lingering at my neck. It was nothing like a movie kiss, her lips ever so soft and gentle against mine, and despite her pinning me down, I found myself gripping at her arm, certain I was about to float away.

Taking her leave from my mouth, she stretched forward to kiss behind my ear, then moved the shoulder of my dress aside and pressed her lips carefully to the bone

245

there—places a stray lipstick mark would never be seen—and I caught a gasp in my throat, my free hand curling against the mirror as my head fell back.

Then my breath stopped for another reason. "The door—"

She looked up at me, cocking an eyebrow and saying, "You didn't lock it?"

I stared at her, then laughed and shook my head, pressing my fingers into her stomach as I gently pushed her off of me. "I don't know why you might think I was coming in here. Anyway, you were here first."

"True enough," she said, letting her hand slip down my arm to curl around my palm as she backed toward the door and pulled me along with her. I followed easily enough, even as I stumbled slightly, unable to break her persistent eye contact—until the wall loomed behind her and I knew she'd hit the bench first. Lunging forward, I steered her by her shoulders to my right, and the momentum sent us colliding into the door, my hands braced on either side of her head as her back made contact.

She blinked for a second, her focus broken, then smiled and wrapped her arms around my waist, pulling my body snug against hers and saying coyly, "Why, Miss Evie."

I couldn't help but blush at my clumsiness, though I let my hands fall to rest on the bare skin at the nape of her neck as she leaned forward to press her lips to my heated cheek and then turn her cool cheek to rest against my own.

"I do have to go, though," she murmured near my ear, before resting back against the door, her expression serious for the first time that I'd seen.

"Yes, you do," I replied, cupping her face in my hands and watching as her eyes scanned my face, once; then I kissed her, allowing the moment to freeze around us as I savoured her taste, the pressure of her body against mine, the desperation in her fingers as they twisted in the fabric of my dress.

A moment later, without a pause, I pried the door open and slipped through, my heels clicking loudly in the empty hallway as I made my way quickly back to the exit door. Before emerging into the sunlight once more, I took a glance around and flipped up the hem of my dress, tugging the bottom of my slip up toward my face so I could scrub off any remaining traces of lipstick. I would borrow Judy's compact as soon as I popped up at her side, but for now a lack of lipstick would be far less conspicuous than full lips worn half off.

Having done what I could, I straightened my dress, put my hand on the doorknob, and froze.

My other hand rose, pressing the pads of my fingertips to my lips. It felt now as if I'd scrubbed her away, too; not that I'd had a choice. Would I ever see her again? Had that moment been real, had it meant anything?

Well, one thing, certainly: a confirmation, an assurance; a removal of doubt. I was the way I was—the way I had always known I was—and that was that. It almost felt a relief to acknowledge it. Even though I would never be normal. Even though the white picket fence was out of my grasp permanently. Even if some part of me had to mourn it—it was a new beginning, still. A life to live.

At least, that was my hope, now, as I heaved open the door and stepped back out into the sunlight.

A week later, a postcard arrived in the mail—*Hope to see you when I'm back in town, xoxo*—and two months after that her wedding was splashed across the front page of every rag the newsstand carried. *Starlet Lillie Madison Weds Fellow Actor Jacob Wilding in Surprise Courthouse Ceremony!* I grabbed the last copy of the only paper to publish a photo—Lillie and the young man standing together in front of an austere bell tower, their smiles so stiff I glanced automatically into the background for a father holding a shotgun. A strip blared *EXCLUSIVE!* over the top left corner of the photo, and when I looked close enough I could read the words *DAVIDSON TOWN HALL* carved into the stone of the building's face.

Where the devil was that? Walking back to the residence, my nose practically pressed to the newsprint, I read the photo's caption with no concern for my next step. *Lillie Madison and Jacob Wilding wed at Davidson Town Hall, Davidson, Saskatchewan. Why they simply couldn't wait for the end of her bond drive! What nobody knew about their hush-hush courtship! Where the Canadian-American couple will make their home!*

I practically ran up the residence stairs, bursting into our room and dropping the paper in front of Judy's face where she lay on her stomach reading on the bed. As I waited for her reaction, I began to pace the insubstantial width of the room.

After three-and-a-half laps, she pushed the paper away and said quietly, "How sad."

I stopped in my tracks, did a slow three-sixty, then sat down on my bed, all the nervous energy deflating out of me. We sat in silence for a moment and then I said, "What if it's better than being alone?"

Shutting her book, Judy sat up and turned to mirror me, facing me across the space between our beds. She stared at me for a long time, before finally saying in the same quiet tone, "You're the most honest person I know. It would kill you."

I looked down at my hands in my lap. "It is sad. I don't suppose I can do anything for her."

Next thing I knew, Judy was on the bed next to me, wrapping her arms around me and squeezing tight. "You know you're my most favourite person in the entire world, right?"

"Well, at least there's that."

GOODWIN, Evelyn "Evie" Rosemary, 94, passed away peacefully in her home Saturday, September 15, 2014, in Uxbridge. Known as one of the leading proponents of same-sex marriage in the 60s and 70s, Evelyn and her partner of 32 years, Josephine "Jo" Avery, were legally married on June 14, 2003, four days after same-sex marriage was legalized in Ontario. Survived by a chosen family of many, Evie looked forward to joining her wife Jo and countless old friends "wherever the heck they ended up."

With Ball Due Respect

Allison Fradkin

"That strawberry you got there is a real peach," Peggy remarks, admiring the rouge bruise I'm sporting on the outside of my left thigh. "And you said playing ball in a dress was fruitless."

"At least I didn't say it was painless," I retort, watching my face contort at the contusion as I turn sideways in the full-length mirror to get a better view.

"That's right—show it off."

"What, you want me to model my mottle?"

"Sure do! It's our lesions that have won us legions of fans, you know."

"You know it all, don't you?"

Peggy blinks at me, a counterfeit Gracie Allen with Kewpie doll eyes.

I roll mine. "I had no idea these injuries were so popular. In that case, they can't possibly hurt the League."

"Nah, just the players." Having successfully lobbed insult at injury, Peggy laughs. There's nothing specifically spectacular about the sound. It's just your basic homerun-of-the-mill pitch-perfect titter. Nothing special. "Now come on, Lynette, make like Ruth and be a babe."

I lift my skirt to *show some leg*, like some of the spectators hooted last year, the first time they experienced the spectacle of women playing a man's game. We still get guff sometimes, but I'm not bothered by it. It's not like they're saying that stuff to me. They mean it for the other girls: the dames, the dollies. That's not me, although I got to say—on the field, when I'm a ballplayer, I feel...well, I feel womanly, I guess. Off the field, when I'm just a plain old person, I might as well change my name to Bob Hopeless or maybe something a little more feminine, like Irene Dunderhead. If I were a pin-up girl, they'd pull the pin on me.

I'm surprised Peggy hasn't. I guess she likes a little oddball with her baseball. "Just wait 'til the transformation starts," she enthuses, adjusting to a more comfortable cross-legged position on the floor, which is the color of a catcher's mitt and almost as hard. "Then I can serenade you with that Sinatra song, 'In the Blue of Evening,' and it'll match your uniform."

"From batter's box to mailbox. The next time we go downtown, make sure I don't stand in any one place for too long. And make sure I don't open my mouth if I do—someone might put something in it."

"Like a tongue?"

"How about a letter, knucklehead?"

"Your guess wasn't nearly as good as mine," Peggy opines, and reclines on her elbows. "By the way, I like you in blue. I also like you in lavender, which is why I think you should wear your new blouse when we take those publicity shots tomorrow."

"The photos won't be in color, so why should I?"

Having posed the question, I pause mid-pose. In the mirror is a bugbear—a jitterbugbear, to be factual, its arms and legs akimbo, a disgrace to grace. "Whose brainchild was it to include me in publicity pictures?" I mumble, returning my arms to my sides and my feet to the floor.

"You mean you've never wanted to be in pictures?" Peggy rags, and pats my knee. Then she gets up on both of her own and chugs over to the dresser in our room.

Well, it isn't *our* room, really. It belongs to the daughters of the Holbrooks, our host family here in South Bend, Indiana, where our team the Blue Sox is based. Like us, the girls are doing their part for the war effort: one's a WAVE, the other's a WASP.

Their room is real nice—all coral and floral and sunlight—and their parents are even nicer. They dote on us, wait on us, cheer us on. And even though we're only twenty, they treat us like we're much more mature. They say they're glad we're here, that we remind them of their girls because of the "sisterly spirit" of our relationship.

But I would never kiss my sis the way I want to kiss Peggy. Not that I would, or could, because if I did, I'm sure I can kiss my spot on this team goodbye. It's unlikely that the League would consider such behavior feminine, much less all-American. Worse, kissing would divest us of our lip paint, which would taint not only our image, but the League's as well.

If the team chaperone suspected there was something untoward going on, she would not have approved of us living together this season. It wouldn't have mattered that Peggy and I are compatible in other ways: we're both from Chicago, both early risers, both teetotalers (now *that* the League loves). We're also two of few girls who don't have a loved one stationed overseas. The only person I have to worry will come back to me is Peggy.

When she does return, she's accompanied by a bottle of iodine, a couple of cotton balls, a fresh patch of gauze, first aid tape, and lastly, something pointy. What on earth?

"Is that an eyebrow pencil?"

"You're sharp," Peggy quips, pressing a soggy clump of cotton to the wound.

"Is there such a thing as a sore winner?" I wince.

"Yes, and her name is Lynette, although her teammates call her—"

"She knows what her teammates call her, thank you."

A diamond in the rough who gets rough on the diamond: Masculynette, that's what they call her. Me. That's what they call me. Behind my back. Inside their heads. Or maybe it's all in my head.

I hope it's not in hers. Her head, with its hair the color of buttered popcorn and its tresses folded into bony braids—the only thing scrawny about her—is at my hip.

From there, her face forms a frown. "They call you The Bat's Meow," she informs me.

"Since when?"

"Since I told them that's what you are."

If I were some dopey sap, my insides would be mushier than a rained-out field right about now. But I'm not, so they aren't.

Besides, it's not as though she thinks I'm...pleasing to look at or some such gobbledygook. I'm as flat as a paper doll, my nose belongs on an A-20 bomber plane, and while I don't exactly put the *man* in *sportsmanship*—I wouldn't have made the team if I did—unlike Peggy, I'm...well, I'll be kind to myself for once: I'm batting average.

The looker in this room is Peggy: a cross between Alice Faye and Fay Wray, with a little Eve Arden to harden the bold mold she's cut from. But she's more than pretty. She's also witty and gritty and the most proficient professional I've ever had the privilege of playing with.

I'd better stop spewing my guts out or I might say something I shouldn't. Heck, I've said too much already. Thank goodness she didn't hear any of that. She might think I was...strange or...or queer or...I don't know. I don't normally feel this way about girls.

No, that's a lie. Sheesh, I'm more underhanded off the field than I am when I'm on the pitcher's mound. These feelings didn't come right out of left field and smack me in the kisser. But I don't normally feel this way about girls this strongly. That's the truth. When the feelings are...weaker, I can conceal them easier. I just yank the blackout curtains closed, like we're supposed to do during an air raid, to avoid detection by enemies and traitors—people who can hurt me.

"Ouch!" I exclaim, at the same time she claims, "Oops!"

Peggy peers around the corner of my freshly bandaged thigh. "Sorry," she simpers. "It's hard to stay straight."

"Are you writing on me?"

"I'm tracing the seams on your stockings," she states, and waits for me to stop scowling.

"Is that a League-sanctioned use of an eyebrow pencil?"

"I don't know and I don't care. That's one of many bases they neglected to cover in the Rules of Conduct."

"But I'm not wearing stockings," I protest, more relieved than aggrieved. I own them, because League management wants us to. But I'll never forget the day that I delightfully deposited my old ones inside the collection bin in the unmentionables department of Marshall Field's.

It wasn't long after our country entered the War, and the rationing of nylon was one sacrifice I was eager to make. If the parachutes want them, the parachutes can have them. And anyway, "You're the one who wants to leave a legacy in the vein of Betty Grable, don't you, Leggy Peggy?"

"The only cracks you ought to be making are of the bat," Peggy huffs, but it's in vain. However, when I don't slide the smirk off my face, she smacks the back of my thigh. "Coach gave me that nickname the first time I legged out a triple," she insists. "It's got nothing to do with my gams. You of all people know for a fact that my eyelashes are not the only thing I can bat. And who even needs million-dollar legs when you're batting a thousand-watt smile?" she gloats, and flashes one.

It really is a miracle that Peggy got recruited instead of discovered. She could have gone straight from the sandlot to the studio lot, just like Carole Lombard did. Instead, she's here in South Bend, knocking the Blue Sox right off my feet.

"—you've got a killer-diller figure too," Peggy is telling me.

After one and a half seasons together, I've finally gotten the hang of all the slang she uses, so I'm confident that's a compliment. "I guess my looks aren't...completely crummy," I concede.

"Atta girl. Now you're cooking with gas." She whacks my buttocks. "Get a load of those bases."

I don't know whether to turn red or drop dead from embarrassment.

In our doubleheader of a reflection, I see Peggy press her thumb to her lips, right between them, as if she's just stabbed her thumb with a sewing needle. And then the moisture from her mouth is on my skin, on the back of my thigh, in place of the possibly inappropriately-used eyebrow pencil. Her thumb circles near the bases but doesn't round them, thank goodness.

Please, underpants, I implore, *don't make like a pop fly and fall straight down.* Thanks to rubber rationing, my girlie garments have no elastic at the waist. Instead, they're tied in place with a string not unlike that found on a yo-yo.

Mercifully, my underwear goes nowhere. Neither does Peggy's hand, which is now splayed across the back of my thigh. I can feel the length and strength of every finger, and I feel myself cracking open like the shell of a peanut.

Peggy has me sauced. Bonkers. She makes my ticker flicker, sparks all these sloppy soppy sensations in me.

I feel like I'm not supposed to have these feelings for her, but they're the only kinds of feelings I've ever had, and it takes ball kinds to make a world, doesn't it?

I should just lay it on the baseline. After all, who knows how long this freedom will last? If we win the War, will we lose the game? Each other?

But I'm no brave WAVE. Of course, you don't have to be in the Navy to experience women's reserve. And as reserved as this woman is, I'm sure I'll hit a grounder and flounder, probably spook her too. So I shouldn't say anything. They taught us in charm school that the eyes *bespeak our innermost thoughts.* Maybe I should simply—

"Let me take a crack at it, Lynette."

Peggy has lifted herself off the floor and shifted to my side. She turns me toward her. One hand moves to the base of my spine, the other to the base of my neck.

My hands take the same base paths.

"Instead of publicity photos," Peggy says, her voice pleasingly low, like the etiquette expert says it should be, "I wish we could take one of those paper moon portraits. My folks had one made on their honeymoon."

I picture Peggy and me, cradled carefully by a cardboard crescent, and smile. "Is there somebody you're mooning over?" I tease.

"Some teammate of mine, but just once in a blue moon. You?"

"Perhaps, Peg o' my heart," I reply, and she moves nearer to it.

"I like being the leadoff batter," Peggy murmurs, "but I'd like you to be the contact hitter, Lynette. So I'll be looking at the gal who hung the moon, but I'll be seeing you shooting your snoot to me for a smooch."

"Okay," I say, and line up our lips until they're closer than the spikes on our cleats and the dirt on our skirts.

I make contact, our mouths connecting like a bat with a ball—but with a smack instead of a crack. The kiss, more seamless than my stockings, hurtles my heart right out of the park and over the rainbow. I feel like a Blue star shining bright, a picture-perfect moonstruck patriot.

Afterward, dizzy with a dame, I blink blankly at her.

"You look like Little Orphan Annie," Peggy needles. "What's the matter? Does the batter taste bitter?"

My head moves from side to side, like a pennant flapping in the breeze. When I joined the League, I got my first taste of freedom, my first taste of independence. But no taste can compare to or compete with the taste of my first kiss. "No," I assure her. "No, I just feel like I've been hit with a beanball is all."

"So do I, Lynette," she commiserates, and grins at me. Then she hides her smug mug in a hug, nestling against me like a ball in the pocket of a glove. "That's what happens when a gal experiences a change of base. Now come on, we've got a game to get ready for. Because when the boys are away, the girls will play ball, and we'll have a gay old time doing it."

—⚓—

"Batter up and at 'em! Let's cream those Peaches!"

Peggy makes her way from the dugout to the batter's box, swishing past me in her Sonja Henie hemline. "You know I'll South Bend over backward for you, Lynette!" she shouts over her shoulder.

I feel my face turn redder than the seams on a baseball, but I just roll my eyes and clap my hands.

A flare of fanfare follows Peggy all the way to home base. My gal's got more than enough brass for that bugle. She's wearing the same visage of victory she put on after our first kiss two weeks ago, only it's even more dazzling on the field than it is off, if you can believe that.

Peggy steps up to the plate. Even from the dugout, I can make out the ferocious focus on her face. She treats each period of play not as an inning but as a femininning, and thanks to her, I now know what it really means to be feminine.

It doesn't mean being gentle or genteel. It doesn't mean adherence to an appearance that's pleasing to men. It means that when those cleats go on, our clout comes out. It means we vaunt our valor and flaunt our curveballs, and we don't let anything daunt our dedication. It means making great strides—and even greater slides—with ballplayers who have pride of place and pride of base.

And there's no base like home, where Peggy waits at the plate—like Goldilocks, until the pitch is just right: not too low, not too high, not too wide.

When it comes, her stoic stamina cracks along with the bat and it's a hit.

Leggy Peggy catapults across Bendix Field like a batter out of hell, her legs churning with yearning, inevitably earning her safety on first base.

The stadium bursts into cheers. Who's on first is what it's about. Peggy exemplifies everything that's best about baseball: the skill, the will, the thrill. The fans know it just as well as I do.

Speaking of me, I'm next in the lineup.

I swing into action—well actually, for Peggy's benefit so she can move into scoring position, I bunt, but the sentiment is the same.

And pretty soon, the game itself is in full swing. We put each other on the bases and through the paces. I'm not Peggy's bat girl. She can hold her own and so can I. We're teammates, we're equals, we're...sweethearts.

But I can't dwell on the swell stuff right now. I've got to keep my eye on the ball, not the ballplayer. Swifter than my feet, I switch gears. It's a good thing, too, or I would've gotten tagged out.

With a firm grip on my feelings and, when necessary, my bat, I play the rest of the game with a fighting chance, a sturdy stance, and the occasional stolen glance to complement a stolen base.

Confident in our competence and in each other, we—all of us Blue Sox— through every out and run and inning, never lose steam or team spirit or that gleam in our eye.

Even with the elements—the heat, the wind, the dirt—there's nothing elementary about the way we play the game.

We're in our element.

And when we win, we're in all our glory.

Peggy flings her arms around me, and I press her to my body like a chest protector. I pretend we're also wearing catcher's masks, because if I let myself forget there's nothing between us, I'll kiss her right here on the field. Then the cheering will turn to jeering and something will come between us.

"You've got a real nice swing, you know that?" I remark, as we embark on our walk off to the locker room.

"It don't mean a thing if it ain't got that," Peggy hoots. "But were you referring to my bat or my hips?"

"You're batty. Your bat."

"You flatter the batter so." Peggy swoons in time with her rhyme, and it's clear that I'm rubbing off on her even more than the dirt on my uniform is. "You deserve a grandstanding ovation yourself," she declares, clapping me on the back in a fraternal fashion, "especially for the way you were busting the ump's chops out there."

"Got to keep the home umpires burning."

"I have to hand it to you, Lynette," Peggy says, and hands me a towel for the showers, "you play cornball better than any woman in this country." She sighs, a dramatic performance that rivals the one she's just given on the field. "Sadly, you are the one ham I just can't can."

I wind the towel around my hands until I've practically coiled it into a pin curl. "So I'm safe?" I venture.

"With me?" Peggy thumps my rump with her own towel. "You bet your bases."

<hr/>

"There's something I'd like to touch base with you about."

261

Beside me, in the sweater section of Robertson's Department Store—fitting, given the perspiration that's presenting an exhibition game on my forehead—Peggy pivots on her kitten heels and gives me her full attention.

So, too, do two teen-aged female fans.

Actually, they're aiming their fountain pens at both of us. "Would you sign our magazine?" the taller one implores.

The smaller one giggles and goggles, her eyes rounder than canteens.

"You're so pretty in person," her elder companion comments. "Up close, I mean."

By the time I figure out that she's speaking to me, Loretta Young can no longer claim the accuracy of her surname.

I hold the magazine at one end and Peggy holds it at the other. It's opened to an article about the League, entitled "Dames on the Diamond," and with only a modicum of mortification, I recognize Peggy and me in the publicity photos.

In one picture, my teammates and I are masquerading as manicurists. The League managers delight in letting the public know they've given their players polish.

In the foreground of the photo, Peggy is painting my nails. I remember the delicate way she held my hand, as if at any moment she would lift it to her lips and kiss it. I must admit, I do look mildly enchanting in that picture—my lovely lavender blouse photographs beautifully in black-and-white.

In another photo, players are playing beauty parlor. I'm shown sitting between Peggy's knees while she puts thingamabobs in my hair, the result of which was a Victory Roll. That day, my hair experienced more winding-up than my pitching arm ever has, and I enjoyed—endured—several hours of having a great big blob thicker than my bat hover over my hairline like the bill of a ball cap.

Needless to say, this is not my favorite photo. That honor is bestowed upon the image of our team engaged in batting practice, and shared with the team picture next to it. Even in the latter, Peggy and I are together. I'm down on South Bended knee and she's seated on a bench behind me, her hands touching—clutching—my shoulders. On top of my uniform, I'm wearing a winning smile. In fact, with those chipper choppers I'm flashing, I'm surprised the Blue Sox haven't traded me to Pepsodent.

I sign my name across my knees with the inspiring inscription: *You're aces on bases!* Peggy writes across her chest the equally edifying: *Don't play the field—play on it!* We return the magazine to our fans.

Each young lady thanks us by seizing the sides of her skirt and executing a pinch-perfect Shirley Temple curtsy from before their time.

"Did you notice they got our team name right in the article?" I inquire, having no desire to return to the conversation I initiated. "Remember when *Time* did that story on us at the start of the first season? Perhaps one day we'll get to play against the always-instructive Rockford Teachers and the happy-go-lucky Kenosha Shamrocks. I'm surprised they didn't call us the South Bend Goulash or something equally distasteful."

"Yep," Peggy concurs, and laughs. Almost immediately, her smile crimps like piecrust and she turns bobby pin-brown eyes on me. "You said you wanted to touch base with me about something," she reminds me.

I couldn't feel more uncomfortable if I were wearing a

wool sweater, but there aren't too many of those, I don't think, because wool fabric is rationed, isn't it? I can't remember just now. But just because we have to ration our fabrics and our food and our fun doesn't mean we also have to ration our happiness, or, for that matter, rationalize our unhappiness.

I'm rambling—I realize that. And even though I'm not rambling out loud, I know Peggy can read my mindless meandering because she's looking at me like I'm one pitch short of a shutout.

Okay, Lynette, The Bat's Meow, take a deep breath and then it's off to the bases.

Mind you, slow and steady may not win the base, but maybe, just maybe, it'll win the winsome woman who's on it.

I open my mouth, breathe in, breathe out, then snap my lips shut like a compact mirror. What if she thinks I'm lousy with lunacy? What if she makes like a shortstop and stops me short?

Try to Ty Cobble together some courage, would you? Jeez, why the heck do I have a man on my mind at a time like this?

"You're more riveting than Rosie," I blurt.

"And you're more joltin' than Joe," she flirts.

I could go on—tell her she's got more steel than a mill, more sand than an hourglass, more craft than an airplane factory; tell her how I admire everything about her, from her stride to her slide; tell her I love her when she's scrappy, when she's snappy, even when she's just a little bit yappy. We could toss the ball around all day. But if I don't get a homerun today, I'll end up running home tomorrow.

And so, finally, I fold like a spectator seat. "I don't

want to just play with you. I want to stay with you this year—here, when the season's over. We don't know how long the League or the War will last. We've only played two seasons, but the War could end and send the men—"

"Men don't send me," Peggy cuts in. "They can pitch woo all they like, but they'll score a no-hitter every time. So if you're asking me to stick around, then right off the bat my answer is yes, because I'm not just rooting for our team; I'm rooting for us."

And then, right there between the stacks of sweaters, she stacks our hands together. As part of our beauty routine, every All-American Girl is exhorted to *exercise practical good sense in preserving the hands that serve her so faithfully and well in her activities.* Let it never be said that Peggy and I don't play by the rulebook.

"Maybe we can stay together with the Holbrooks," I suggest, "if they'll let us stay on. We can get jobs in town—selling concessions at the Palace, where we can wear slacks to work! I would even be willing to work here, at Robertson's, but please—not at the Leg Make-up Bar downstairs."

Peggy chuckles, then chucks me under the chin. "I don't think ours is the sort of war bond the government had in mind, so we'll have to exercise the utmost discretion," she advises, and surprises me with a kiss on the cheek. "But then, if it were going to be easy, they'd have to call it something other than hardball."

"You know me—I never take the base path of least resistance."

Being with Peggy, it...well, it will be laborious and glorious, I bet, just like playing ball. I'll have a base to call home, and someone to come home to.

"You think it'll last through the War?" I ask, with only

a minimum of reserve.

"I think it'll outlast it," Peggy answers, with a maximum of certainty. "No matter what, I'll always go to bat for you."

We can do it, I tell myself, getting cozy with words of encouragement from Rosie.

After all, it's a woman's patriotic prerogative to embrace a man's job.

But right now, I'd rather hug Peggy, so I do.

It's brief, but it's also a relief—because while I'm wrapped around my sweetheart like foil on a stick of chewing gum, I realize there's a pastime and a place for everything.

And everyone.

Even a couple of dames on the diamond with stars in their eyes and strawberries on their thighs.

Beebo Brinker (Excerpt)

Ann Bannon

She was almost as surprised to find herself on the street as Jack would have been to see her there. And yet the cool night air washed gratefully over her face and cleared her thoughts. She wandered aimlessly a while, as if trying to ignore the one place she wanted to visit: the Colophon.

But her feet took her there anyway, and she found herself ringing the bell. The owner opened the peek-through in the door and nodded to her. She felt a momentary country-girl shame at being recognized at such a place. But she was glad enough to gain entrance. The glow inside was the color of fluorescent Merthiolate. It seemed almost antiseptic to Beebo, who had painted the undersides of countless cows and sows with disinfectants the same shade prior to delivery.

She took a seat at the bar. "Scotch and water," she said.

While the barman got it, she gazed idly into the mirror

behind him, picking out the interesting girls surrounding her. She felt uncomfortable here in the pants she usually wore to work; in her hair that had just been cut and was too short again.

Do they think I'm funny? She wondered. Or—*exciting?* She drank in silence and ordered another, thinking the solitude and uncertainty she felt now were worse than those she felt with Jack. For a minute, almost anything seemed better than having to leave Jack, with only fifty bucks a week to spend, no friends, and no place to live.

The bartender brought her another drink while she searched for the last cigarette in her pack. It was empty. The girl sitting next to her immediately offered her one, but Beebo declined. It was partly her shyness, partly knowledge that it was better to be hard-to-get in the Colophon.

"Do you have cigarettes?" she asked the bartender.

"Machine by the wall," he said.

She got up and sauntered over, ignoring the outrage on the face of the girl at the bar. The machine swallowed her coins and spit out a pack of filter-tips. Beebo noticed the jukebox, looked at her change, and fed it a quarter, good for three dances. She liked to watch the girls move around the floor together, now that the initial revolt had worn off.

But when she regained her seat, she found most of the patrons paying attention to her, not the tunes. She looked back at them, surprised and wary. The cigarettes in her hand were an excuse to look away for a minute and she did, lighting one while the general conversation died away like a weak breeze. She lowered her match slowly and glanced up again, her skin prickling. What in the hell were they trying to do? Scare her out? Show her they didn't like her?

Had she been too aloof with them, too remote and hard to know?

She had started the music, and it was an invitation to dance. They were waiting for her to show them. It wasn't hostility she saw on her faces as much as "Show us, if you're so damned big and smart. We've been waiting for a chance to trap you. This is it."

She had to do something to humanize herself. There was an air of self-confidence and sensual promise about Beebo that she couldn't help. And when she felt neither confident nor sensual, she looked all the more as if she did: tall and strong and coolly sure of herself. She had turned the drawback of being young and ignorant into a deliberate defense.

It didn't matter to the sophisticated girls judging her now that she was a country girl fresh from the hayfields of Wisconsin, or that she had never made love to a woman in her life. They didn't know that and wouldn't have believed it anyway.

Beebo recognized quickly that she had to start acting the way she looked. She had established a mood of expectation about herself, and now it was time to come across. The music played on. It was Beebo's turn.

The match she held was burning near her finger, and because she had to do something about *it* and all the eyes on her, she turned to the girl beside her and held out the match.

"Blow," she said simply, and the girl, with a smile, blew.

Beebo returned the smile. "Well," she said in her low voice, which somehow carried even into the back room and the dance floor, "I'm damned if I'm going to waste a good quarter." She got up and walked across the room toward the prettiest girl she could see, sitting at a table with her lover and two other couples. It was exactly the way she would have reacted to student-baiting at Juniper Hill High. The worse it got, the taller she walked. Her heart was beating so hard she wanted to squeeze it still. But she knew no one could hear it through her chest.

She stopped in front of the pretty girl and looked at her for a second in incredulous silence. The she said quietly, "Will you dance with me, Mona?"

Mona Petry smiled at her. Nobody else in Greenwich Village would have flouted the social code that way: walked between two lovers and taken one away to dance. Mona took a leisurely drag on her cigarette, letting her pleasure show in a faint smile. Then she stood up and said, "Yes. I will, Beebo." Her lover threw Beebo a keen, hard look and then relapsed into a sullen stare.

Beebo and Mona walked to the floor single file, and Mona turned when she got clear of any tables, lifting up her arms to be held. The movement was so easy and natural that it excited Beebo and made her bold—she who knew nothing about dancing. But she was not lacking in grace or rhythm. She took Mona in a rather prim embrace at first and began to move her over the floor as the music directed.

Mona disturbed her by putting her head back and smiling up at her. At last she said, "How did you know my name?"

"Pete Pasquini told me," Beebo said. "How did you know mine?"

"Same answer," Mona laughed. "He gets around, doesn't he?"

"So they say," Beebo said.

"You mean you don't know from personal

270

experience?"

"Me?" Beebo stared at her. "Should I?"

Mona chuckled. "No, you shouldn't," she said.

"Did I—take you away from something over there?" Beebo said.

"From some*body*, "Mona corrected her. "But it's all right. She's deadly dull. I've been waiting for you to come over."

Beebo felt her face get warm. "I didn't even see you until I stood up," she said.

"I saw you," Mona murmured. They danced a moment more, and Beebo pulled her closer, wondering if Mona could feel her heart, now bongoing under her ribs, or guess at the racing triumph in her veins.

"Did you ask Pete about me?" Mona prodded.

"A little," Beebo admitted. And was surprised to find that the admission felt good. "Yes," she whispered.

"What did he say?"

"He said you were a wonderful girl."

"Did you believe him?"

Beebo hesitated and finally said, huskily, "Yes."

"You're a good dancer, Beebo," Mona said, knowing, like an expert, just how far to go before she switched gears.

"I dance like a donkey." Beebo grinned, strong enough in her victory to laugh at herself.

"No, you're a natural," Mona insisted. "A natural dancer, I mean."

"I don't care what you mean, just keep dancing," Beebo said.

Mona put her head down against Beebo's shoulder and laughed, and Beebo felt the same elation as a man when he has impressed a desirable girl and she lets him know it with her flattery. Mona—so elusive, so pretty, so dominant in Beebo's dreams lately. Beebo was holding her tighter than she meant to, but when she tried to loosen her embrace, Mona put both arms around her neck and pulled her back again.

For the first time, Beebo had the nerve to look straight at her. It was a long, hungry look that took in everything: the long dark square-cut hair and bangs; the big hazel eyes; the fine figure, slim and exaggeratedly tall in high heels. But it was still necessary for her to look up at Beebo.

"It's nice you're so tall," Mona told her.

"Who's that girl you're with?" Beebo said. "I think she wants to drown me."

"No doubt. Her name's Todd."

"Is she a friend?"

"She was, till you asked for this dance." Mona smiled.

Beebo didn't want to make trouble. "I'm sorry," she said.

"Are you?" Mona was forward as only a world-weary girl with nothing to learn—or lose—could be. And yet she seemed too young for such ennui—still in her twenties. "Are you sorry about Todd?" she pressed Beebo.

"I'm not sorry I'm dancing with you, if that's what you mean," Beebo said.

"That's what I mean." Mona smiled. "Would you like to dance without an audience, Beebo?"

Beebo frowned at her. "You mean ditch your friends?"

Mona could see that Beebo was offended by such a suggestion of two-timing; and Mona was interested enough in this big, beautiful, strange girl not to want her offended. "They aren't true friends," Mona said plaintively, "that you could count on, anyway. It's all over between Todd and me, too. We just came here to bury the corpse tonight. This is where we met five months ago."

"Five months? That not very long to be in love with somebody," Beebo said.

"I wasn't," Mona said.

"Was she?" It seemed indescribably sad to Beebo that one partner be in love and the other feel nothing. She wanted everyone to be happy on this night full of sequin-lights and clouds of music: even Todd.

"I never meant much to Todd," Mona said. "Talk about ditching, Beebo. I'm the one who's getting ditched."

"You?" Beebo held her tightly, glad for the excuse. "How could anyone ever do that to you?"

Mona swayed against her, smiled with her eyes shut, and Beebo was too immersed in her to notice the look on Todd's face.

"She likes to torment her lovers," Mona whispered. "She uses them, as if they were things. When she gets tired of them, she puts them in a drawer and pulls them out to show off, like trophies. That's all she does—collect broken hearts."

"She sounds like a female dog," Beebo commented. And yet the little speech recalled disturbingly some of Jack's remarks about Mona; as if Mona were amusing herself by describing her own faults to Beebo and pretending they were Todd's.

The music ended and they stood on the floor for a moment, arms still clasped about each other. "Wait at the bar," Mona whispered into Beebo's ear. "I'll get my coat." Beebo glanced doubtfully at the table, but Mona said, "It'll be better if I tell her alone. Go on."

Beebo released her reluctantly, went to her seat, and sipped her drink until Mona came up. She let Mona lead the way, feeling a sudden wild exhilaration as she followed, lighting a cigarette, holding the door for Mona, taking the street side when they reached the sidewalk.

"Was Todd angry?" she asked.

"No one wants to look the fool," Mona said tightly, with a smile.

"I'm sorry. I wouldn't like to get you up the creek, Mona," Beebo said. "I didn't want trouble."

"I make my own trouble, Beebo. I thrive on it. The way I see it—" she paused to give Beebo her arm, and Beebo took it smoothly with a sense of power and burgeoning desire, "—life is flat and dreary without trouble." Mona dodged a puddle, then continued. "Good trouble. Exciting trouble. You can't just walk across the Flats forever, doing what's expected of you. Excitement. That's everything to me." Mona stopped her in her tracks to look at Beebo with bright sly eyes. "Being good isn't exciting. Right?"

"I'm not a philosopher," Beebo said.

"I'll prove it to you. You're a good person, aren't you? You felt bad about Todd. You've been good all your life. But are you happy?"

"I am right now. Are you telling me to be bad?" Beebo said, laughing.

"Would making love to me be bad?" Mona asked her, so directly that Beebo wondered if she were being made fun of. There was no respect in Mona for the innate privacy and mystery of every human soul. She saw them all as part of the Flats—unless they could make beautiful trouble with her. Then, she was interested. Then, she saw an individual.

"Making love to you," Beebo said slowly, "would have to be good."

"I'll make it better than good." Mona reached up for Beebo's shoulders, pulling her back into the dusk of a doorway. They stood there a moment, Beebo in a fever of need and fear, til Mona's hand slid up behind her head, cupped it downward, and brought their lips together.

Beebo came to life with a swift jerking movement. Mona's kiss had been light and brief until Beebo caught her again in a violent embrace and imprisoned her mouth. She forgot everything for a few minutes, holding Mona there in her arms and kissing her lips, pressing her back against the doorway and feeling the whole length of her body against Beebo's own.

It wasn't until she became aware that Mona was protesting that she let her go. She stood in front of Mona, still trembling and weak-kneed, her breath coming fast and her head spinning, and she felt oddly apologetic. Mona had started it, but Beebo had carried it too far. "I'm sorry," she panted.

"Stop saying you're sorry all the time," Mona told her in a sulky voice. And, with a briskness that all but shattered the mood, she turned and started walking off, her heels snapping against the asphalt. Beebo stared after her, shocked. Was this the end of it?

But Mona turned back after a quarter of a block and called her. "You aren't going to spend the night there, are you?" she said crisply.

Beebo hurried after her, and they walked two more blocks without exchanging a word. Beebo could only suppose she had done something wrong. Yet she didn't know what, or how to make amends.

Mona stopped at a brownstone house with six front steps. "I live here," she said.

Beebo glanced up at it. "Shall I leave?" she said.

"Do you want to?"

"Don't answer my questions with more questions!" Beebo said, a tide of anger releasing her tongue. "Damn it, Mona, I don't like evasions."

275

"All right. Don't go," Mona said and smiled at the outburst. She went up the steps with Beebo coming uneasily behind her, opened the door, and went to the first-floor apartment in the back. At her door, she pulled out her key and waited. Beebo was looking around at the hall, old and modest, but cleanly kept. The apartments in a place like this could be astonishingly chic. She had seen some belonging to Jack's friends.

Mona let her take it in til Beebo became aware of the silence and turned to her quizzically.

"Approve?" Mona said.

Beebo nodded, and Mona, as if that were the signal, turned the key in the lock. She walked over the threshold, switched on a light, and abruptly backed out again, preventing Beebo from entering.

"What's wrong?" Beebo said, surprised.

"There's someone in there," Mona said.

Without thinking, Beebo made a lunge for the door. She had thrown prowlers out of her father's house before. A situation like this scared her far less than being alone with Mona—much as she wanted it.

But Mona caught her arm. "It's a friend of mine!" She hissed. "Beebo, please!" Beebo stopped, irritated, waiting for an explanation. "It's a girl. I told her Todd and I were breaking up," Mona shrugged. "I guess she came over to cheer me up. We've been friends a long time. Oh, it's nothing romantic, Beebo."

"Well, send her home," Beebo said. It was one thing to be afraid of Mona, but another entirely to forfeit the whole night in honor of a hen party.

"I can't." Mona looked up at her in pretty distress. "She's my one real friend and I owe her a lot. She's had some bad times in her own life lately. Beebo, look—here's my phone number. Call me in an hour. Maybe we can still make it." She took a scratch pad from her purse and scribbled on it.

Beebo took it, feeling rebuffed and insulted. But Mona stood on her tiptoes and kissed her lips again. And when Beebo refused to embrace her, Mona took her wrists and pulled them around her and gave Beebo a luxurious kiss. "Forgive me," she said. "It would be tough if she knew I'd brought someone home—it really would." She slipped out of Beebo's arms and put a hand on the doorknob. "Be sure to call me," she said. And then she disappeared inside the apartment.

Beebo stood in the hall a while, leaning on the dingy plaster and trying to make sense out of Mona. There was no sound from the apartment. Perhaps Mona and the girl had gone into the bedroom to talk. The idea made Beebo angry and jealous. She went slowly down the front hall. There was a pay phone by the entrance. Beebo went outside and sat on the front stoop for about forty-five minutes, then went in to call.

She had lifted the telephone receiver and was about to drop in a dime, when she heard a bang from the end of the hall, as if someone had dropped something heavy. It seemed to come from Mona's door, and Beebo rushed toward it. But at the threshold, she froze.

Mona's voice, muffled as if through the walls of several rooms, but discernable, penetrated the wood. "And you! You sneak in here like a rat with the plague! God damn, how many times do I have to say it? *Call first.* Are you deaf or just stupid?"

Beebo's mouth opened as she strained to hear the answer. It came after a slight pause: "Rats don't scare you, doll. You already got the plague."

Beebo whirled away from the door as if she had been burned and stood with her knuckles pressed angrily against her temples.

The voice belonged to a man.

Honeydew Moon

Lee Lynch

You know that song about the moon hitting your eye like a big pizza pie, how that's amore? That's what the moon was like on our honeymoon, only it wasn't a pizza pie, it was honeydew. A fat juicy honeydew, perfect, like I sometimes get for my fruit stand, almost white, with the tiniest bit of yellow to remind you about the sun that grew it, hanging loud in that night sky, looking like it would fall right into our laps. If it did, it'd pop right open, split clean in half—half for her, half for me. We rolled back on the cool night grass on the edge of that sand cliff like we were the only people in the world, lay back for a while on the edge of our lives together, practically sucking sugar from that honeydew moon.

Now what got me started? Right, you want to take your girl away for the weekend. You definitely should. New York might be the greatest city in the world, and Queens the greatest borough in the city. Still, fresh air and the ocean you remember all your life, am I right, Beanpole? Okay, okay, I'll tell you the whole story of my honeymoon. First, it's late already, hand me the broom. You start weeding out the fruit that's too manhandled to sell full price like I showed you. Ouch—stooping's not as easy as it was back when we took our honeymoon, Kathy and me—here's a crate to put the bad stuff in. Those berries, they're too far gone to save. Would you look at that sky? I swear, if they made syrup out of gold, this is what it'd look like, the way the sunrays come in these little windows in the late afternoon. Did you ever see anything prettier? Gold syrup. That's why I need you to keep the windows clean; everything looks prettier, more open, with all the little panes clear as air for the gold-syrup to pour on the fruit. My dad had this all closed in, all wood. I put in plenty of windows, maybe from that taste of open air markets I got on our honeymoon. I wanted something that resembled the country, where fruit comes from. Not food factories like the supermarkets.

You're thinking about taking her to Atlantic City? The beach is okay down there, if crowded. No place to cuddle in some lonely spot. No place to get away from it all. How about the Cape? Or out on the Island? I hear there's a lot of good restaurants on the Cape, and you need them. Never mind you want to do *that* with your girl all weekend. You take her to a good restaurant and feed yourself. Skinny as a rail. I don't know how you lift these crates, except you have to if you want to keep your job. Am I right? Little dykes like you are a dime a dozen, Beanpole. You put some weight on your bones or you'll keel over someday and I'll sweep you out with the old straw.

Yeah, me and Kathy went to Long Island for our honeymoon. Way out near Montauk, the Hamptons. Of course they let us in, there's working people out there. Who do you think makes life easy for the rich people? We stayed with friends—stop asking questions! I'm not telling you another story until this place is clean. Look how the light's shining on those red apples, like they're going to catch on fire any minute. What a sight.

I'll tell you what, why don't you come have supper with us and I'll tell you the story of the honeymoon—Kathy can fill in what I leave out—and we'll feed you. No, don't worry; we're practically vegetarians too. I'll make you something nice and fattening right out of this store, what do you think of that?

———

Okay, Beanpole, how does dinner look? Is Kathy talking your ear off? Ah, she's boring you with the picture albums already? No, we didn't have a camera on our honeymoon. They weren't as easy to come by back then. Now I have two. Wait, let me get the Polaroid and take your picture with Kathy and the fruit salad. I'll call it Fattening the Beanpole. You don't like me calling you that? Too bad. Let the kids use cool nicknames, you're Beanpole to me.

Look, I made strawberries in gold-syrup—or the closest I could get with the sun already down. Soaked in honey instead of sugar water. Over chunks of watermelon, cantaloupe, fresh coconut, pineapple rings, banana slices. And here in the middle, (I cheated) this isn't from my store, some sherbet. Now that ought to fatten you up a little. Let's eat before it melts!

She wants to hear about our honeymoon, Kath, you want to help me tell it? Wish we had some May wine. Kathy makes good May wine, learned from Monica, one of the women we visited on our honeymoon. She died real soon after her lover. Don't look sad, Beanpole. They had a good long life. Am I right, Kath? They lived into their eighties. That made them, what, sixty-something when we stayed there.

This was after my folks died and left me with the fruit stand. Kathy was determined on a honeymoon. Said she was tired of falling in love and breaking up in a month or a year. She had this idea that when she found the girl she wanted to spend her life with, if we did some of the things straight people do to tie the knot, maybe we'd have a chance of staying tied forever. You know, since the religions won't bless us, she thought up other ways to make what we promised each other real important so we'd take it seriously when things got rough.

You bet it worked. Twenty-five years! I'm glad you're impressed. Some of these little dykes today think it's not such a hot idea to stay together, to have a rock in your life you can lean on. As far as I'm concerned, except for my stand and my girl, life wouldn't be worth living. I couldn't enjoy it and I'd probably die on a barstool. It's rough out there. Didn't you find that out yet? Wait, you'll see what I mean. Me, I wanted the whole package including Niagara Falls. Kath was right, as usual. Hey! What's with the dirty look? Can't I pinch my girl?

Maybe Long Island wasn't the perfect honeymoon spot. At least we weren't stuck in the middle of thousands of squares showing off how straight they can be and staring at us because we weren't like them.

See, we visited Monica and Johnnie. They lived right on the beach and we rented a cabin nearby. Who were they? How can I explain them to you? In the old days, queers had it even worse than now. Johnnie had a really bad time of it and had to do things different.

You ever hear about women who dressed like men, pretended they were men? No, it's not disgusting. Sometimes that was the only way you could be queer and get along. Our friend Johnnie did it when she couldn't get a job any other way. The story she told, through Monica, was about looking just like a man—I guess you'd describe her as burly, and she had these rough features. She'd be called ugly if she dressed like a girl, and she was mean-looking in men's clothes. Had a scar on her chin that healed all red and ugly because she didn't have money for a doctor. She hated doctors from listening to their comments when she had to strip to get examined. Professional? No, there's something about a woman who looks like a man that makes otherwise nice doctors get nasty. On top of all that, she had a beard. Really, she had to shave. Dressed as a woman, she'd shave every day to hide it—not when she pretended to be a man.

The worst thing for Johnnie? She was mute. Could hear, didn't talk. She couldn't explain herself. You see why she had a hard time? Yes, she really was a woman. It was only the world said she wasn't. Monica told us the older Johnnie got the gladder she was to be a woman. Acting like a man, she saw a lot of stuff men do that women wouldn't usually see. She hated them. Wanted to start a woman's army and someday take over the world.

Meantime, she had to earn a living and kind of fell into the gardening business. She was from a city upstate and didn't know much about growing things. She looked for any kind of work at all, got knocked around by the men who found out she was a woman, laughed at by the women who found out she wasn't a man. She heard about a job assisting a gardener. It didn't pay much, but it didn't need any talking and the guy let her bunk in his garage.

He thought she was a mute boy and took a liking to her. She learned everything he had to teach and would have stayed on except it turned out he was gay. He was married, see, and pretty soon Johnnie figured out why he went downtown one night a week. He showed up at the garage drunk, looking for a guy and discovered Johnnie wasn't one. He's the one gave her that red scar, when she snuck back for her belongings. She got away with only a picture of her and her mother wrapped in some underwear.

Johnnie hit the road again, spent a bad winter cleaning johns and ended up on Long Island, doing odd jobs at a mansion. It was spring, and with no friends, Johnnie wandered the grounds, taking care of the plants and trees out of love. Her luck changed when the gardener quit. The rich people from the mansion noticed her skill. To keep her around, they let her fix up an unused cottage on the beach. She wouldn't make a salary off-season—she wouldn't have rent either. All around the cottage she grew her own garden, and she learned from the cook how to preserve fruits and vegetables. This was the second happy season of her life. She had a job, a home, and nobody bothered the strange mute gardener who lived all by himself in the cottage on the beach. Hey, Beanpole, eat up, your sherbet's melting. No, you didn't have enough. What's the matter? The story's upsetting you? Hey, this is the way it was, count your blessings.

Anyways, here's Johnnie living on the beach in back of this mansion, happy as a peach pit about to grow a tree, lonely as the last apple in an orchard. She thinks about a girl back home who used to walk with her in the woods. And kiss her.

Then, on a trip to town, she notices the new girl at the hardware store. They always had a man before, now all the sons were off fighting the war. Johnnie used to dread visiting town once a month; now she now went weekly. There was something about this girl.

Next thing Johnnie knows, she's sitting outside her cottage after dinner, watching the birds fish, when the girl comes walking up the beach. She's in pants, like Johnnie, and that was unusual then. Johnnie pulls her kitchen chair out of the cabin and they sit together awhile, the girl chattering enough for the two of them and making Johnnie laugh. The girl returns the night after and Johnnie pulls the chair out again. By the third night, Johnnie's bought a beach chair at the junkshop in town. She's suffering, wondering if this girl is like the one back home. By the flush on her cheeks when she looks Johnnie's way, she might be. Does she have a chance with a pants-wearing girl who thinks Johnnie's a man?

One night the girl, Monica, shows up early. Johnnie's still inside washing her dinner plate. Monica wanders around the cabin. She picks up a picture of Johnnie as a young girl, bow in her hair, holding her mother's hand. Johnnie figures it's now or never and points first to the little girl in the picture, then to herself.

Monica smiles, sets the picture back, and walks over to Johnnie. She puts her arms around Johnnie's neck and presses herself to her. "I know," the girl says, kissing Johnnie.

Will you look at this table? Picked clean. Beanpole could do with a good feeding once in a while, am I right, Kathy? Let's clear it off and put up coffee. You want what? Herb tea? No, we don't have any of that stuff. What's the matter with you, Beanpole, you've got to be different? Yeah, I heard caffeine's bad for you—I need my fix. Wait, I know what we'll do. How about fresh mint leaf tea with honey for gold syrup? Go sit. This kitchen's not big enough for three. And yes, I'm getting to the honeymoon. You had to know the whole story.

No, Monica's folks weren't upset. Johnnie and her ran off to New York City and came back saying they were married. Nobody asked to see a license. Monica's folks were disappointed she didn't get a man with money and looks instead of a mute gardener, but Monica was happy as a robin on a spring lawn. She thought her mother envied her, living such a simple life right on the water instead of taking care of five sons and an ambitious husband.

They never did find out Johnnie was a girl. Monica worked at the hardware store til the war ended and her brothers took back their jobs. She did housekeeping for the people in the mansion. Years later, when Johnnie and Monica were too old to work like they had, they got a small pension and the cottage for life. What more could they ask?

Give me the dishtowel. Kath, I'll dry. Your coffee's almost ready. Beanpole, this tea's pretty weak stuff; no wonder it's good for you.

How we got to honeymoon out there, Kathy met Johnnie and Monica through some friends. It seems Monica was not exactly innocent when she put her arms around Johnnie that night. She knew a couple of women like us through work. Those women knew a couple more and on like that til there was a circle of them having parties at their homes. Monica and Johnnie didn't let on about Johnnie except to a very few who visited on the q.t. One of them brought Kath and—how could they resist her?

Umm. Gold mint-water. I think I'll start a company: Henny's Mint Syrup. Healthy, refreshing, dull as a hothouse tomato. You don't think it'll catch on?

When we met, Kathy hadn't seen Monica and Johnnie for months. We decided to honeymoon on Long Island. Besides, you kind of thought of them as your family by then, am I right, Kath? She wanted their approval. Goodness knows I was nervous.

I closed up the stand that Saturday night. We didn't want to spend the money calling long distance for a room, so we slept outside Johnnie and Monica's in the panel truck I used for hauling fruit. Kathy thought to toss a couple of blankets in the back.

Yes, that's where we spent our first honeymoon night, Beanpole, locked in the dark truck, lying on the ridged metal floor, covered by smells like cantaloupe rind, strawberry juice, lemons and limes and bananas, all gone a little musty, like in a dream. I called the truck Cornucopia. Kathy was my new treat and I had a feast. Oh, stop blushing, Kath, I didn't mean that. Beside, Beanpole knows the facts of life.

In the morning, we met two of the finest human beings on earth. I thought Kathy was a magician to have found them. Monica was this grandmother type in a faded bib apron with flour up to her elbow and hairpins sticking out of her grey hair. Johnnie was still pretty solid, though stooped from gardening. She had a kind of rough way about her like people get when they have a hard time being understood. Once you caught on to how she talked—with her hands, with Monica's help, with scraps of paper and shaky, old-fashioned printing—she was shy and gentle as could be. Birds would pick crumbs off her big palm, am I right, Kath?

The grounds around their cottage, despite the sandy soil and salt water, were a picture postcard. Johnnie had flowering vines trailing all up and around their porch, rose trellises, fruit trees. You could see why the rich people were letting her live out her life in that cottage: she'd planted much of herself in it.

And the way they were together! Their eyes still shone when they looked at each other. They were so patient and appreciative you would have thought they were the ones on a honeymoon. I mean, who ever thought of two old ladies loving each other? All of a sudden, I could see me and Kathy twenty, fifty years down the road. Being gay had always meant being young, fooling around, going out. Now I was looking at the happiest people I ever met and they didn't fit any of that. We had a future!

What a week it was. The pretty cabin we stayed in down the road was all open to the wind and sun. It was painted white outside; inside was rough wood that, warm, smelled fresh cut. One whole side of the beach bordered the monastery next door. We had it all to ourselves and, mornings, ran along the water's edge as far as our breath held, holding hands and hugging. There were little sand cliffs above the beach with short trees and tall grasses and we'd lie there making out, always alert because we would've killed ourselves if we gave Johnnie away.

Since they'd given up driving, we made a big shopping trip into town to save them the bus ride. Johnnie put on a tie and Monica a hat and dress. It was a small, shady town after all that white beach, and we carried their packages. Along the roads were produce stands. I had to stop at all of them. That's where I got some ideas for my place: straw on the floor, the light, bushel baskets. Little tricks like that make people feel they're in the country, think the fruit is fresher.

In town, I saw for myself what Johnnie gained by playing a man. I was like you, because though I liked her a lot, it really bothered me: the shaving, the haircut, men's clothes down to the boxer shorts Monica hung on the line. It seemed perverted. I suspected Johnnie liked playing a man and Monica didn't really want a woman. Then I saw everybody they met on the street stop and say hello, smiling and passing the time of day. I could see the appeal for shy Johnnie.

I mean, twenty-five years ago Kathy and I were careful not to be seen on the street too much, afraid people would put two and two together and quit shopping at the fruit's fruit stand. Lucky Monica leaned on her lover's arm, wore a matching wedding band, all in a small, stuffy-rich town.

So don't put Johnnie down, Beanpole. If she looked like you, they might have killed her, wouldn't have employed her for sure. Her life would have been barebones. They compromised back then. You may not be afraid with your marches and your bookstores. Don't forget, there are plenty of Johnnies left.

That day, the four of us were happy as bananas grinning on a tree—us two on our honeymoon, those two enjoying the fruit of their long years of hard work and caution.

We got back to their cottage exhausted, and sat around talking. You'd think me and Kathy would want to be by ourselves for a while. No, we had a whole lifetime to do that, and every minute with those old people was too precious to waste. They gave our honeymoon something nobody who goes to Niagara Falls will ever get. We even talked about setting up a farmers market and lunch counter near them. Kathy was waitressing and knew the ropes. Now and then, Johnnie's eyes would brighten and she'd put in her two cents, her hands going a mile a minute in her own kind of sign language, and keep up with her.

After a while, when the ideas were flying fast and it really seemed like me and Kathy might move out of the city, this big silver car pulled up in the driveway.

Monica threw her hands up. "It never rains, but it pours."

Though she hadn't mentioned any problems to us, we recognized their fear. Johnnie sat tight and tense. The lawyer talked smooth and polite and slimy at Monica, said he represented the monastery.

Monica hadn't wanted to worry Kathy on her honeymoon. The rich people from the estate died, and their kids planned to cash out to the monastery. Monica and Johnnie said there were signed papers saying the cottage was theirs to live in all their lives, rent free. Nobody gave them copies of the papers, the church people claimed there never were any such papers, and the lawyer was there to tell them they had to leave.

Me and Kathy sat there speechless while the lawyer said he'd be back with the final papers ordering them out. The Brothers offered to put them in a senior citizen project.

Monica cried. "Johnnie accepted the cottage instead of enough money to pay rent! We won't be able to grow our own food and stretch our dollars."

Until this afternoon, they hadn't been too worried. One of the things pretending to be straight had done for them was to make the church respect them like the townspeople did. They figured the priests were too naive to see past what the world thought. They'd been praying up a storm, sure they'd be saved in the end. Now it looked like religion wasn't all it was cracked up to be.

Didn't they have a lawyer, we asked? No, they didn't want to make a scene with the church, lawyer talk was over their heads, they weren't the kind to hire lawyers, how would they pay him? What if, somehow, in all this, Johnnie got found out?

We four spent the rest of the day trying to find a solution.

Nothing worked or suited them. The threat of the monastery was over us all night, like evil. After the lies and pretending, the hard work and fear, this would wipe out all their efforts toward a decent life. They might as well have been out in the open from the start.

"That's okay, girls," Monica said. "All we ever had was each other. And the good will of the people on the hill."

By the time the lawyer showed up the next day, I was mad as hell.

"What's the matter with the Brothers?" I shouted at him as he got out of his slimy silver car. Someone had to speak up for these women. "Are they afraid of the real world? Let them come throw the old people out themselves."

Monica and Johnnie watched me, Monica's eyes frightened, Johnnie's face creased with worry.

"Why can't your so-called Christians let these old people stay? The priests don't need the damn cottage."

He claimed they'd love to let them stay, but their insurance made it impossible.

"What you mean," Kathy says, "is they don't want to spend the money insuring these owners who've always lived on the water and now might all of a suddenly fall in?"

Monica managed to laugh.

Silverslime didn't like our tone at all. He pulled himself up and said he could make them one final offer.

"We're listening."

He wanted to move them into the caretaker cottage on

the monastery grounds. If they were employees, and not as endangered by hurricanes, the problem would be solved.

The old people looked interested, but not happy. Seeing that, I couldn't help myself, I risked everything because I knew they were right. Except for being queer, they lived a godlier life than anyone I knew. Their world was full of peace and love and kindness and, with the little they had, charity. The god of flowers and fruit and sea and sun had claimed this little piece of land for them, and big old Henny was their appointed priestess. I couldn't help it.

"No, they're not going to settle for changing their whole lives this late, mister. Johnnie paid for his home with years of his labor. It's not much reward. You know how little pension he gets. He and Monica own something here. You can keep them from selling it, from passing it on. Take it away? Wrong. I own my business in the city and I know about your games. They've me got in their corner now. Get yourself and your papers back in that car and get out of here. Their lawyer will contact you."

Silverslime huffed up, looked like he was either going to give me a speech or have a heart attack, and I didn't much care which. At the last minute he oozed back into his slimemobile and roared off.

Maybe I was being hasty and getting involved where I didn't belong. Maybe I was bluffing a little to prove to the priests that I could match their firepower. Maybe it was my sense of fair play that was offended. What did I have to offer them if we lost? My parents' old apartment where Kathy and I already lived? Damn it, I wanted that home for them. For all those years they'd had to swallow their pride and their own natural ways, for all the things they did without to get what they had, for all the queers who lived half-lives to get any peace at all, l wanted that home.

So our honeymoon took an unexpected turn. We didn't run along the beach that day, or make love that night. I wanted to call my lawyer. Monica said she'd call the one who first drew up the papers on their house. I said we'd pay him, and she accepted with tears in her eyes, despite Johnnie's gruff head shake no. Monica kept putting off calling, like she was still waiting for that church to fix things up.

When two of the brothers from the monastery came to the front door that night, as Johnnie was building a fire in the woodstove, I wondered if Monica's faith was paying off. How could priests order such frail good people out of their home, once they met them? An hour later they were gone, whining at not getting their way.

"Faggots," Kathy declared, and we all laughed except Johnnie, whose eyes laughed for her.

In the morning, we found a formal letter in the mailbox. The sheriff was coming to evict them.

Kathy persuaded Monica to call the lawyer immediately. I paced around outside watching to see if any busybody sheriff dared stick his nose into our business. Kathy called me in. Another setback: the old lawyer had been dead for several months. His daughter took over his practice. A woman! She'd care. Monica and Johnnie were old-fashioned. They were dead-set against using a "lady lawyer." Things were at a standstill again. Hell, I decided, I'd gotten them that far against their obstinate wills. I called that lady lawyer. Once she heard who was involved, she got very interested. Their benefactor's daughter had been her best childhood friend, and she remembered the family's affection for the old couple. She would check father's files.

We sat down to a cold supper of homegrown

vegetables and baked chicken, worried this might be the last dinner on the beach, the last homegrown vegetables ever. Would it kill Monica and Johnnie to move up to the monastery? It would be better than wandering around Queens, living a new life among strangers, depending on us.

After they went to bed, Kathy and I sat on the front porch, watching the dark waters. Near midnight we were startled—there was a sound inside the cabin. It was like a child's cry, or the whimpering of a hurt animal. Kathy put her hand on my arm.

We heard Monica ask, "Johnnie, are you crying?" The bedroom was right behind the porch and light burst into the night. They must have thought we'd gone to our cabin.

"I don't want to leave this place," said a dry, rasping, high voice. I went cold with shock. Kathy's hand leapt across her open mouth. It was Johnnie. Talking.

"Something will happen." Monica was trying to comfort her. "If we do have to move to the city with the kids, why then you can be yourself at last. No one will know us or care about the way we are."

"Have we been wrong to live like this? Maybe we're being punished. If only I could use my voice! I'm ashamed, Henny having to do this for me. If anyone fights for our home, it should be me."

"Johnnie, say it with me." Like a prayer they must have prayed many times, they said, "Don't you forget, whatever happens, we still have each other."

There was a smile in Johnnie's little voice. "That's most important, I know." The light went out.

Kathy and I held hands in the dark. The voices went on for a while, Johnnie's breathy, unused. It gave me the chills because it was female as could be in a body I didn't think of that way, and because we never guessed she had a voice at all.

We waited about an hour after the voices faded and very carefully snuck off the porch, down the road to our cottage. Too stunned to talk, we held each other and cried over Johnnie's girlish sobs, her few rusty words. How terrible it had been for Johnnie: she'd given up her voice to mute the ordeal of living in her body. I was bowled over thinking how awfully, awfully strong she'd been all those years, how she'd stayed as true to herself as she could, and kept loving Monica, and lived the whole time like a tomato plant without a stake, holding herself up by sheer will. If she lost everything she'd earned by giving up her voice—

By eight o'clock that morning, I was at the lady lawyer's office. The sheriff might come any time I told her, and I insisted on helping in some way.

She was a pretty lady, very straight, and looked at me like I was a new kind of beetle about to attack her rose garden. "No need," she said, waving a folder. "I found this in Dad's personal files at home with a few closed cases."

She handed me a sheet of paper. It was the original notarized statement giving Johnnie and Monica the cottage and a half acre of land around it. "Hot dog!" I yelled and before she knew what hit her, I hugged her.

The lawyer dropped out of my arms to her seat. She produced two copies. "Dad got sick and never made it back to the office; these were never mailed out."

She thanked me for calling her, both for the old couple and for her father's reputation. She would deliver the papers to the monastery lawyer. "The brothers might still fight it, since the cottage wasn't mentioned in the sale of the property to the monastery. We'll work something out."

She smiled big and I ran off to show Monica and

Johnnie that beautiful piece of paper.

They clapped their hands and, arm in arm, did the tiniest bit of a square dance swing, crying in relief—Monica loudly, Johnnie silently, though Kathy and I listened hard for a familiar whimper. The lady lawyer called later to say their problems were over. Out of respect for their parents' wishes, out of a sense of responsibility because her father's office was at fault, the children of the rich people and the lady lawyer would make a donation to the monastery to be used to pay insurance on the beach cottage.

Hey, Kathy, will you look at the grin on Beanpole's face. What's the matter with friends like me and Kathy, you needed to worry?

Our honeymoon? Oh sure, we got back in the mood, what with all the celebrating we did that night. We were exhausted from our scare and from the royal battle. We collapsed the last two days.

I kept hoping Johnnie would thank us by breaking her silence. It was okay that she didn't; they gave plenty. Like what? Their example: staying together, enduring. It was like having parents to look up to. We wanted to live like them, to be as decent as they were in spite of what they went through. We wanted to stay together forever, like they did, because we could see how happy they were.

Yeah, Beanpole, like me and Kath are now. Like you're going to be someday.

Don't get me misty-eyed about it, though. I saw you and Kathy looking for tissues. Here, it's late anyway. Take these pastries and get home to your girlfriend. Don't stay up late looking for honeymoon dew. I need your eyes open at work tomorrow.

What's honeymoon dew? Look at Kathy winking at me

over there. It's something we discovered on our honeymoon. You'll figure it out.

AUTHOR BIOS

Ann Bannon has been called "The Queen of Lesbian Pulp Fiction" for her landmark "Beebo Brinker Chronicles," five original novels about lesbian lives in Greenwich Village in the mid-20th Century. These stories created the iconic young butch, Beebo, and provide a glimpse into the world of young women in love that continues to engage and inspire in the present day.

Jean Copeland is an English teacher and the author of *The Revelation of Beatrice Darby.* Her short fiction and essays appear in online and print journals including *A Family by Any Other Name, Sharkreef.org, The Connecticut Review, Texas Told 'Em, Best Lesbian Love Stories,* and *The First Line.* www.jeancopeland.wordpress.com, www.boldstrokesbooks.com/Author-Jean-Copeland.html

R.G. Emanuelle's published works include *Twice Bitten, Add Spice to Taste,* and short stories in numerous anthologies. She co-edited the Lambda Award Finalist anthology *All You Can Eat: A Buffet of Lesbian Erotica & Romance,* as well as *Unwrap These Presents,* and *Skulls and Crossbones.* www.rgemanuelle.com, https://www.facebook.com/RGEmanuelle

Allison Fradkin believes the "L" in AAGPBL ("All-American Girls Professional Baseball League") is open to interpretation. They don't call it fantasy baseball for nothing. In addition to appreciating ballpark figures,

299

Allison has a gay old time editing the yearly queerly *Off the Rocks: An Anthology of GLBT Writing* for NewTown Writers Press. She also goes to bat for Pride Films & Plays as Literary Manager, Bella Books as Editorial Consultant, and *Curve Magazine* as Book Reviewer. Touch base at allisonfradkin.blogspot.com.

Patty G. Henderson, when she's not writing or thinking of plot lines in her head, loves spending time with her family, friends, and coffee shops. An avowed Pluviophile, rain and thunderstorms feed her soul. She also creates book covers and offers other book services for the indie author via her Boulevard Photografica business services.
www.pattyghenderson.com,
www.boulevardphotografica.yolasite.com,
https://www.facebook.com/pg.henderson.94,
http://thehendersonfiles.blogspot.com/

Heather Rose Jones writes in the intersection of history and fantasy, including the Alpennia series: *Daughter of Mystery* and *The Mystic Marriage*. This story was inspired by her research on lesbian themes in history and literature, which she blogs as the Lesbian Historic Motif Project. Website: alpennia.com

Lee Lynch wrote the classic novels *Toothpick House* and *The Swashbuckler*. Her newest book is Lammy finalist *An American Queer*. She is namesake and first recipient of the Golden Crown Literary Society Lee Lynch Classic Award for her novel *The Swashbuckler*. She is also a recipient of the James Duggins Mid-Career Award in Writing and many more honors. Books by Lee Lynch are available at <u>boldstrokesbooks.com</u>.

Megan McFerren enjoys exploring queer history through erotic romance, and illuminating the love that once dared not speak its name. Texan by birth and New Yorker by choice, she has contributed stories to anthologies from Torquere Press and Love Slave.

Cara Patterson is an Edinburgh-based Scottish writer. She has been telling stories since before she can remember, and progressed onto writing them down as soon as she had a grasp of the alphabet. She's delighted to be able to say she is now a published author.

Aliisa Percival lives in Ajax, Ontario, and is a font of useless knowledge about the Ajax munitions plant. She has a Bachelor's degree in English from the University of Toronto, and this is her first published work. Find her on twitter @aliiisamooose for triple the vowels.

Doreen Perrine's third novel has just been released through Bedazzled Ink and her stories have appeared in numerous anthologies and ezines. A finalist in South Africa's *Bloody Parchment Literary Festival*, Doreen's plays have been performed throughout New York. She is also an artist and teacher. http://www.doreenperrine.com/

Priscilla Scott Rhoades's work has appeared in *Harrington Lesbian Literary Quarterly, Mississippi Review, The Iowa Review, The San Francisco Bay Guardian, The San Francisco Sentinel*, and *Plexus—A Bay Area Women's Newspaper*. She lives now in the mountains of North Carolina where she writes erotica under the pseudonym Pascal Scott.

Susan Smith is a writer and librarian. Smith's work is steeped in mythology, identity, gender, art, and sexuality. Her novels *Of Drag Kings and the Wheel of Fate, Burning Dreams*, and *Put Away Wet* were published by Bold Strokes Books, and the novella "Billy Boy" is in the *Outsiders* anthology from Brisk Press.

Lexy Wealleans lives in Wiltshire, England, with her partner and their imaginary dog Heathcliff. She spends most of her day struggling with spreadsheets and wishing she lived in an Enid Blyton novel instead. Her previous story, "Counting Down the Seconds", was selected for inclusion in *Heiresses of Russ 2014*.

Connie Wilkins is the real-life alter-ego of editor Sacchi Green. Connie started with science fiction and fantasy, and still writes the occasional historical or fantasy story under her own name, but Sacchi gets most of the fun, editing ten lesbian anthologies, including two Lambda Award winners. Connie has only edited two anthologies, both speculative fiction. Find them on Facebook (under Sacchi's name, of course) or at sacchi-green.blogspot.com.

MJ Williamz is the author of seven books, including Goldie award winning *Initiation by Desire*. She has also had over thirty short stories published, most of them erotica with a few romances and a couple of horrors thrown in for good measure. Her newest book, *Summer Passion,* is now available as eBook and paperback.

302

www.ingramcontent.com/pod-product-compliance
Lightning Source LLC
Chambersburg PA
CBHW071246170626
46809CB00001B/92